GREAT EXPECTATIONS

Published by Priory Books,
© Peter Haddock Publishing,
United Kingdom, YO16 6BT.

wo iv

GREAT EXPECTATIONS

CHAPTER 1

My father's family name being Pirrip, and my Christian name Philip, my infant tongue could make out only Pip. I therefore called myself Pip, and came to be called Pip.

I give Pirrip as my father's family name, on the authority of his tombstone and my sister – Mrs Joe Gargery, who married the blacksmith. I took it from the shape of the letters on my father's tombstone, that he was a square, dark man, with curly black hair. From the inscription, "Also Georgiana Wife of the Above," I concluded that my mother was freckled and sickly. There were also five little stone lozenges, in a row beside their grave, sacred to the memory of my five little brothers.

Ours was the marsh country, down by the river, within twenty miles of the sea. I think my first most vivid and broad impression was gained on a memorable raw afternoon. At such a time I found out that this bleak place was the churchyard; and that Philip Pirrip, Georgiana, Alexander, Bartholomew, Abraham, Tobias, and Roger, infant children of the aforesaid, were also dead and buried; and that the dark flat wilderness beyond the churchyard was the marshes; and that the low leaden line beyond, was the river; and that the small bundle of shivers growing afraid of it all and beginning to cry, was Pip.

"Hold your noise!" cried a terrible voice, as a man started up from among the graves. "Keep still, you little devil, or I'll cut your throat!"

A fearful man; all in coarse grey, with a great iron on his leg. A man with no hat, and broken shoes, and an old rag tied round his head. A man smothered in mud and lamed by stones, and torn by briars; who limped, shivered and growled.

"Oh! Don't cut my throat, sir," I pleaded in terror.

"Tell us your name!" said the man. "Quick!"

"Pip, sir."

"Show us where you live," said the man. "Pint out the place!"

I pointed to where our village lay, a mile from the church.

The man looked at me for a moment, turned me upside down, and emptied my pockets. There was nothing but a piece of bread. When upright again, I was seated on a high tombstone, trembling, while he ate the bread ravenously.

"You young dog," said the man, licking his lips, "what fat cheeks you ha' got."

I believe they were fat, though I was then small for my years.

"Darn me if I couldn't eat 'em," said the man, with a threatening shake of his head, "and if I han't half a mind to't!"

I held tighter to the tombstone on which he had put me; partly, to keep myself upon it; partly, to keep myself from crying.

"Now lookee here!" said the man. "Where's your mother?"

"There, sir!" said I.

He started, and looked over his shoulder.

"There, sir!" I timidly explained. "Also Georgiana. That's my mother."

"Oh!" said he. "And is that your father alonger your mother?"

"Yes, sir," said I; "him too; late of this parish."

"Ha!" he muttered then, considering. "Who d'ye live with – supposin' I let you live, which I han't decided?"

"My sister, sir – Mrs Joe Gargery – wife of Joe Gargery, the blacksmith, sir."

"Blacksmith, eh?" said he. And looked down at his leg.

He looked at me several times, and then he took me by both arms, and tilted me back as far as he could hold me.

"Now lookee here," he said. " You know what a file is?"

"Yes, sir."

"And you know what wittles is?"

"Yes, sir."

"You get me a file." He tilted me. "And you get me wittles, and you bring 'em both to me." He tilted me again. "Or I'll have your heart and liver out."

I clung to him with both hands.

He then gave me a most tremendous dip and roll, then held me upright, and continued: "You bring me, tomorrow morning early, that file and them wittles, at that old Battery over yonder, and never dare to say a word that you have seen such a person as me, and you shall be let to live. You fail, or go from my words in any partickler, and your heart and your liver shall be tore out, roasted and ate. Now, I ain't alone. There's a young man

4

hid with me, in comparison with whom I am a Angel. That young man hears the words I speak. It is in wain for a boy to attempt to hide himself. A boy may lock his door, and think himself safe, but that young man will creep in and tear him open. I am a-keeping that young man from harming you at the present moment, with great difficulty. Now, what do you say?"

I said that I would get him the file, and what food I could, and would come to him at the Battery, early in the morning.

"Now," he pursued, "you remember what you've undertook, and that young man, and you get home!"

"Goo-good night, sir," I faltered.

"Much of that!" said he, glancing about him over the cold wet flat. "I wish I was a frog. Or a eel!"

At the same time, he hugged his shuddering body and limped towards the wall. I watched him go, picking his way among the nettles. When he came to the wall, he got over it, his legs numbed and stiff, then turned round to look for me. I set my face towards home, but looked back to see him nearer the river, picking his way among the stepping stones dropped into the marshes here and there.

I ran home without stopping.

CHAPTER 2

My sister, Mrs Joe Gargery, was more than twenty years older than I, and had established a great reputation for herself because she had brought me up "by hand".

She was not good-looking, my sister; and I had a general impression that she must have made Joe Gargery marry her. Joe was a fair man, with curls of flaxen hair, and with eyes of a very undecided blue. He was a mild, good-natured, sweet-tempered, easy-going, foolish, dear fellow – a sort of Hercules in strength, and also in weakness.

My sister, Mrs Joe, had black hair and eyes, and very red skin. She was tall and bony, and almost always wore a coarse apron, fastened over her figure behind with two loops, with a square impregnable bib in front, stuck full of pins and needles.

5

Joe's forge adjoined our house. When I ran home from the churchyard, the forge was shut, and Joe sat alone in the kitchen. Joe and I were fellow-sufferers, and being such, Joe said, the moment I raised the door latch and peeped in at him, "Mrs Joe is out now, looking for you, Pip."

"Is she?"

"Yes, Pip," said Joe.

"Has she been gone long, Joe?" I always treated him as a larger species of child, and as no more than my equal.

"Well," said Joe, glancing up at the Dutch clock; "she's been on the Ram-page, this last spell, about five minutes, Pip. She's a-coming! Get behind the door, old chap."

I took the advice. My sister, Mrs Joe, throwing the door wide open, and finding an obstruction, immediately divined the cause. She threw me at Joe, who passed me on into the chimney and quietly fenced me up there with his great leg.

"Where have you been, you young monkey?" said Mrs Joe, stamping her foot. "What have you been doing to wear me away with fret and fright?"

"I have only been to the churchyard," said I, from my stool.

"Churchyard!" repeated my sister. "If it warn't for me you'd have been there long ago, and stayed. Who brought you up by hand?"

"You did," said I.

"And why did I do it?" exclaimed my sister.

I whimpered, "I don't know."

"I don't!" said my sister. "I'd never do it again! I may truly say I've never had this apron off since born you were. It's bad enough to be a blacksmith's wife (and him a Gargery) without being your mother."

My thoughts strayed from that question as I looked disconsolately at the fire. The fugitive on the marshes, the mysterious young man, the file, the food, and the dreadful pledge I had made to steal under this sheltering roof, rose before me in the coals.

"Hah!" said Mrs Joe. "Churchyard, indeed! You may well say churchyard. You'll drive me to the churchyard betwixt you, one of these days, and oh, a pr-r-recious pair you'd be without me!"

As she applied herself to set the tea-things, Joe peeped down at me over his leg, as if calculating what kind of pair we should make. After that, he sat following Mrs Joe about with his blue eyes.

On the present occasion, though I was hungry, I dared not eat my slice of bread. I felt that I must save it for my dreadful friend. I resolved to put my hunk of bread-and-butter down the leg of my trousers.

I took advantage of a quiet moment, when Joe had just looked at me, and got my bread-and-butter down my leg.

The guilty knowledge that I was going to rob Mrs Joe – I never thought I was going to rob Joe, for I never thought of any of the housekeeping property as his – together with having to hold the bread-and-butter as I sat, almost drove me out of my mind.

It was Christmas Eve, and I had to stir the pudding for next day. I found the bread kept slipping out of my trousers, so I quickly slipped away, and left the bread in my bedroom.

"Hark!" said I, having finished stirring, and was warming up in my corner before going to bed; "was that the great guns, Joe?"

"Ah!" said Joe. "There's another conwict off."

"What does that mean, Joe?" said I.

Mrs Joe, who always took explanations upon herself, said snappishly, "Escaped."

I mouthed to Joe, "What's a convict?"

"There was a conwict off last night," said Joe, aloud. "They fired warning of him. And now, it appears another's gone."

"Who's firing?" said I.

"The Hulks!" exclaimed my sister.

"Oh-h!" said I, looking at Joe. "Hulks! And please what's Hulks?"

"That's his trouble!" exclaimed my sister, and shaking her head at me. "Answer him one question, and he'll ask a dozen. Hulks are prison-ships, right 'cross th' meshes."

"I wonder who's put into prison-ships, and why they're put there?" said I, in a general way, and with quiet desperation.

It was too much for Mrs Joe. "I didn't bring you up by hand to badger people," said she. "People are put in the Hulks because they murder, and rob, and do all sorts of bad; and they always begin by asking questions. Now, you get to bed!"

I went upstairs in the dark. I was clearly on my way to the Hulks. I had begun by asking questions, and I was going to rob Mrs Joe.

I was afraid to sleep, for I knew that at the first light of morning I must rob the pantry. There was no doing it at night, for I would have to strike a light, and make such a noise.

As soon as the sky was shot with grey, I went downstairs; every board upon the way calling, "Stop thief!" and "Get up, Mrs Joe!" The pantry was far fuller than usual, owing to the season. I swiftly stole some bread, cheese, half a jar of mincemeat, some brandy from a stone bottle – replacing the difference with water from a jug – and a beautiful round pork pie. It was carefully put away in a covered dish in a corner. I hoped that it would not be missed for some time.

There was a door to the forge from the kitchen; I unbolted it, and got a file from Joe's tools. Then, I relocked the door and went out through the house door and ran for the misty marshes.

CHAPTER 3

It was a damp morning. The damp lay on the bare hedges and spare grass, like a coarser sort of spiders' webs. The marsh-mist was so thick, that the wooden finger on the post to our village was invisible until I was under it.

The mist was heavier yet upon the marshes. The cattle came upon me with like suddenness, steaming out of their nostrils, "Holloa, young thief!"

One black ox stared at me, and moved his blunt head round in such an accusatory manner that I blubbered out to him, "I couldn't help it, sir! It wasn't for myself!" Upon which he put down his head and blew smoke out of his nose.

I drew closer to the river. I knew my way to the Battery, pretty straight; but, in the confusion of the mist, I found myself too far to the right, and consequently had to head back along the riverside. I had just crossed a ditch near to the Battery, and scrambled up the mound, when I saw the man sitting before me. His back was towards me, and he was nodding forward, heavy with sleep.

I went forward softly and touched him on the shoulder. He instantly jumped up, and I saw it was not the same man, but another man!

And yet he was dressed in coarse grey, too, with a great iron on his leg; and was lame, and hoarse, and cold, and everything that the other man was; except that he had not the same face, and wore a flat broad-brimmed felt hat. He swore at me, made a hit at me – a weak blow that missed me – and then he ran into the mist.

"It's the young man!" I thought, feeling my heart shoot as I identified him.

I was soon at the Battery, and there was the right man – hugging himself – waiting for me. He was awfully cold. His eyes looked so hungry, too. I opened the bundle and emptied my pockets.

"What's in the bottle, boy?" said he.

"Brandy," said I.

He left off eating to take some of the liquor, shivering violently all the while.

"I think you have the ague," said I.

"I'm much of your opinion, boy," said he.

He was gobbling mincemeat, bread, cheese, and pork pie, all at once: staring distrustfully while he did so into the mist, and often stopping to listen.

"You brought no one with you?"

"No, sir! No!"

"Nor giv' no one the office to follow you?"

"No!"

"Well," said he, "I believe you. You'd be but a fierce young hound indeed, if at your time of life you could help to hunt a wretched warmint!"

He smeared his ragged rough sleeve over his eyes.

Watching him settle down to the pie, I made bold to say, "I am glad you enjoy it."

"Thankee, my boy. I do."

The man took strong sudden bites, swallowing each mouthful.

"I am afraid you won't leave any for him," said I, timidly.

"Leave any for him? Who's him?" said my friend, stopping in his crunching of pie-crust.

"The young man that was hid with you."

"Oh ah!" he returned, with a gruff laugh. "He don't want no wittles."

"I thought he looked as if he did," said I.

The man stopped eating, regarding me with scrutiny and the greatest surprise. "Looked? When?"

"Just now."

"Where?"

9

"Yonder," said I, pointing; "where I found him nodding asleep, and thought it was you."

He held me by the collar and stared at me.

"Dressed like you, only with a hat," I explained, trembling; "and – and with – the same reason for needing a file. Didn't you hear the cannon last night?"

"Then, there was firing!" he said to himself. "This man – did you notice anything in him?"

"He had a badly bruised face," said I, recalling what I hardly knew I knew.

"Not here?" exclaimed the man, striking his left cheek.

"Yes, there!"

"Where is he?" He crammed the remaining food into his grey jacket. "Show me the way. I'll pull him down, like a bloodhound. Curse this iron on my sore leg! Give us hold of the file, boy."

I indicated in what direction the mist had shrouded the other man, and he looked up at it for an instant. But he was filing at his iron like a madman, and not minding me. I told him I must go, but he took no notice, so I thought the best thing I could do was to slip off. The last I saw, his head was bent over his knee and he was working hard at his fetter. The last I heard, the file was still going.

CHAPTER 4

I fully expected to find a Constable in the kitchen. But there was no Constable, and no discovery of the robbery. Mrs Joe was busy getting the house ready for the festivities, and Joe sat upon the kitchen doorstep.

"And where the deuce ha' you been?" was her Christmas salutation.

I said I had been to hear the Carols. "Ah well!" observed Mrs Joe. "You might ha' done worse." Not a doubt of that, I thought.

"Perhaps if I warn't a blacksmith's wife, and a slave with her apron never off, I should have been to hear the Carols," she said.

Joe, venturing into the kitchen after me, secretly crossed his two forefingers, as our sign that Mrs Joe was cross. This was so normal, that we would often have our fingers crossed for weeks.

We were to have a superb dinner, consisting of a leg of pickled pork and greens, and a pair of roast stuffed fowls. A handsome mince pie had been made yesterday morning, and the pudding was already on the boil.

Mrs Joe put clean white curtains up, and tacked a new flowered-flounce across the wide chimney to replace the old one, and uncovered the little state parlour across the passage, which was never uncovered at any other time.

My sister having so much to do was going to church vicariously; that is, Joe and I were going. In his working clothes, Joe was a characteristic-looking blacksmith; in his holiday clothes, he more closely resembled a scarecrow in good circumstances. Nothing seemed to fit him or belong to him. On the present festive occasion he emerged from his room the picture of misery. As for me, when my sister took me for a new suit of clothes, it seemed the tailor had orders to make them so that I had no free use of my limbs.

Joe and I going to church, therefore, must have been a moving sight. But, the terrors that had assailed me whenever Mrs Joe had gone near the pantry, were only to be equalled by the remorse I felt for what I had done. Under the weight of my wicked secret, I pondered whether the Church would be powerful enough to shield me from the terrible young man, if I divulged to that establishment.

Mr Wopsle, the clerk at church, was to dine with us; and Mr Hubble the wheelwright and Mrs Hubble; and Uncle Pumblechook (Joe's uncle, but Mrs Joe appropriated him), a well-to-do corn-chandler in the nearest town. The dinner hour was half-past one. When Joe and I got home, we found the table laid, and Mrs Joe dressed, and the front door unlocked (it never was at any other time) for the company to enter by, and everything most splendid. And still, no word of the robbery.

I opened the door to the company – first to Mr Wopsle, next to Mr and Mrs Hubble, and last of all to Uncle Pumblechook. N.B., *I* was not allowed to call him uncle, under the severest penalties.

"Mrs Joe," said Uncle Pumblechook: a large hard-breathing middle-aged slow man, "I have brought you, as the compliments of the season – a bottle of sherry wine – and a bottle of port wine."

Every Christmas Day he arrived, carrying two bottles. Every Christmas Day, Mrs Joe replied, as she now replied, "Oh, Un-cle Pum-ble-chook! This *is* kind!" Every Christmas Day, he retorted, "It's no more than your merits."

We dined in the kitchen, and adjourned, for the nuts and oranges and apples, to the parlour. Mr Wopsle said grace and ended with the very proper aspiration that we might be truly grateful. Upon which my sister fixed me with her eye, and said, "Do you hear that? Be grateful."

"Especially," said Mr Pumblechook, "be grateful, boy, to them which brought you up by hand."

Joe's station and influence were somewhat feebler when there was company, than when there was none. But he always aided me when he could, and he always did so at dinner-time by giving me gravy. There being plenty today, Joe spooned into my plate, at this point, about half a pint.

"He was a world of trouble to you, ma'am," said Mrs Hubble, commiserating my sister.

"Trouble?" echoed my sister; "trouble?" and then entered on a fearful catalogue of all the illnesses I had been guilty of; and all the acts of sleeplessness I had committed; and all the high places I had tumbled from; and all the injuries I had done myself; and all the times she had wished me in my grave, and I had refused to go there. I was granted a severe look at the end of her speech.

She then turned to Mr Pumblechook.

"Have a little brandy, uncle," she said.

O Heavens, it had come at last! He would say it was weak, and I was lost! I held tight to the leg of the table, with both hands, and awaited my fate.

My sister came back with the stone bottle, and poured his brandy out: no one else taking any. The wretched man trifled with his glass – took it up, looked at it through the light, put it down – prolonging my misery.

I couldn't keep my eyes off him. Holding tight to the leg of the table, I saw the miserable creature finger his glass playfully, take it up, smile, throw his head back, and drink the brandy off. Instantly afterwards, he sprang to his feet, turned round several times in an appalling whooping-cough dance, and rushed out the door; he then became visible through the window, violently expectorating, making the most hideous faces, and apparently out of his mind.

I held on tight, while Mrs Joe and Joe ran to him. I had no doubt I had murdered him somehow. It was a relief when he was brought back, and, surveying the company all round, sank into his chair and gasped, "Tar!"

I had filled up the bottle from the tar-water jug. I knew he would be worse by-and-by.

"Tar!" cried my sister, in amazement. "Why, how could Tar come there?"

But, Uncle Pumblechook wouldn't hear of the subject, waved it all away with his hand, and asked for hot gin-and-water. My sister, who had begun to be alarmingly thoughtful, got the gin, hot water, sugar, and lemon-peel, and mixed them. For the time being, I was saved.

Then came pudding. Mr Pumblechook partook of pudding. All partook of pudding. The course terminated, and Mr Pumblechook had begun to beam under the genial influence of gin-and-water. I began to think I should get over the day, when my sister said to Joe, "Clean plates – cold."

I clutched the leg of the table again. I foresaw what was coming, and I felt that this time I really was gone.

"You must taste," said my sister, addressing the guests, "to finish with, such a delicious present of Uncle Pumblechook's!"

Must they! Let them not hope to taste it!

"It's a savoury pork pie," said my sister, rising.

The company murmured their compliments. Uncle Pumblechook said – "Well, Mrs Joe, let us have a cut at this same pie."

My sister went to get it. I heard her proceed to the pantry. I saw Mr Pumblechook balance his knife. I heard Joe say, "You shall have some, Pip." I have never been absolutely certain whether I actually cried out, or just imagined I did. I felt that I could bear no more, and that I must run away. I ran for my life.

But, I got no further than the house door, for there I ran headlong into a party of soldiers: one of whom held out a pair of handcuffs to me, saying, "Here you are, look sharp, come on!"

CHAPTER 5

The sudden sight of soldiers on our doorstep caused the dinner-party to stand in confusion, and caused Mrs Joe re-entering the kitchen empty-handed, to stop short and stare, in her wondering lament of "Gracious me, what's gone – with the – pie!"

13

The sergeant and I were in the kitchen. It was the sergeant who had spoken, and he now looked round at the company, holding out the handcuffs in his right hand, his left on my shoulder.

"Excuse me, ladies and gentleman," said the sergeant, "but as I mentioned at the door to this young shaver," (which he hadn't) "I want the blacksmith."

"And what might you want with him?" retorted my sister.

"Missis," returned the gallant sergeant, "speaking for myself, the honour and pleasure of his fine wife's acquaintance; speaking for the king, I have to say, a little job done."

This was received as rather neat in the sergeant.

"You see, blacksmith," said the sergeant, who had by this time picked out Joe, "I find the lock of one of these's gone wrong. As they are wanted immediately, will you throw your eye over them?"

Joe said he would need to light his forge fire, and it would take nearer two hours than one. "Will it? Then will you set about it at once, blacksmith?" said the off-hand sergeant, "as it's on his Majesty's service." With that, he called to his men, who came trooping into the kitchen, piling their arms in a corner. And then they stood about, as soldiers do.

Realising that the handcuffs were not for me, and that the pie was far in the background, I collected a little more of my scattered wits.

"Would you give me the time?" said the sergeant.

"It's just gone half-past two," Mr Pumblechook replied.

"That's not so bad," said the sergeant, reflecting. "Even if I had to stay here two hours, that'll do. How far are you from the marshes, hereabouts? Not above a mile, I reckon?"

"Just a mile," said Mrs Joe.

"That'll do. We begin to close in upon 'em about dusk, as ordered."

"Convicts, sergeant?" asked Mr Wopsle.

"Ay!" returned the sergeant. "Two. It's fairly certain they won't try to get clear of the marshes before dusk. Anybody here seen anything of any such game?"

Everybody, myself excepted, said no, with confidence. Nobody thought of me.

"Well!" said the sergeant, "they'll find themselves trapped, sooner than they count on. Now, blacksmith! If you're ready, his Majesty the King is."

14

Joe had his leather apron on, and passed into the forge. One soldier opened its windows, another lighted the fire, another turned to at the bellows, the rest stood round the soon roaring blaze. Then Joe began to hammer and clink, while we watched.

My sister drew a pitcher of beer from the cask for the soldiers, and invited the sergeant to take a glass of brandy. But Mr Pumblechook said, sharply, "Give him wine, Mum. There'll be no Tar in that." The sergeant thanked him, saying that as he preferred his drink without tar, he would take wine. He drank his Majesty's health and Compliments of the Season.

I thought about my fugitive friend on the marshes. The soldiers were anticipating "the two villains" being taken.

At last, Joe's job was done. He got on his coat, and mustered courage to propose that some of us should go with the soldiers and see what came of the hunt. Mr Wopsle said he would go, if Joe would. Joe said he was agreeable, and would take me, if Mrs Joe approved. We never should have got leave to go, I am sure, but for Mrs Joe's curiosity to know how it ended. She merely stipulated, "If you bring the boy back with his head blown to bits by a musket, don't expect me to put it together again."

The sergeant took a polite leave of the ladies, and his men fell in. Mr Wopsle, Joe, and I, received strict charge to keep in the rear, and to speak no word after we reached the marshes. When we were all out in the raw air and moving towards the marsh, I treasonably whispered to Joe, "I hope, Joe, we shan't find them."

Joe whispered to me, "I'd give a shilling if they had cut and run, Pip."

No stragglers joined us from the village, for darkness was coming on. A few faces looked after us, but none came out. We passed the finger-post, and held straight on to the churchyard. There, we were stopped by a signal from the sergeant's hand, while a couple of his men searched among the graves. They found nothing, and then we struck out on the open marshes. A bitter sleet came rattling against us, and Joe took me on his back.

I considered for the first time, with great dread, would my particular convict believe that I had brought the soldiers there, that I had betrayed him?

It was no use asking myself this now. I was on Joe's back, and he charged at the ditches like a hunter, and urged Mr Wopsle to keep up with us. The soldiers were in front, extending into a wide line. Under the red glare of sunset, the Battery and the opposite shore of the river, were plain, though all of a watery lead colour.

With my heart thumping, I looked for any sign of the convicts. I could see none, I could hear none. The sheep looked timidly at us; and the cattle stared angrily at us; but, there was no break in the bleak stillness of the marshes.

The soldiers moved in the direction of the old Battery, and we were a little way behind them. All of a sudden, we stopped, for we heard a long shout. It was repeated. It was towards the east, long and loud. Nay, there seemed to be two or more shouts raised together – if one might judge from a confusion in the sound.

The sergeant ordered that the sound should not be answered, but that the course should be changed, and that his men should make towards it "at the double".

It was a run indeed. Down banks and up banks, and over gates, and splashing into dykes: no man cared where he went. As we came nearer to the shouting, it was clear that it was made by more than one voice. Sometimes, it seemed to stop altogether, and then the soldiers stopped. When it broke out again, the soldiers made for it, and we after them. After a while, we could hear one voice clearly calling "Murder!" and another voice, "Convicts! Runaways! Guard! This way for the runaway convicts!"

The sergeant ran in first, with two of his men close behind him. Their pieces were cocked and levelled.

"Here are both men!" panted the sergeant, struggling at the bottom of a ditch. "Surrender, you two! Come asunder!"

Water was splashing, mud was flying, oaths were being sworn, and blows struck. More men went into the ditch to help the sergeant; and dragged out, separately, my convict and the other one. Both were bleeding and struggling; and I knew them both.

"Mind!" said my convict, wiping blood from his face with his ragged sleeves, and shaking torn hair from his fingers: "I took him! I give him up to you! Mind that!"

"It'll do you small good, my man," said the sergeant; "being in the same plight yourself. Handcuffs there!"

"I don't expect it to do me any good," said my convict, with a laugh. "I took him. He knows it. That's enough for me."

The other convict seemed to be bruised and torn all over, in addition to the old bruises on his face. He could hardly catch his breath to speak, until they were both separately handcuffed.

"Take notice, guard – he tried to murder me," were his first words.

"Tried to murder him?" said my convict, disdainfully. "Try, and not succeed? I took him, and giv' him up; that's what I done. I not only prevented him getting off the marshes, but I dragged him back here. He's a gentleman, if you please, this villain. Now, the Hulks has got its gentleman back, through me."

The other one still gasped, "He tried – to – murder me. Bear – bear witness."

"Lookee here!" said my convict to the sergeant. "I got clear of the prison-ship; I made a dash and I done it. I could ha' got clear of these death-cold flats as well – look at my leg: you won't find much iron on it. Only I discovered that he was here. Let him go free? Let him profit by the means as I found out? Let him make a tool of me afresh? No, no. If I had died at the bottom there – " and he pointed at the ditch with his manacled hands; " – I'd have held to him with my dying grip, that you should have found him in my hold."

The other fugitive, evidently in extreme horror of his companion, repeated, "He tried to murder me. I should have been dead if you had not come up."

"He lies!" said my convict, fiercely. "He's a liar born, and he'll die a liar. Look at his face; ain't it written there? Let him turn those eyes of his on me. I defy him to do it."

The other, with an effort at a scornful smile, looked at the soldiers, and looked about at the marshes and at the sky, but certainly did not look at the speaker.

"Do you see?" pursued my convict. "See what a villain he is? Do you see those grovelling and wandering eyes? That's how he looked when we were tried together. He never looked at me."

The other, always working his dry lips, finally looked for a moment on the speaker, with the words, "You are not much to look at." At that point, my convict became so maddened, that he would have rushed upon him but for the soldiers. "Didn't I tell you," said the other convict, "that he would murder me, if he could?" And he shook with fear.

"Enough of this," said the sergeant. "Light those torches."

As one of the soldiers knelt down to open his basket, my convict looked round him for the first time, and saw me. I had alighted from Joe's back and had not moved since. I looked at him eagerly, and slightly

17

moved my hands and shook my head. I had been waiting for him to see me that I might assure him of my innocence. I'm not sure he comprehended, for he gave me a look I did not understand.

The soldier with the basket soon got a light, and lighted three or four torches. Four soldiers then stood in a ring, firing twice into the air. Presently we saw other torches kindled some distance behind us, and others from the opposite bank of the river.

"All right," said the sergeant. "March."

We had not gone far when three cannon were fired ahead of us. "You are expected on board," said the sergeant to my convict. "Don't straggle, my man. Close up here."

The two were kept apart, and each walked surrounded by a separate guard. I held Joe's hand now, and Joe carried one of the torches. There was a reasonably good path now, mostly on the edge of the river. When I looked round, I could see the other lights coming in after us. I could see nothing else but black darkness. We could not go fast, because of their lameness; and they were so spent, that two or three times we had to halt while they rested.

After an hour or so, we came to a rough wooden hut and a landing-place. There was a guard in the hut, and they challenged, and the sergeant answered. Then, we went into the hut. The sergeant made some kind of entry in a book, and then the convict whom I call the other convict was drafted off with his guard, to go on board first.

My convict never looked at me, except that once. While we stood in the hut, he stood before the fire looking thoughtfully at it. Suddenly, he turned to the sergeant, and remarked: "I wish to say something respecting this escape. It may prevent some persons laying under suspicion alonger me."

"You can say what you like," returned the sergeant, looking at him with his arms folded, "but you have no call to say it here. You'll have opportunity enough to say about it, before it's done with, you know."

"I know, but this is a separate matter. A man can't starve; at least I can't. I took some wittles, up at the willage over yonder – where the church stands a'most on the marshes. From the blacksmith's."

"Halloa!" said the sergeant, staring at Joe.

"Halloa, Pip!" said Joe, staring at me.

"It was some broken wittles – and a dram of liquor, and a pie."

"Have you missed such an article as a pie, blacksmith?" asked the sergeant.

"My wife did, at the very moment you arrived."

"So," said my convict, turning his eyes on Joe, and without the least glance at me; "so you're the blacksmith, are you? Than I'm sorry to say, I've eat your pie."

"God knows you're welcome to it," returned Joe. "We don't know what you have done, but we wouldn't have you starved to death for it, poor miserable fellow-creatur'. – Would us, Pip?"

The man turned his back. The boat had returned, and his guard were ready, so we followed him to the landing-place and saw him put into the boat, which was rowed by a crew of convicts like himself. No one seemed surprised or interested to see him. By the light of the torches, we saw the black Hulk lying out a little way from the shore, like a wicked Noah's ark. We saw the boat go alongside, and we saw him taken up the side and disappear.

CHAPTER 6

I had been exonerated from the pilfering but I felt unable to tell the truth to Joe. I loved Joe – perhaps for no better reason in those early days than because he let me love him. It was much upon my mind (particularly when I first saw him looking for his file) that I ought to tell Joe the whole truth. Yet I did not, for fear he would think ill of me. The fear of losing Joe's confidence tied up my tongue. I told myself that if Joe knew, I never afterwards could see him at the fireside without thinking that he was meditating on it. In a word, I was too cowardly to do what I knew to be right, as I had been too cowardly to avoid doing what I knew to be wrong.

As I was sleepy before we were far from the prison-ship, Joe took me on his back again and carried me home.

When we reached home, I staggered on the kitchen floor like a little drunkard, through having been newly set upon my feet, having been fast asleep, and through waking in the heat and lights and noise of tongues. As I came to myself I found Joe telling them about the convict's confession,

19

and all the visitors suggesting different ways by which he had got into the pantry. Mr Pumblechook made out, after carefully surveying the premises, that he must have first got upon the roof of the forge, and then upon the roof of the house, and had then let himself down the kitchen chimney by a rope made of his bedding cut into strips; and as Mr Pumblechook was very positive and drove his own chaise-cart – it was agreed that it must be so.

This was all I heard that night before my sister clutched me, and assisted me up to bed with a strong hand.

CHAPTER 7

When I was old enough, I was to be apprenticed to Joe, and until I could assume that dignity I was not to be pampered. Therefore, I was not only odd-boy about the forge, but if any neighbour needed an extra boy to frighten birds, or pick up stones, or do any such job, I was favoured with the employment. All earnings were dropped in a money-box. I realised very early on that I had no hope of sharing the treasure.

Mr Wopsle's great-aunt kept an evening school in the village; where she used to sleep from six to seven every evening, in the society of youth who paid twopence per week each, for the improving opportunity of seeing her do it. She rented a small cottage, and Mr Wopsle had the room upstairs, where we students used to overhear him reading aloud in a most terrific manner, and occasionally bumping on the ceiling.

Mr Wopsle's great-aunt kept – in the same room – a little general shop. She had no idea what stock there was, or the price of anything; but there was a little greasy book kept in a drawer – a Catalogue of Prices – whereby Biddy arranged all the shop transactions. Biddy was Mr Wopsle's great-aunt's granddaughter; I still can't work out what relation she was to Mr Wopsle. She was an orphan like myself; also brought up by hand. Her hair always wanted brushing, her hands always wanted washing, and her shoes always wanted mending. But on Sundays, she went to church elaborated.

With the help of Biddy, I struggled through the alphabet. After that, I fell among the nine figures, who seemed every evening to do something new to disguise themselves. But, at last I began, in a groping way, to read, write, and cipher, on the very smallest scale.

A year passed in this way.

Mrs Joe made occasional trips with Uncle Pumblechook on market-days, to assist him in buying such goods as required a woman's judgement. This was market-day, and Mrs Joe was out on one of these expeditions.

Joe made the fire and swept the hearth, and then we listened for the chaise-cart. It was a dry cold night, and the wind blew keenly.

"Here comes the mare," said Joe, "ringing like a peal of bells!"

The sound of her shoes upon the hard road was quite musical, as she came along at a much brisker trot than usual. We stirred up the fire that they might see a bright window, and checked the kitchen that nothing might be out of place.

Mrs Joe was soon landed, and Uncle Pumblechook too, covering the mare with a cloth, and we were soon all in the kitchen.

"Now," said Mrs Joe, unwrapping herself with haste and excitement, and throwing her bonnet back, "if this boy an't grateful this night, he never will be!"

I looked as grateful as possible, without knowing why I should be grateful.

"I only hope he won't be Pompeyed," said my sister.

"She an't in that line, Mum," said Mr Pumblechook. "She knows better."

She? I looked at Joe, making the motion with my lips and eyebrows, "She?" Joe looked at me, making a similar expression, "She?" My sister caught him in the act.

"Well?" she snapped. "What are you staring at?"

"You mentioned – she?" Joe politely hinted.

" Unless you call Miss Havisham a he?" said my sister. "And I doubt if you'll go so far as that."

"Miss Havisham, up town?" said Joe.

"Is there any Miss Havisham down town?" returned my sister. "She wants this boy to go and play there. And of course he's going."

I had heard of Miss Havisham up town – everybody for miles round, had heard of Miss Havisham up town – as an immensely rich and grim lady who lived in seclusion in a large and dismal house barricaded against robbers.

21

"Well to be sure!" said Joe, astounded. "I wonder how she come to know Pip!"

"Noodle!" cried my sister. "Who said she knew him?"

" – Which some individual," Joe again politely hinted, "mentioned that she wanted him to go and play there."

"And couldn't she ask Uncle Pumblechook if he knew of a boy to go and play there? And Uncle Pumblechook being a tenant of hers, who sometimes goes there to pay his rent – couldn't she then ask Uncle Pumblechook if he knew of a boy? And couldn't Uncle Pumblechook, being always thoughtful for us – though you may not think it, Joseph," in a tone of the deepest reproach, as if he were the most callous of nephews, "then mention this boy, that I have for ever been a willing slave to?"

"Well put!" cried Uncle Pumblechook. "Prettily pointed! Now Joseph, you know the case."

"No, Joseph," said my sister, still in a reproachful manner, "you do not yet know the case. You may consider that you do, but you do not. For you do not know that Uncle Pumblechook, knowing that, for all we know, this boy's fortune may be made by his going to Miss Havisham's, has offered to take him into town and keep him and take him to Miss Havisham's tomorrow morning. And Lor-a-mussy me!" cried my sister, casting off her bonnet in sudden desperation, "here I stand talking, while Uncle Pumblechook waits, and the mare catches cold at the door."

With that, she pounced upon me, and I was soaped, and kneaded, and towelled, until I really was quite beside myself.

When my ablutions were completed, I was put into clean linen of the stiffest character, and trussed up in my tightest suit. I was then handed to Mr Pumblechook, who formally received me, and who delivered the speech that I knew he had been dying to make all along: "Boy, be for ever grateful to all friends, but especially unto them which brought you up by hand!"

"Good-bye, Joe!"

"God bless you, Pip, old chap!"

I had never parted from him before, and what with my feelings and the soap-suds, I could at first see no stars. But they twinkled out one by one, without throwing any light on why on earth I was going to play at Miss Havisham's, and what on earth I was expected to play at.

22

CHAPTER 8

Mr Pumblechook's premises in the High Street of the market town, was that of corn-chandler and seedsman.

I was sent straight to bed in an attic with a sloping roof, which was so low in the corner where the bedstead was, that I calculated the tiles as being within a foot of my eyebrows.

I breakfasted with Mr Pumblechook at eight o'clock in the parlour behind the shop. I considered Mr Pumblechook wretched company. He had my sister's idea that a mortifying and penitential character ought to be imparted to my diet – so he gave me as much crumb as possible in combination with as little butter, and put such a quantity of warm water into my milk that it would have been better to have left the milk out altogether. And his conversation consisted of nothing but arithmetic. On my politely bidding him Good morning, he began a running sum that lasted all through breakfast. "Seven?"

"And four?"

"And six?"

"And two?"

"And ten?"

And so on. Breakfast was eaten in this way. And after each figure was disposed of, it was as much as I could do to get a bite or a sup, before the next came; while he sat eating bacon and hot roll.

For such reasons I was very glad when ten o'clock came and we started for Miss Havisham's; though I was not at all at my ease regarding the manner in which I should acquit myself under that lady's roof.

Within a quarter of an hour we came to Miss Havisham's house, which was of old brick, and dismal, and had a great many iron bars to it. There was a courtyard in front, and that was barred; so, we had to wait, after ringing the bell, for someone to open it. While we waited, I peeped in, and saw that at the side of the house there was a large brewery. No brewing seemed to have taken place for a long time.

A window was raised, and a clear voice demanded, "What name?" To which my conductor replied, "Pumblechook." The voice returned, "Quite right," and a young lady came across the courtyard, with keys in her hand.

"This," said Mr Pumblechook, "is Pip."

"This is Pip, is it?" returned the young lady, who was very pretty and seemed very proud. "Come in, Pip."

She stopped Mr Pumblechook with the gate. "Did you wish to see Miss Havisham?"

"If Miss Havisham wished to see me," replied Mr Pumblechook, discomfited.

"Ah!" said the girl; "but you see she don't."

She said it so finally, that Mr Pumblechook, though ruffled, could not protest. But he eyed me severely – as if I had done anything to him! And departed with the words: "Boy! Let your behaviour here be a credit unto them which brought you up by hand!"

My young conductress locked the gate, and we went across the courtyard. It was paved and clean; but grass grew in every crevice. The brewery buildings stood open; and all was empty and disused.

She saw me looking at it, and she said, "Better not try to brew beer there now, or it would turn out sour, boy; don't you think so?"

"It looks like it, miss."

"Not that anybody means to try," she added, "for that's all done with. Anyway, there's enough in the cellars already, to drown the Manor House."

"Is that the name of this house, miss?"

"One of its names, boy. Its other name was Satis; which is Greek, or Latin, or Hebrew, or all three – for enough."

"Enough House," said I. "That's a curious name, miss."

"Yes," she replied; "but it meant that whoever had this house, could want nothing else. They must have been easily satisfied in those days, I should think. But don't loiter, boy."

Though she called me "boy" so often, in a way that was far from complimentary, she was of about my own age. She seemed much older than I, of course, being a girl, and beautiful and self-possessed; and she was scornful of me.

We went into the house by a side door – the great front entrance had two chains across it outside – and the first thing I noticed was, how dark it all was and that she had left a candle burning. She took it up, and we went through more dark passages and up a staircase.

At last we came to a door, and she said, "Go in."

I answered, more in shyness than politeness, "After you, miss."

24

To this, she returned: "Don't be ridiculous, boy; I am not going in." And scornfully, she walked away, taking the candle with her.

The only thing to do was knock at the door. I was told from within to enter. I entered, therefore, and found myself in a pretty large room, well lighted with wax candles. No glimpse of daylight was to be seen. It was a dressing room, as I supposed from the furniture. Prominent in it was a draped table with a gilded looking glass, and that I realised at first sight was a fine lady's dressing table.

In an armchair, with an elbow resting on the table and her head on that hand, sat the strangest lady I have ever seen.

She was dressed in rich materials – satins, and lace, and silks – all of white. Her shoes were white. And she had a long white veil, with bridal flowers in her hair, but her hair was white. Bright jewels sparkled on her, and some other lay sparkling on the table. Dresses, less splendid than the one she wore, and half-packed trunks, were scattered about. She had not quite finished dressing, for she had but one shoe on – the other was on the table near her hand – her veil was but half arranged, and some lace for her bosom lay with those trinkets, and with her handkerchief, and gloves, and some flowers, and a prayer-book, all confusedly heaped about the looking-glass.

While my eyes saw these items they also saw that everything that ought to be white, had been white long ago, and was now faded and yellow. I saw that the bride within the bridal dress had withered like the dress and like the flowers; and had no brightness left but the brightness of her sunken eyes. I saw that the dress had been put upon the rounded figure of a young woman, and that the figure upon which it now hung loose, had shrunk to skin and bone.

"Who is it?" said the lady at the table.

"Pip, ma'am."

"Pip?"

"Mr Pumblechook's boy, ma'am. Come to play."

"Come nearer; let me look at you."

It was when I stood before her, avoiding her eyes, that I saw that her watch had stopped at twenty minutes to nine, and that a clock in the room had stopped at twenty minutes to nine.

"Look at me," said Miss Havisham, her hands to her chest. "Do you know what I touch here?"

"Yes, ma'am."

"What do I touch?"

"Your heart."

"Broken!"

She uttered the word with strong emphasis, and with a weird smile that had a kind of boast in it. She kept her hands there for a moment, and slowly took them away as if they were heavy.

"I am tired," said Miss Havisham. "I want diversion, and I have done with men and women. Play."

I think my most argumentative reader would agree, that this was the hardest thing to do under the circumstances.

"I sometimes have sick fancies," she went on, "and I have a sick fancy that I want to see some play. There, there!" with an impatient movement of the fingers of her right hand. "Play, play, play!"

For a moment, I considered starting round the room looking like Mr Pumblechook's chaise-cart. But, I felt myself so unequal to the performance that I gave it up, and stood looking at Miss Havisham.

"Are you sullen and obstinate?"

"No, ma'am, I am very sorry for you, and very sorry I can't play just now. If you complain of me I shall get into trouble with my sister, so I would do it if I could; but it's so new here, and so strange, and so fine – and melancholy – " I stopped, fearing I might say too much, and we took another look at each other.

Before she spoke again, she turned and looked at the dress she wore.

"So new to him," she muttered, "so old to me; so strange to him, so familiar to me; so melancholy to both of us! Call Estella."

As she was still looking at her reflection, I thought she was still talking to herself, and kept quiet.

"Call Estella," she repeated, flashing a look at me. "You can do that. Call Estella. At the door."

To stand in the dark in an unknown house, bawling Estella to a scornful young lady neither visible nor responsive, was almost as bad as playing to order. But, she answered at last, and her light came along the dark passage like a star.

Miss Havisham beckoned her closer, took up a jewel from the table, and tried its effect upon her fair young bosom. "Your own, one day, my dear. Let me see you play cards with this boy."

26

"With this boy? Why, he is a common labouring-boy!"

I thought I overheard Miss Havisham answer – only it seemed so unlikely – "Well? You can break his heart."

"What do you play, boy?" asked Estella, with the greatest disdain.

"Nothing but beggar my neighbour, miss."

"Beggar him," said Miss Havisham to Estella. So we sat down to cards.

It was then I realised that everything in the room had stopped, like the watch and the clock, a long time ago. I noticed that Miss Havisham put the jewel back exactly where she had taken it up. As Estella dealt the cards, I glanced at the shoe upon the dressing table. Once white, now yellow, it had never been worn. I glanced down at the foot where the shoe should be, and saw that the silk stocking on it, once white, now yellow, had been trodden ragged.

So she sat, corpse-like, as we played at cards.

"He calls the knaves, Jacks, this boy!" said Estella with disdain, before our first game was out. "And what coarse hands he has! And what thick boots!"

I had never considered being ashamed of my hands before; but I now thought them a very indifferent pair. Her contempt for me was so strong, it was infectious, and I caught it.

She won the game, and I dealt. I misdealt, as was only natural, when I knew she was waiting for me to do wrong; and she denounced me for a stupid, clumsy labouring-boy.

"You say nothing of her," remarked Miss Havisham to me, as she looked on. "She says many hard things of you, but you say nothing. What do you think of her?"

"I don't like to say," I stammered.

"Tell me in my ear," said Miss Havisham, bending down.

"I think she is very proud," I whispered.

"Anything else?"

"I think she is very pretty. And she is very insulting." (She was looking at me then with a look of supreme aversion.)

"Anything else?"

"I think I should like to go home."

"And never see her again, though she is so pretty?"

"I am not sure that I shouldn't like to see her again, but I should like to go home now."

"You shall go soon," said Miss Havisham, aloud. "Play the game out."

Saving for the one weird smile at first, I was almost sure that Miss Havisham's face could not smile. It had dropped into a watchful and brooding expression and it looked as if nothing could ever lift it again. Her chest had dropped, so that she stooped; she had the appearance of having dropped, body and soul, within and without, under the weight of a crushing blow.

I played the game to an end with Estella, and she beggared me. She threw the cards down on the table when she had won them all, as if she despised them for having been won of me.

"When shall I have you here again?" said Miss Havisham. "Let me think. Come again after six days. You hear?"

"Yes, ma'am."

"Estella, take him down. Let him have something to eat, and let him roam and look about him while he eats. Go, Pip."

I followed the candle down, and she stood it where we had found it. Until she opened the side entrance, I had fancied, without thinking about it, that it must be night time. The bright daylight made me feel as if I had been in the candlelit room many hours.

"Wait here, boy," said Estella, disappearing and closing the door.

I took the opportunity to look at my coarse hands and my common boots. My opinion was not favourable. They had never troubled me before, but they troubled me now, as vulgar appendages. I would ask Joe why he had taught me to call those picture cards, Jacks, instead of knaves. I wished Joe had been more genteelly brought up, and then I should have been so too.

She came back, with some bread and meat and a little mug of beer. She put the mug down, and gave me the bread and meat without looking at me, as if I were in disgrace. I was so humiliated, hurt, spurned, offended, angry, sorry – I cannot find the right name for the feeling – that tears welled. The girl looked at me with a quick delight in having been their cause. This gave me power to keep them back and to look at her: so, she gave a contemptuous toss and left me.

But, when she was gone, I looked about me for a place to hide and got behind a gate in the brewery-lane, and leaning against the wall there, put my forehead on it and cried. As I cried, I kicked the wall, twisting at my hair; so bitter were my feelings.

My sister's bringing up had made me sensitive. I had known, from the time when I could speak, that my sister, in her capricious and violent coercion, was unjust to me. I had cherished a profound conviction that her bringing me up by hand, gave her no right to bring me up by jerks. Through all my punishments, disgraces, fasts and vigils, I had nursed this assurance.

I got rid of my injured feelings by kicking them into the brewery wall, and twisting them out of my hair, and then I smoothed my face with my sleeve, and came from behind the gate. The bread and meat were acceptable, and the beer was warming and tingling, and I was soon in spirits to look about me.

In a by-yard, there was a wilderness of empty casks, which had a certain sour remembrance of better days lingering about them.

Behind the furthest end of the brewery, was a rank garden with an old wall. I could struggle up and hold on long enough to look over it, and saw that the rank garden was the garden of the house, and that it was overgrown with tangled weeds. There was a track along the paths, as if some one sometimes walked there. Estella was walking away from me even then. But she seemed to be everywhere. For, when I first went into the brewery, and, rather oppressed by its gloom, stood near the door looking about me, I saw her pass among the extinguished fires, and ascend some light iron stairs, and go out by a gallery high overhead, as if going out into the sky.

It was in this place, and at this moment, that a strange thing happened. I thought it strange then, and I thought it a stranger thing long afterwards. I turned my eyes – a little dimmed by looking up at the frosty light – towards a great wooden beam in a low nook, and I saw a figure hanging there by the neck. A figure all in yellow white, with but one shoe to the feet; and it hung so, that I could see the faded trimmings of the dress, and that the face was Miss Havisham's. In the terror of seeing the figure, and in the terror of being certain that it had not been there a moment before, I at first ran from it, and then towards it. And my terror was greatest of all, when I found no figure there.

Nothing less than the frosty light of the cheerful sky, the sight of people passing beyond the bars of the courtyard gate, and the reviving influence of the rest of the bread and meat and beer, would have brought me round. Then I saw Estella approaching with the keys, to let me out. She would have some fair reason for looking down upon me, I thought, if she saw me frightened; and she should have no fair reason.

She gave me a triumphant glance, as if rejoicing that my hands were so coarse and my boots were so thick, and she opened the gate, and stood holding it. I was passing out without looking at her, when she touched me.

"Why don't you cry?"

"Because I don't want to."

"You do," said she. "You have been crying till you are half blind, and you are near crying again now."

She laughed contemptuously, pushed me out, and locked the gate upon me. I went straight to Mr Pumblechook's, and was immensely relieved to find him not at home. So, leaving word with the shopman on when I was wanted at Miss Havisham's again, I set off on the four-mile walk to our forge. I pondered on all I had seen – the fact that I was a common labouring-boy; that my hands were coarse and my boots were thick; that I had fallen into a despicable habit of calling knaves Jacks; and that I was much more ignorant than I had considered myself last night.

CHAPTER 9

When I reached home, my sister was very curious to know all about Miss Havisham's, and asked a number of questions. I found myself heavily bumped from behind, and having my face ignominiously shoved against the kitchen wall, because I did not answer those questions at sufficient length.

I felt convinced that if I described Miss Havisham's as my eyes had seen it, I should not be understood. And also that Miss Havisham too would not be understood. Although she was perfectly incomprehensible to me, I felt that there would be something coarse and treacherous in my dragging her as she really was (to say nothing of Miss Estella) before the contemplation of Mrs Joe. Consequently, I said as little as I could, and had my face shoved against the kitchen wall.

The worst of it was that that bullying old Pumblechook, greedily wishing to be informed of all I had seen and heard, came at tea-time, to have the details divulged to him. And the mere sight of him made me vicious in my reticence.

"Well, boy," Uncle Pumblechook began, as soon as he was seated in the chair of honour by the fire. "How did you get on up town?"

I answered, "Pretty well, sir," and my sister shook her fist at me.

"Pretty well?" Mr Pumblechook repeated. "Pretty well is no answer. Tell us what you mean, boy?"

I reflected for some time, and then answered as if I had discovered a new idea, "I mean pretty well."

My sister was about to fly at me – I had no defender, for Joe was busy in the forge. But Mr Pumblechook interposed: "No! Don't lose your temper. Leave this lad to me, ma'am."

"Boy! What like is Miss Havisham?" Mr Pumblechook began again, folding his arms tight on his chest and applying the screw.

"Very tall and dark," I told him.

"Is she, uncle?" asked my sister.

Mr Pumblechook winked assent; from which I instantly gathered that he had never seen Miss Havisham, for she was nothing of the kind.

"Good!" said Mr Pumblechook conceitedly. "Now, boy! What was she a-doing, when you went in today?"

"She was sitting," I answered, "in a black velvet coach."

Mr Pumblechook and Mrs Joe stared at one another and both repeated, "In a black velvet coach?"

"Yes," said I. "And Miss Estella – that's her niece, I think – handed her in cake and wine at the coach-window, on a gold plate. And we all had cake and wine on gold plates. And I got up behind the coach to eat mine, because she told me to."

"Was anybody else there?" asked Mr Pumblechook.

"Four dogs," said I.

"Large or small?"

"Immense," said I. "And they fought for veal cutlets out of a silver basket."

Mr Pumblechook and Mrs Joe stared at one another again, in utter amazement. I was frantic and would have told them anything.

"Where was this coach?" asked my sister.

"In Miss Havisham's room." They stared again. "But there weren't any horses to it." I added this saving clause, and rejected four richly caparisoned coursers.

31

"Can this be possible, uncle?" asked Mrs Joe. "What can he mean?"

"I'll tell you, Mum," said Mr Pumblechook. "My opinion is, it's a sedan-chair. She's flighty enough to pass her days in a sedan-chair."

"Did you ever see her in it, uncle?" asked Mrs Joe.

"How could I," he returned, forced to the admission, "when I never see her in my life? Never clapped eyes upon her!"

"Goodness, uncle! And yet you have spoken to her?"

"Why, don't you know," said Mr Pumblechook, testily, "that when I have been there, I have been on the outside of her door, and she has spoke to me from the inside. Howsoever, the boy went there to play. What did you play at, boy?"

"We played with flags," I said.

"Flags!" echoed my sister.

"Yes," said I. "Estella waved a blue flag, and I waved a red one, and Miss Havisham waved one sprinkled all over with little gold stars, out at the coach-window."

If they had asked me any more questions I should undoubtedly have betrayed myself. They were so much occupied, however, in discussing the marvels I had already presented for their consideration, that I escaped. The subject still held them when Joe came in to have a cup of tea. My sister related my pretended experiences to him.

Now, when I saw Joe open his blue eyes and roll them all round the kitchen in helpless amazement, I was overtaken by penitence; but only towards him. Only with Joe did I consider myself a young monster; while they sat debating what would happen as a result of Miss Havisham's acquaintance and favour. They were convinced that Miss Havisham would "do something" for me; but what form would that something take? My sister stood out for "property". Mr Pumblechook was in favour of a handsome premium for an apprenticeship to some genteel trade – say, the corn and seed trade, for instance. Joe fell into the deepest disgrace with both, for suggesting that I might only be presented with one of the dogs that had fought for the veal-cutlets. "If a fool's head can't express better opinions than that," said my sister, "and you have got work to do, you had better go and do it." So he went.

After Mr Pumblechook had driven off, I stole into the forge to Joe, and stayed until he had done for the night. Then I said, "Before the fire goes out, Joe, I should like to tell you something."

"Should you, Pip?" said Joe. "Then tell us. What is it, Pip?"

"Joe," said I, taking hold of his rolled-up shirt sleeve, and twisting it between my finger and thumb, "you remember all that about Miss Havisham's?"

"Remember?" said Joe. "I believe you! Wonderful!"

"It's a terrible thing, Joe; it ain't true."

"What are you telling of, Pip?" cried Joe, falling back in the greatest amazement. "You don't mean to say it's – "

"Yes I do; it's lies, Joe."

"But not all of it? Why, do you mean to say, that there was no black welwet coach?" For I stood shaking my head. "But at least there was dogs, Pip."

"No, Joe."

"A dog?" said Joe. "A puppy? Come?"

"No, Joe, there was nothing at all of the kind."

As I fixed my eyes hopelessly on Joe, Joe contemplated me in dismay. "Pip, old chap! This won't do, old fellow! I say! Where do you expect to go to?"

"It's terrible, Joe; an't it?"

"Terrible?" cried Joe. "What possessed you?"

"I don't know, Joe," I replied, letting his shirt sleeve go, hanging my head; "but I wish you hadn't taught me to call Knaves at cards, Jacks; and I wish my boots weren't so thick nor my hands so coarse."

And then I told Joe that I hadn't been able to explain myself to Mrs Joe and Pumblechook who were so rude to me, and that there had been a beautiful young lady at Miss Havisham's who was dreadfully proud, and that she had said I was common, and that I knew I was common, and that I wished I was not common, and that the lies had come of it somehow, though I didn't know how.

"There's one thing you may be sure of, Pip," said Joe, after some rumination, "namely, that lies is lies. Howsoever they come, they didn't ought to come. Don't you tell no more of 'em, Pip. That ain't the way to get out of being common, old chap. Anyway – you are oncommon in some things. You're oncommon small. Likewise you're a oncommon scholar."

"No, I am ignorant and backward, Joe. I have learnt next to nothing. You think much of me. It's only that."

"Well, Pip," said Joe, "be it so or be it son't, you must be a common scholar afore you can be a oncommon one, I should hope!"

There was some hope in this piece of wisdom, and it rather encouraged me.

"You are not angry with me, Joe?"

"No, old chap. But bearing in mind that they were of a stunning and outdacious sort – alluding to weal-cutlets and dog-fighting – a sincere well-wisher would adwise, Pip, their being dropped into your meditations, when you go upstairs to bed. That's all, old chap, and don't never do it no more."

When I got up to my little room and said my prayers, I did not forget Joe's recommendation, but my young mind was in that disturbed and unthankful state, that long after I laid me down, I thought how common Estella would consider Joe, a mere blacksmith: how thick his boots, and how coarse his hands. I thought how Joe and my sister were then sitting in the kitchen, and how I had come up to bed from the kitchen, and how Miss Havisham and Estella never sat in a kitchen.

It was a memorable day, for it made great changes in me. But, it is the same with any life. Imagine one selected day struck out of it, and think how different its course would have been.

CHAPTER 10

A morning or two later I woke with the idea, that the best step I could take towards making myself uncommon was to get out of Biddy everything she knew. To achieve this I mentioned to Biddy when I went to Mr Wopsle's great-aunt's, that I had a particular reason for wishing to get on in life, and that I should feel very much obliged to her if she would impart all her learning to me. Biddy, who was the most obliging girl, said she would, and indeed began within five minutes.

That very evening Biddy began by imparting some information from her little Catalogue of Prices, under the head of moist sugar, and lending me, to copy at home, a large old English D which she had copied from some newspaper, and which I supposed, until she told me what it was, to be a design for a buckle.

There was a public house in the village, and Joe liked sometimes to smoke his pipe there. I had received orders from my sister to call for him at the Three Jolly Bargemen, that evening, on my way from school, and bring him home at my peril. To the Three Jolly Bargemen, therefore, I directed my steps.

I wished the landlord good evening, and passed into the common room, where there was a large kitchen fire, and where Joe was smoking his pipe with Mr Wopsle and a stranger. Joe greeted me as usual with "Halloa, Pip, old chap!" and the moment he said that, the stranger turned and looked at me.

He was a secret-looking man whom I had never seen before. He took a pipe from his mouth, and, after slowly blowing all his smoke away and looking hard at me all the time, nodded. So, I nodded, and then he nodded again, and made room on the settle that I might sit down.

But, as I sat beside Joe whenever I entered that place, I said "No, thank you, sir," and fell into the space Joe made for me. The strange man, after glancing at Joe, and seeing that he was looking elsewhere, nodded to me again, and then rubbed his leg – in a very odd way, as it struck me.

"You was saying," said the strange man, turning to Joe, "that you was a blacksmith."

"Yes, and this other gentleman," observed Joe, by way of introducing Mr Wopsle, "is our clerk at church."

"Aha!" said the stranger, quickly, and cocking his eye at me. "The lonely church, right out on the marshes, with graves round it!"

"That's it," said Joe.

The stranger, with a comfortable kind of grunt, put his legs up on the settle. He wore a broad-brimmed traveller's hat. As he looked at the fire, I thought I saw a cunning expression, followed by a half-laugh, come into his face.

"I am not acquainted with this country, gentlemen, but it seems a solitary country towards the river."

"Most marshes is solitary," said Joe.

"No doubt, no doubt. Do you find any gipsies, now, or tramps, or vagrants of any sort, out there?"

"No," said Joe; "none but a runaway convict now and then. And we don't find them, easy. Eh, Mr Wopsle?"

Mr Wopsle assented; but not warmly.

"Seems you have been out after such?" asked the stranger.

"Once," returned Joe. "Not that we wanted to take them, you understand; we went out as lookers on; me, and Mr Wopsle, and Pip. Didn't us, Pip?"

"Yes, Joe."

The stranger looked at me again – still cocking his eye – and said, "He's a likely young parcel of bones that. What is it you call him?"

"Pip," said Joe.

"Christened Pip?"

"No."

"Surname Pip?"

"No," said Joe, "it's a kind of family name what he gave himself when a infant, and is called by."

"Son of yours?"

"Well," said Joe, meditatively, "well – no. No, he ain't."

"Nevvy?" said the strange man.

"Well," said Joe, "he – he is not – my nevvy."

"What the Blue Blazes is he?" asked the stranger. Which appeared to me to be an inquiry of unnecessary strength.

Mr Wopsle interposed here, expounding the ties between me and Joe.

All this while, the strange man looked at nobody but me. But he said nothing after offering his Blue Blazes observation, until three glasses of rum-and-water were brought; and then he made his shot, and a most extraordinary shot it was. It was not a verbal remark. Instead, he stirred his rum-and-water pointedly at me. But not with a spoon that was brought to him, but with a file.

He did this so that nobody but I saw the file; and when he had done it he wiped the file and put it in a breast pocket. I knew it was Joe's file, and I knew that he knew my convict, the moment I saw the instrument. I sat gazing at him, spell-bound. But he now took very little notice of me, and talked principally about turnips.

Joe always stayed out half an hour longer on Saturdays than at other times. The half hour and the rum-and-water running out together, Joe got up to go, and took me by the hand.

"Stop half a moment, Mr Gargery," said the strange man. "I think I've got a bright new shilling somewhere in my pocket, and if I have, the boy shall have it."

He looked it out from a handful of small change, folded it in some crumpled paper, and gave it to me. "Yours!" said he. "Mind! Your own."

I thanked him, staring at him, while holding tight to Joe. He gave Joe good-night, and he gave Mr Wopsle good-night (who went out with us), and he gave me only a look with his aiming eye.

On the way home, I was so stupefied by this turning up of my old misdeed and old acquaintance that I could think of nothing else.

My sister was not in a very bad temper when we arrived in the kitchen, and Joe was encouraged by that unusual circumstance to tell her about the bright shilling. "A bad un, I'll be bound," said Mrs Joe triumphantly, "or he wouldn't have given it to the boy! Let's look at it."

I took it out of the paper, and it proved to be a good one. "But what's this?" said Mrs Joe, throwing down the shilling and catching up the paper. "Two One-Pound notes?"

There they were – two fat sweltering one-pound notes that seemed to have travelled via all the cattle markets in the county. Joe caught up his hat again, and ran with them to the Jolly Bargemen to restore them to their owner. While he was gone, I sat down on my stool and looked vacantly at my sister, feeling pretty sure that the man would not be there.

Presently, Joe returned, saying that the man was gone, but that he, Joe, had left word at the Three Jolly Bargemen concerning the notes. Then my sister sealed them up in a piece of paper, and put them in an ornamental teapot in the state parlour. There they remained, a nightmare to me, many a day.

I had sadly broken sleep when I got to bed, through thinking of the strange man and of the guiltily coarse and common thing it was, to be on secret terms of conspiracy with convicts. I coaxed myself to sleep by thinking of Miss Havisham's, next Wednesday; and in my sleep I saw the file coming at me, without seeing who held it, and I screamed myself awake.

CHAPTER 11

At the appointed time I returned to Miss Havisham's, and my hesitating ring at the gate brought out Estella. She locked it after admitting me, as she had done before, and again led me through the house. She took no notice of me until she had the candle, when she looked over her shoulder, superciliously saying, "You are to come this way today," and took me to quite another part of the house.

The passage was a long one, seeming to stretch the length of the Manor House. At the end of it she stopped, and put her candle down and opened a door. Here, the daylight reappeared, and I found myself in a small courtyard, the opposite side of which was a detached dwelling house, that looked as if it had once belonged to the manager or head clerk of the extinct brewery.

We went into a gloomy room with a low ceiling. There was some company in the room, and Estella said to me as she joined it, "You are to stand there, boy, till you are wanted."

"There" being the window, I crossed to it, and stood "there", in a very uncomfortable state of mind, looking out.

It opened to the ground, and looked into a most miserable corner of the neglected garden, upon a rank ruin of cabbage-stalks.

I divined that my coming had stopped conversation in the room, and that its other occupants were looking at me. I could see nothing of the room except the shining fire in the window glass, but I stiffened in the knowledge that I was under close inspection.

There were three ladies and one gentleman. Before I had been standing there five minutes, they somehow conveyed to me that they were all toadies and humbugs, but that each of them pretended not to know that the others were toadies and humbugs: because the admission that he or she did know it, would have made him or her out to be a toady and a humbug.

They all had a listless air of waiting somebody's pleasure, and the most talkative lady had to speak quite rigidly to repress a yawn. This lady, Camilla, very much reminded me of my sister, except that she was older.

"Poor dear soul!" said this lady, with an abruptness of manner quite my sister's. "Nobody's enemy but his own!"

"It would be much more commendable to be somebody else's enemy," said the gentleman; "far more natural."

"Poor soul!" Camilla presently went on (I knew they had all been looking at me in the mean time), "he is so very strange! Would anyone believe that when Tom's wife died, he actually could not see the importance of the children's having the deepest of trimmings to their mourning? 'Good Lord!' says he, 'Camilla, the poor bereaved little things are in black?' So like Matthew! The idea!"

"Good points in him," said the man; "Heaven forbid I should deny good points in him; but he never will have any sense of the proprieties."

"You know, Raymond," said Camilla, "I was obliged to be firm. I said, 'It *will not do*, for the credit of the family.' I told him that the family was disgraced. I cried about it from breakfast till dinner. And at last he said, with a D, 'Then do as you like.' Thank Goodness it will always be a consolation to me to know that I instantly went out in a pouring rain and bought the things."

"He paid for them, did he not?" asked Estella.

"It's not the question, my dear child, who paid for them," returned Camilla. "I bought them. And I shall often think of that with peace, when I wake up in the night."

The ringing of a distant bell interrupted the conversation and Estella said to me, "Now, boy!" On my turning round, they all looked at me with the utmost contempt, and, as I went out, I heard one say, "Well I am sure! What next!" and Camilla add, with indignation, "Was there ever such a fancy! The i-de-a!"

Estella stopped all of a sudden with the candle, and, facing round, said in her taunting manner with her face quite close to mine: "Well?"

"Well, miss?" I answered, almost falling over.

She stood looking at me, and, of course, I stood looking at her.

"Am I pretty?"

"Yes; I think you are very pretty."

"Am I insulting?"

"Not so much as you were last time," said I.

"Not so much?"

She slapped my face with such force, when I answered her.

"Now?" said she. "You little coarse monster, what do you think of me now?"

39

"I shall not tell you."

"Because you are going to tell, upstairs. Is that it?"

"No," said I, "that's not it."

"Why don't you cry again, you little wretch?"

"Because I'll never cry for you again," said I. Which was a lie, for I was inwardly crying for her then.

We went on our way upstairs; and, as we were going up, we met a gentleman groping his way down.

"Whom have we here?" asked the gentleman, stopping and looking at me.

"A boy," said Estella.

He was a burly man of an exceedingly dark complexion, with an exceedingly large head and a correspondingly large hand. He turned up my face to have a look at me by the light of the candle. He was prematurely bald on the top of his head, and had bushy black eyebrows. His eyes were set very deep in his head, and were disagreeably sharp and suspicious. He had a large watch chain. He was nothing to me, and I could have had no foresight then, that he ever would be anything to me, but it happened that I had this opportunity of observing him well.

"Boy of the neighbourhood? Hey?" said he.

"Yes, sir," said I.

"How do you come here?"

"Miss Havisham sent for me, sir," I explained.

"Well! Behave yourself. I have a pretty large experience of boys, and you're a bad set of fellows. Now mind!" said he, biting the side of his great forefinger as he frowned at me, "you behave yourself!"

He then went his way downstairs. I wondered whether he could be a doctor; but no, I thought; he couldn't be a doctor, or he would have a quieter and more persuasive manner. There was not much time to consider the subject, for we were soon in Miss Havisham's room, where she and everything else were just as I had left them. Estella left me standing near the door, until Miss Havisham cast her eyes upon me from the dressing table.

"So!" she said, without being startled or surprised; "the days have worn away, have they?"

"Yes, ma'am. Today is – "

She gave an impatient movement of her fingers. "I don't want to know. Are you ready to play?"

I was obliged to answer in some confusion, "I don't think I am, ma'am."

"Not at cards again?" she demanded, with a searching look.

"Yes, ma'am; I could do that, if I was wanted."

"Since this house strikes you old and grave, boy," said Miss Havisham, impatiently, "and you are unwilling to play, are you willing to work?"

I could answer this inquiry with a better heart and I said I was quite willing.

"Then go into that opposite room," said she, pointing at the door behind me with her withered hand, "and wait there till I come."

I crossed the staircase landing, and entered the room she indicated. Again that room was dark, and it had an airless smell that was oppressive. A fire had been lately kindled in the damp old-fashioned grate and the reluctant smoke that hung in the room seemed colder than the clearer air. Certain wintry branches of candles on the high chimney-piece faintly lighted the chamber. It was spacious, and I dare say had once been handsome, but every discernible thing in it was covered with dust and mould. The most prominent object was a long table with a tablecloth spread on it, as if a feast had been in preparation when the house and the clocks all stopped together. A centrepiece of some kind was in the middle of this cloth; it was so heavily overhung with cobwebs that its form was quite undistinguishable; and, as I looked along the yellow expanse out of which I remember its seeming to grow, like a black fungus, I saw speckled-legged spiders with blotchy bodies running home to it, and running out from it.

I heard the mice too, rattling behind the panels, as if the same occurrence were important to their interests. But, the black beetles took no notice, and groped about them as if shortsighted and hard of hearing, and not on terms with one another.

These crawling things fascinated me and I watched them from a distance, when Miss Havisham laid a hand upon my shoulder. In her other hand she had a crutch-headed stick on which she leaned, and she looked like the Witch of the place.

"This," said she, pointing to the long table with her stick, "is where I will be laid when I am dead. They shall come and look at me here."

With some vague misgiving that she might get upon the table then and there and die at once, I shrank under her touch.

"What do you think that is?" she asked me, again pointing with her stick; "where those cobwebs are?"

41

"I can't guess, ma am."

"It's a great cake. A bride-cake. Mine!"

She looked all round the room in a glaring manner, and then said, leaning on my shoulder, "Come, come! Walk me, walk me!"

I gathered that the work I had to do, was to walk Miss Havisham round and round the room. Accordingly, I started at once, and she leaned upon my shoulder, and we went away.

She was not physically strong, and after a little time said, "Slower!" After a while she said, "Call Estella!" so I went out on the landing and roared that name as I had done on the previous occasion. When her light appeared, I returned to Miss Havisham, and we started away again round the room.

If just Estella had come to watch, I should have felt sufficiently discontented; but, as she brought with her the three ladies and the gentleman whom I had seen below, I didn't know what to do. In my politeness, I would have stopped; but, Miss Havisham twitched my shoulder, and we posted on – with a shame-faced consciousness on my part that they would think it was all my doing.

"Dear Miss Havisham," said Miss Sarah Pocket. "How well you look!"

"I do not," returned Miss Havisham. "I am yellow skin and bone."

Camilla brightened when Miss Pocket met with this rebuff; and she murmured, as she plaintively contemplated Miss Havisham, "Poor dear soul! Certainly not to be expected to look well, poor thing. The idea!"

"And how are you?" said Miss Havisham to Camilla. As we were close to Camilla then, I thought we would stop, but Miss Havisham wouldn't stop. We swept on, and I felt that I was highly obnoxious to Camilla.

"Thank you, Miss Havisham," she returned, "I am as well as can be expected."

"What's the matter with you?" asked Miss Havisham, sharply.

"Nothing worth mentioning," replied Camilla. "I don't wish to make a display of my feelings, but I have habitually thought of you more in the night than I am quite equal to."

"Then don't think of me," retorted Miss Havisham.

"Very easily said!" remarked Camilla, repressing a sob, while a hitch came into her upper lip, and her tears overflowed. "Raymond is a witness what ginger and sal volatile I am obliged to take in the night. Raymond is a witness what nervous jerkings I have in my legs. Chokings and nervous jerkings, however, are nothing new to me when I think with anxiety of those I love. To not thinking of you in the night – The idea!" Here, a burst of tears.

The Raymond referred to was the gentleman present, and him I understood to be Mr Camilla. He came to the rescue at this point, and said, "Camilla, my dear, it is well known that your family feelings are gradually undermining you."

"I am not aware," observed the grave lady whose voice I had heard but once, "that to think of any person is to make a great claim upon that person, my dear."

Miss Sarah Pocket, whom I now saw to be a little dry brown corrugated old woman, with a small face, supported this position by saying, "No, indeed, my dear. Hem!"

"Thinking is easy enough," said the grave lady.

"What is easier, you know?" assented Miss Sarah Pocket.

"Oh, yes, yes!" cried Camilla. "It's a weakness to be so affectionate, but I can't help it. No doubt my health would be much better if it was otherwise, still I wouldn't change my disposition if I could." Here another burst of feeling.

Miss Havisham and I had never stopped all this time, but kept going round and round the room: now, brushing against the skirts of the visitors: now, giving them the whole length of the dismal chamber.

"There's Matthew!" said Camilla. "Never mixing with any natural ties, never coming here to see how Miss Havisham is! I have taken to the sofa with my staylace cut, and have lain there hours, insensible, with my head over the side – for hours and hours, on account of Matthew's inexplicable conduct, and nobody has thanked me."

"Really I must say I should think not!" interposed the grave lady.

"You see, my dear," added Miss Sarah Pocket (a blandly vicious personage), "the question to ask yourself is, who did you expect to thank you, my love?"

"Without expecting any thanks, or anything of the sort," resumed Camilla, "I have remained in that state, hours and hours, and Raymond is a witness of the extent to which I have choked, and what the total inefficacy of ginger has been." Here Camilla put her hand to her throat.

When this same Matthew was mentioned, Miss Havisham stopped, and stood looking at the speaker.

43

"Matthew will come and see me at last," said Miss Havisham, sternly, "when I am laid on that table. That will be his place – there," striking the table with her stick, "at my head! And yours will be there! And your husband's there! And Sarah Pocket's there! And Georgiana's there! Now you all know where to take your stations when you come to feast upon me. And now go!"

At the mention of each name, she had struck the table with her stick. She now said, "Walk me, walk me!" and we went on again.

"I suppose there's nothing to be done," exclaimed Camilla, "but comply and depart. It's something to have seen the object of one's love and duty, for even so short a time. I shall think of it with a melancholy satisfaction when I wake up in the night. I wish Matthew could have that comfort, but he sets it at defiance. I will not make a display of my feelings, but it's very hard to be told one wants to feast on one's relations – as if one was a Giant – and to be told to go. The bare idea!"

Mr Camilla interposed, and Mrs Camilla kissed her hand to Miss Havisham, and was escorted forth. Sarah Pocket and Georgiana contended who should remain last; but, Sarah ambled round Georgiana so that the latter was obliged to take precedence. Sarah Pocket then made her departing with "Bless you, Miss Havisham dear!" and a smile of forgiving pity on her walnut-shell countenance for the weaknesses of the rest.

While Estella was away lighting them down, Miss Havisham still walked with her hand on my shoulder, but more slowly. At last she stopped before the fire, and said, after muttering and looking at it some seconds: "This is my birthday, Pip."

I was going to wish her many happy returns, when she lifted her stick.

"I don't suffer it to be spoken of. I don't suffer those who were here just now, or any one, to speak of it. They come here on the day, but they dare not refer to it."

Of course I made no further effort to refer to it.

"On this day of the year, long before you were born, this heap of decay," stabbing with her crutched stick at the pile of cobwebs on the table, "was brought here. We have worn away together. The mice have gnawed at it, and sharper teeth than teeth of mice have gnawed at me."

She held the head of her stick against her heart as she looked at the table; she in her once white dress; the once white tablecloth; everything around, ready to crumble at a touch.

"When the ruin is complete," said she, with a ghastly look, "and when they lay me dead, in my bride's dress on the bride's table – which shall be done, and which will be the finished curse upon him – so much the better if it is done on this day!"

She looked at the table as if she looked at her own figure lying there. I remained quiet. Estella returned, and she too remained quiet. We stayed thus for a long time. In the heavy air of the room, I even had an alarming fancy that Estella and I might presently begin to decay.

At length, coming out of her distraught state in an instant, Miss Havisham said, "Let me see you two play cards; why have you not begun?" With that, we returned to her room, and sat down as before; I was beggared, as before; and again, as before, Miss Havisham watched us all the time, directed my attention to Estella's beauty, and made me notice it the more by trying her jewels on Estella's breast and hair.

Estella, for her part, likewise treated me as before; except that she did not speak. After playing some half-dozen games, a day was appointed for my return, and I was taken down into the yard to be fed in the former dog-like manner. There, too, I was again left to wander about as I liked.

A gate stood open, and as I knew that Estella had let the visitors out – for, she had returned with the keys in her hand – I strolled into the garden and strolled all over it. It was quite a wilderness.

Having exhausted the garden, and a greenhouse with nothing in it, I found myself in the dismal corner upon which I had looked out of the window. I looked in at another window, and found myself, to my great surprise, exchanging a broad stare with a pale young gentleman with red eyelids and light hair.

This pale young gentleman quickly disappeared, and re-appeared beside me. He had been at his books and I now saw that he was inky.

"Halloa!" said he, "young fellow!"

I answered in the same vein: "Halloa!" politely omitting young fellow.

"Who let you in?" said he.

"Miss Estella."

"Who gave you leave to prowl about?"

"Miss Estella."

"Come and fight," said the pale young gentleman.

What could I do but follow him? I have often asked myself the question since: but, what else could I do? His manner was so final and I was so astonished, that I followed where he led.

"Stop a minute, though," he said, wheeling round. "I ought to give you a reason for fighting. There it is!" He slapped his hands together, daintily flung one of his legs up behind, pulled my hair, slapped his hands again, dipped his head, and butted into my stomach.

This bull-like proceeding, besides being somewhat of a liberty, was particularly disagreeable just after bread and meat. I therefore hit out at him and he said, "Aha! Would you?" and began dancing backwards and forwards in a manner quite unknown to me.

"Laws of the game!" said he, skipping from foot to foot. "Regular rules! Come to the ground, and go through the preliminaries!" Here, he dodged backwards and forwards, and did all sorts of things while I looked helplessly at him.

I was secretly afraid of him when I saw him so dextrous; but, I was convinced that his head had no business in the pit of my stomach. Therefore, I followed to a retired nook of the garden. He then begged my leave to absent himself for a moment, and quickly returned with a bottle of water and a sponge dipped in vinegar. "Available for both," he said, placing these against the wall. And then fell to pulling off his jacket and waistcoat, and his shirt too, in a manner at once light-hearted, businesslike, and bloodthirsty.

Although he did not look very healthy – having pimples on his face – these dreadful preparations quite appalled me. He was about my own age, but much taller. He was a young gentleman in a grey suit with his elbows, knees, wrists, and heels, considerably in advance of the rest of him as to development.

My heart failed me when I saw him squaring at me and eyeing my anatomy as if minutely choosing his bone. I never have been so surprised in my life, as I was when I let out the first blow, and saw him lying on his back, looking up at me with a bloody nose.

But, he was on his feet directly, and after sponging himself began squaring again. The second greatest surprise was seeing him on his back again, looking up at me out of a black eye.

His spirit inspired me with great respect. He seemed to have no strength, and he never once hit me hard, and he was always knocked down; but, he got up again in a moment, sponged himself, and then came

46

at me with an air that made me believe he really was going to do for me at last. He got heavily bruised, for I am sorry to record that the more I hit him, the harder I hit him; but, he came up again and again, until at last he had a bad fall with the back of his head against the wall. Even after that, he got up and turned round and round confusedly a few times, not knowing where I was; but finally went on his knees to his sponge and threw it up: at the same time panting out, "That means you have won."

He seemed so brave and innocent, that although I had not proposed the contest I felt only gloomy satisfaction in my victory. I got dressed, and I said, "Can I help you?" and he said "No thankee," and I said "Good afternoon," and he said "Same to you."

When I got into the courtyard, I found Estella waiting. But, she neither asked me where I had been, nor why I had kept her waiting; and there was a bright flush upon her face, as though something had happened to delight her. Instead of going straight to the gate, she beckoned me.

"Come here! You may kiss me, if you like."

I kissed her cheek as she turned it to me. I think I would have gone through a great deal to kiss her cheek. But, I felt that the kiss was worth nothing.

What with the birthday visitors, and the cards, and the fight, my stay had lasted so long, that when I neared home the light from Joe's furnace was flinging a path of fire across the road.

CHAPTER 12

I made many visits to Miss Havisham during the course of the next twelve months; and on the last occasion she announced that I had better be apprenticed to Joe. It was a trial to my feelings, to see him dressing in his Sunday clothes to accompany me to Miss Havisham's on my next visit. However, it was not for me to tell him that he looked far better in his working dress, because I knew he made himself so dreadfully uncomfortable, entirely on my account.

At breakfast time my sister declared her intention of going to town with us, and being left at Uncle Pumblechook's and called for "when we had done with our fine ladies". The forge was shut up for the day, and Joe inscribed in chalk upon the door (as was his custom on such very rare occasions) the monosyllable HOUT.

We walked to town, my sister leading the way in a very large beaver bonnet. When we came to Pumblechook's, my sister bounced in and left us. As it was almost noon, Joe and I held straight on to Miss Havisham's house. Estella opened the gate as usual.

She took no notice of either of us, but led the way that I knew so well. I followed, and Joe came last.

Estella told me we were both to go in, so I took Joe by the coat-cuff and conducted him into Miss Havisham's presence. She was seated at her dressing table, and looked round at us immediately.

"Oh!" said she to Joe. "You are the husband of the sister of this boy?"

I could hardly have imagined dear old Joe looking so unlike himself or so like some extraordinary bird; standing, as he did, speechless, with his mouth open, as if he wanted a worm.

"You are the husband," repeated Miss Havisham, "of his sister?"

"I hup and married your sister, and I were at the time what you might call a single man," Joe now observed. Throughout Joe persisted in addressing me instead of Miss Havisham.

"Well!" said Miss Havisham. "And you have reared the boy, intending to take him as your apprentice; is that so, Mr Gargery?"

It was quite in vain for me to endeavour to get him to speak to Miss Havisham. The more I made faces and gestures to him to do it, the more confidential, argumentative, and polite, he persisted in being to me.

"Have you brought his indentures with you?" asked Miss Havisham.

"Well, Pip, you know," replied Joe, "you yourself see me put 'em in my 'at." With which he took them out, and gave them, not to Miss Havisham, but to me. I am afraid I was ashamed of the dear good fellow when I saw that Estella was behind Miss Havisham's chair, and that her eyes laughed mischievously. I took the indentures and gave them to Miss Havisham.

"You expected," said Miss Havisham, as she looked them over, "no premium with the boy?"

"Joe!" I remonstrated; for he made no reply at all. "Why don't you answer – "

"Pip," returned Joe, cutting me short as if he were hurt; "that were not a question requiring a answer betwixt yourself and me, and which you

48

know the answer to be full well No. You know it to be No, Pip, and wherefore should I say it?"

Miss Havisham glanced at him as if she understood what he really was, better than I had thought possible, seeing what he was there; and took up a little bag from the table beside her.

"Pip has earned a premium here," she said. " There are five-and-twenty guineas in this bag. Give it to your master, Pip."

As if absolutely out of his mind with the wonder awakened in him, Joe, even at this pass, persisted in addressing me.

"This is wery liberal on your part, Pip," said Joe, "and it is as such received and grateful welcome, though never looked for. And now, old chap, may we do our duty! May you and me do our duty, both on us by one and another, and by them which your liberal present – have – conweyed to be – for the satisfaction of mind – of – them as never – " here Joe showed that he felt he had fallen into frightful difficulties, until he triumphantly rescued himself with the words, "and from myself far be it!" These words had such a convincing sound for him that he said them twice.

"Good-bye, Pip!" said Miss Havisham. "Let them out, Estella."

"Am I to come again, Miss Havisham?" I asked.

"No. Gargery is your master now. Gargery! One word!"

Thus calling him back as I went out of the door, I heard her say to Joe, in a distinct emphatic voice, "The boy has been a good boy here, and that is his reward. Of course, as an honest man, you will expect no other and no more."

How Joe got out of the room, I have never been able to determine; he was deaf to all words until I laid hold of him and led him out. In another minute we were outside the gate, and it was locked, and Estella was gone.

When we stood in the daylight alone again, Joe backed up against a wall, and said to me, "Astonishing!" And there he remained so long, saying "Astonishing" so often, that I began to think his senses were never coming back. But by degrees, he became conversational and was able to walk away.

I have reason to think that Joe's intellects were brightened by the encounter they had passed through, and that on our way to Pumblechook's he invented a subtle and deep design. My reason is to be found in what took place in Mr Pumblechook's parlour: where my sister sat with that detested seedsman.

"Well?" cried my sister, addressing us both at once. "And what's happened to you? I wonder you condescend to come back to such poor society as this, I am sure I do!"

"Miss Havisham," said Joe, staring at me, as if trying to remember, "made it wery partick'ler that we should give her – were it compliments or respects, Pip?"

"Compliments," I said.

"Which that were my own belief," answered Joe, "her compliments to Mrs J. Gargery – "

"Much good they'll do me!" observed my sister; but rather gratified too.

"And wishing," pursued Joe, with another look at me, "that the state of Miss Havisham's elth were sitch as would have – allowed, were it, Pip?"

"Of her having the pleasure," I added.

"Of ladies' company," said Joe. And drew a long breath.

"Well!" cried my sister, with a mollified glance at Mr Pumblechook. "She might have had the politeness to send that message at first, but it's better late than never. And what did she give young Rantipole here?"

"She giv' him," said Joe, "nothing."

Mrs Joe was going to break out, but Joe went on.

"What she giv'," said Joe, "she giv' to his friends. 'And by his friends,' were her explanation, 'I mean into the hands of his sister Mrs J. Gargery'. Them were her words; 'Mrs J. Gargery'. She mayn't have know'd," added Joe, with a look of reflection, "whether it were Joe, or Jorge."

My sister looked at Pumblechook: who nodded at her and at the fire, as if he had known all about it beforehand.

"And how much have you got?" asked my sister, laughing. Positively, laughing!

"What would present company say to ten pound?" demanded Joe.

"They'd say," returned my sister, curtly, "pretty well. Not too much, but pretty well."

"It's more than that, then," said Joe.

That fearful Impostor, Pumblechook, immediately nodded, and said, "It's more than that, Mum."

"Why, you don't mean to say– " began my sister.

"Yes I do, Mum," said Pumblechook; "but wait a bit. Go on, Joseph!"

"What would present company say," proceeded Joe, "to twenty pound?"

"Handsome would be the word," returned my sister.

"Well, then," said Joe, "It's more than twenty pound."

That abject hypocrite, Pumblechook, nodded again, and said, with a patronising laugh, "It's more than that, Mum!"

"Then to make an end of it," said Joe, delightedly handing the bag to my sister; "it's five-and-twenty pound."

"It's five-and-twenty pound, Mum," echoed that basest of swindlers, Pumblechook, rising to shake hands with her; "and it's no more than your merits (as I said when my opinion was asked), and I wish you joy of the money!"

If the villain had stopped here, his case would have been sufficiently awful, but he blackened his guilt by proceeding to take me into custody, with a right of patronage that left all his former criminality far behind.

"Now you see, Joseph and wife," said Pumblechook, as he took me by the arm above the elbow, "I am one of them that always go right through with what they've begun. This boy must be bound, out of hand. That's my way. Bound out of hand."

"Goodness knows, Uncle Pumblechook," said my sister (grasping the money), "we're deeply beholden to you."

"Never mind me, Mum," returned that diabolical corn-chandler. "A pleasure's a pleasure, all the world over. But this boy, you know; we must have him bound."

The Justices were sitting in the Town Hall, and we at once went over to have me bound apprentice to Joe in the Magisterial presence. I say, we went over, but I was pushed over by Pumblechook, as if I had that moment picked a pocket – indeed, it was the general impression in Court that I had been taken red-handed, for, as Pumblechook shoved me before him through the crowd, I heard some people say, "What's he done?" and others, "He's a young 'un, too, but looks bad, don't he?"

The Hall was a queer place, I thought, but here, in a corner, my indentures were duly signed and attested, and I was "bound"; Mr Pumblechook holding me all the while.

When we had come out again, we went back to Pumblechook's. And there my sister became so excited by the twenty-five guineas, that nothing would serve her but we must have a dinner out of that windfall, at the Blue Boar, and that Pumblechook must go over in his chaise-cart, and bring the Hubbles and Mr Wopsle.

The most melancholy day I passed. That swindling Pumblechook, exalted as the beneficent contriver of the whole occasion, actually took the top of the table.

My remembrances of the great festival are, that they wouldn't let me go to sleep, but whenever they saw me dropping off, woke me up and told me to enjoy myself. That they were all in excellent spirits on the road home, and sang O Lady Fair!

Finally, I remember that when I got into my little bedroom I was truly wretched, with the strongest conviction that I should never like Joe's trade. I had liked it once, but once was not now.

CHAPTER 13

It is a most miserable thing to feel ashamed of home.

Home had never been a very pleasant place to me, because of my sister's temper. But, Joe had sanctified it, and I had believed in it. I had believed in the best parlour as a most elegant saloon; I had believed in the front door, as a mysterious portal of the Temple of State whose solemn opening was attended with a sacrifice of roast fowls; I had believed in the kitchen as a chaste though not magnificent apartment; I had believed in the forge as the glowing road to manhood and independence. Within a single year, all this was changed. Now, it was all coarse and common, and I would not have had Miss Havisham and Estella see it on any account.

How much of my ungracious condition of mind may have been my own fault, how much Miss Havisham's, how much my sister's, is now of no moment to me or to any one. The change was made in me; the thing was done.

Once, it had seemed to me that when I should at last roll up my shirt-sleeves and go into the forge, as Joe's 'prentice, I should be distinguished and happy. Now came reality. There have been occasions in my later life (I suppose as in most lives) when I felt for a time as if a thick curtain had fallen on all that was interesting and romantic. Never has that curtain dropped so heavy and blank, as when my way in life lay stretched out straight before me through the newly entered road of apprenticeship to Joe.

I remember I was quite as dejected on the first working day of my apprenticeship as in that after-time; but I am glad to know that I never breathed a murmur to Joe while my indentures lasted. It is about the only thing I am glad to know of myself in that connection.

It was not because I was faithful, but because Joe was faithful, that I never ran away and went for a soldier or a sailor. It was not because I had a strong sense of the virtue of industry, but because Joe had a strong sense of the virtue of industry, that I worked with tolerable zeal against the grain.

What I wanted, who can say? How can I say, when I never knew? What I dreaded was, that in some unlucky hour I, being at my grimiest and commonest, should lift up my eyes and see Estella looking in at one of the wooden windows of the forge. I was haunted by the fear that she would, sooner or later, find me out, with a black face and hands, doing the coarsest part of my work, and would exult over me and despise me.

CHAPTER 14

As I was getting too big for Mr Wopsle's great-aunt's room, my education under that preposterous female terminated. Not, however, until Biddy had imparted to me everything she knew.

Whatever I acquired, I tried to impart to Joe. I wanted to make Joe less ignorant and common, that he might be worthier of my society and less open to Estella's reproach.

The old Battery out on the marshes was our place of study, and a broken slate and a short piece of slate pencil were our educational implements. I never knew Joe to remember anything from one Sunday to another, or to acquire, under my tuition, any piece of information whatever.

It was pleasant and quiet, out there with the sails on the river passing beyond the earthwork. Whenever I watched the vessels standing out to sea with their white sails spread, I somehow thought of Miss Havisham and Estella; and whenever the light struck upon a cloud or sail or green hill-side or water-line, it was just the same. Miss Havisham and Estella

53

and the strange house and the strange life appeared to have something to do with everything that was picturesque.

One Sunday when Joe, greatly enjoying his pipe, had so plumed himself on being "most awful dull", that I had given him up for the day, I lay on the earthwork with my chin on my hand, seeing traces of Miss Havisham and Estella all over the prospect, in the sky and in the water.

"Joe," said I at last; "don't you think I ought to make Miss Havisham a visit?"

"Well, Pip," returned Joe, slowly considering. "What for?"

"What is any visit made for?"

"There is some wisits, p'r'aps," said Joe, "as for ever remains open to the question, Pip. But in regard to wisiting Miss Havisham. She might think you wanted something – expected something of her."

"Don't you think I might say that I did not, Joe?"

"You might, old chap," said Joe. "And she might credit it. Similarly she mightn't."

Joe felt, as I did, that he had made a point there.

"You see, Pip," Joe pursued, "Miss Havisham done the handsome thing by you. And she called me back to say to me as that were all."

"Yes, Joe. I heard her."

"*All*," Joe repeated, very emphatically.

"Yes, Joe. I tell you, I heard her."

"Which I meantersay, Pip, it might be that her meaning were – Make a end on it! – As you was! – Me to the North, and you to the South!"

I had thought that too, and it was not comforting to find that Joe had thought of it. "But, Joe."

"Yes, old chap."

"Here am I, in the first year of my time, and, since the day of my being bound, I have never thanked Miss Havisham, or asked after her, or shown that I remember her. As we are rather slack just now, if you would give me a half-holiday tomorrow, I think I would go up-town and make a call on Miss Est-Havisham."

"Her name," said Joe, gravely, "ain't Estavisham, Pip, unless she have been rechris'ened."

"I know, Joe, I know. It was a slip of mine. What do you think, Joe?"

In brief, Joe thought that if I thought well of it, he thought well of it. But, he was particular in stipulating that if I were not received with cordiality, then this experimental trip should have no successor. By these conditions I promised to abide.

The next day I found myself at Miss Havisham's. I passed and repassed the gate many times before I could make up my mind to ring.

Miss Sarah Pocket came to the gate. No Estella.

"How, then? You here again?" said Miss Pocket. "What do you want?"

I said that I only came to see how Miss Havisham was. Sarah evidently deliberated whether or no she should send me about my business. But, unwilling to hazard the responsibility, she let me in, and presently brought the sharp message that I was to "come up."

Everything was unchanged, and Miss Havisham was alone.

"Well?" said she, fixing her eyes upon me. "I hope you want nothing? You'll get nothing."

"No, indeed, Miss Havisham. I only wanted you to know that I am doing very well in my apprenticeship, and am always much obliged to you."

"There, there!" with the old restless fingers. "Come now and then; come on your birthday. – Ay!" she cried suddenly, turning to me. "You are looking round for Estella? Hey?"

I had been looking round for Estella – and I stammered that I hoped she was well.

"Abroad," said Miss Havisham. "Educating for a lady; far out of reach; prettier than ever; admired by all who see her. Do you feel that you have lost her?"

There was such a malignant joy in the last words, and she broke into such a disagreeable laugh, that I was at a loss what to say. She spared me the trouble, by dismissing me. When the gate closed behind me, I felt even more dissatisfied with my home and with my trade and with everything.

As I loitered along the High Street, looking in at the shop windows, and thinking what I would buy if I were a gentleman, who should come out of the bookshop but Mr Wopsle. Our way back through the village took us past the Three Jolly Bargemen, which we were surprised to find – it being late – in a state of commotion. Mr Wopsle dropped in to ask what was the matter, but came running out in a great hurry.

"There's something wrong," said he, without stopping, "up at your place, Pip. Run all!"

"What is it?" I asked, keeping up with him.

"I can't quite understand. The house seems to have been violently entered when Joe Gargery was out. Somebody has been hurt."

We didn't stop until we reached our kitchen. It was full of people; the whole village was there, or in the yard; and there was a surgeon, and there was Joe, and there was a group of women, all on the floor in the midst of the kitchen. They drew back when they saw me, and so I saw my sister – lying unmoving on the bare boards where she had been knocked down by a tremendous blow on the back of the head, dealt by some unknown hand when her face was turned towards the fire – destined never to be on the Rampage again, while she was the wife of Joe.

CHAPTER 15

Joe had been at the Jolly Bargemen, smoking his pipe. While he was there, my sister had been seen standing at the kitchen door, and had exchanged Good Night with a farm-labourer going home just before nine. When Joe went home at five minutes before ten, he found her struck down on the floor, and promptly called in assistance. The fire had not then burnt unusually low, nor was the snuff of the candle very long; the candle, however, had been blown out.

Nothing had been taken. And there was no disarrangement of the kitchen, excepting such as she herself had made, in falling and bleeding. But, there was one remarkable piece of evidence. She had been struck with something blunt and heavy, a filed leg iron; after the blows were dealt, it had been thrown down at her with considerable violence, as she lay on her face.

Now, Joe, examining this iron with a smith's eye, declared it to have been filed some time ago. People came from the Hulks to examine the iron, and Joe's opinion was corroborated.

Knowing what I knew, I believed the iron to be my convict's iron, but I could not accuse him of having put it to its latest use. For, I believed one of two other persons had used it so cruelly. Either Orlick, Joe's journeyman, or the strange man who had shown me the file.

56

Orlick had no liking for me. When I was very small, he told me that the Devil lived in a black corner of the forge, and that once in seven years, a live boy was needed for his fire, and that I might consider myself fuel. When I became Joe's 'prentice, Orlick probably assumed that I should displace him; so he liked me still less. Not that he ever said anything, or did anything, openly importing hostility; I only noticed that he always beat his sparks in my direction.

Orlick had been seen about town all evening, in divers companies in several public houses. There was nothing against him, save a recent quarrel with my sister. And she had quarrelled with him, and with everybody else about her, ten thousand times. As to the strange man; if he had come back for his two bank notes there was no dispute, because my sister was fully prepared to restore them. Besides, the assailant had come in so silently and suddenly, that she had been felled before she could look round.

It was horrible to think that I had provided the weapon, however unknowingly, but I could hardly think otherwise. I suffered unspeakable trouble while I considered and reconsidered whether I should at last tell Joe the story. For months afterwards, I every day settled the question finally in the negative, and reopened and reargued it next morning. The argument boiled down to this – the secret was old now, and had become a part of myself. In addition to the dread that, it would be now more likely than ever to alienate Joe from me if he believed it, I had a further restraining dread that he would not believe it, but would assort it with the fabulous dogs as a monstrous invention. However, I resolved to make a full disclosure if I should see any such new occasion as a new chance of helping in the discovery of the assailant.

The Constables, and the Bow Street men from London, were about the house for a week or two, and did pretty much what I have heard and read of like authorities doing in other such cases. They took up several obviously wrong people, and persisted in trying to fit the circumstances to their ideas. Also, they stood about the door of the Jolly Bargemen, with such knowing looks that filled the whole neighbourhood with admiration. But they never found the culprit.

My sister lay very ill in bed for a long time. Her sight was disturbed; her hearing was greatly impaired; her memory also and her speech was unintelligible. When, at last, she came round so far as to be helped downstairs, she kept my slate always by her, that she might indicate in writing what she could not indicate in speech. As she was a more than indifferent speller, and as Joe was a more than indifferent reader, extraordinary complications arose between them. The administration of mutton instead of medicine, the substitution of Tea for Joe, and the baker for bacon, were among the mildest of my own mistakes.

However, her temper was greatly improved, and she was patient. We were at a loss to find a suitable attendant for her, until Mr Wopsle's great-aunt conquered a confirmed habit of living, and Biddy became a part of our establishment.

It may have been about a month after my sister's reappearance in the kitchen, when Biddy came to us and became a blessing to the household. Above all, she was a blessing to Joe as she instantly took the cleverest charge of my sister as though she had studied her from infancy. Joe became able in some sort to appreciate the greater quiet of his life, and to get down to the Jolly Bargemen now and then for a change that did him good.

Biddy's first triumph in her new office was to solve a difficulty that had completely vanquished me. I had tried hard to solve it, but had made nothing of it. Thus it was:

Again and again, my sister had traced upon the slate, a character looking like a curious T, and then with utmost eagerness called our attention to it as something she particularly wanted. I had in vain tried everything that began with a T, from tar to toast and tub. At length realising that it looked like a hammer, and calling that word in my sister's ear, she had begun to hammer on the table, expressing a qualified assent. So I had brought in all our hammers, to no avail. Then I thought of a crutch, the shape being much the same, and I borrowed one in the village. We displayed it to my sister with considerable confidence. But she shook her head.

When my sister found that Biddy was very quick to understand her, this mysterious sign reappeared on the slate. Biddy looked thoughtfully at it, heard my explanation, looked thoughtfully at my sister and Joe (who was always represented on the slate by his initial letter), and ran into the forge, followed by Joe and me.

"Why, of course!" cried Biddy, with an exultant face. "Don't you see? It's him!"

Orlick, without a doubt! She had lost his name, and could only signify him by his hammer. We told him why we wanted him to come into the kitchen, and he slowly laid down his hammer, wiped his brow with his apron, and came slouching out.

I confess that I expected to see my sister denounce him, and that I was disappointed by the different result. She wanted to be on good terms with him, was pleased by his being finally produced, and motioned that she would have him given something to drink. After that day, a day rarely passed without her drawing the hammer on her slate, and without Orlick's slouching in and standing doggedly before her, as if he knew no more than I did what to make of it.

CHAPTER 16

I now fell into a regular routine of apprenticeship life, which was varied, beyond the limits of the village and the marshes, by no more remarkable circumstance than the arrival of my birthday and my paying another visit to Miss Havisham. I found Miss Sarah Pocket still on duty at the gate, I found Miss Havisham just as I had left her, and she spoke of Estella in the very same way, if not in the very same words. The interview lasted but a few minutes, and she gave me a guinea, and told me to come again on my next birthday. This became an annual custom. I tried to decline taking the guinea on the first occasion, but with no better effect than causing her to ask me very angrily, if I expected more? Then, and after that, I took it.

So unchanging was the dull old house, the yellow light in the darkened room, the faded spectre in the chair by the dressing-table glass, that I felt as if the stopping of the clocks had stopped Time in that mysterious place, and, while I and everything else outside it grew older, it stood still. Daylight never entered the house. It bewildered me, and under its influence I continued at heart to hate my trade and to be ashamed of home.

I gradually became conscious of a change in Biddy, however. Her shoes came up at the heel, her hair grew bright and neat, her hands were always clean. She was not beautiful – she was common, and could not be like Estella – but she was pleasant and wholesome and sweet-tempered. She had not been with us more than a year when I noticed one evening that she had curiously thoughtful and attentive eyes; eyes that were pretty and good.

I laid down my pen, and Biddy stopped in her needlework without laying it down.

"Biddy," said I, "how do you manage it? Either I am very stupid, or you are very clever."

"What is it that I manage?" returned Biddy, smiling.

She managed our whole domestic life, and wonderfully too; but I did not mean that.

"How do you manage, Biddy," said I, "to learn everything that I learn, and always to keep up with me?"

"I might as well ask you," said Biddy, "how you manage?"

"I come in from the forge of a night, any one can see me turning to at it. But you never turn to at it, Biddy."

"I suppose I must catch it – like a cough," said Biddy, quietly; and went on with her sewing.

Pursuing my idea, I called to mind now, that she was equally accomplished in the terms of our trade, and the names of our different sorts of work, and our various tools. In short, whatever I knew, Biddy knew. Theoretically, she was already as good a blacksmith as I, or better.

"You are one of those, Biddy," said I, "who make the most of every chance. You never had a chance before you came here, and see how improved you are!"

Biddy looked at me for an instant, and went on with her sewing. "I was your first teacher though; wasn't I?" said she, as she sewed.

"Biddy!" I exclaimed, in amazement. "Why, you are crying!"

"No I am not," said Biddy, looking up and laughing. "What put that in your head?"

What could have put it in my head, but the glistening of a tear as it dropped on her work? I recalled the hopeless circumstances of the miserable little shop and the miserable little noisy evening school, with that miserable great-aunt of Mr Wopsle always to be dragged and shouldered. Biddy sat quietly sewing, shedding no more tears, and it occurred to me that perhaps I had not been sufficiently grateful to Biddy.

"Yes, Biddy," I observed, when I had done turning it over; "you were my first teacher, when we little thought of ever being together like this, in this kitchen."

"Ah, poor thing!" replied Biddy. It was like her self-forgetfulness, to transfer the remark to my sister, "that's sadly true!"

"Well!" said I, "we must talk together a little more, as we used to do. And I must consult you a little more, as I used to do. Let us have a quiet walk on the marshes next Sunday, Biddy, and a long chat."

My sister was never left alone now; but Joe said he would care for her that Sunday afternoon, and Biddy and I went out together. It was summertime, and lovely weather. When we had passed the village and the church and the churchyard, and were out on the marshes and began to see the sails of the ships as they sailed on, I began to combine Miss Havisham and Estella with the prospect, in my usual way. When we came to the riverside I resolved that it was a good time and place tell Biddy my true thoughts.

"Biddy," said I, after binding her to secrecy, "I want to be a gentleman."

"Oh, I wouldn't, if I was you!" she returned. "I don't think it would answer."

"Biddy," said I, with some severity, "I have particular reasons for wanting to be a gentleman."

"You know best, Pip; but don't you think you are happier as you are?"

"Biddy," I exclaimed, impatiently, "I am not at all happy as I am. I am disgusted with my calling and with my life. I have never taken to either, since I was bound. Don't be absurd."

"Was I absurd?" said Biddy, quietly raising her eyebrows; "I didn't mean to be. I only want you to do well, and to be comfortable."

"Well then, understand that I never shall or can be comfortable – or anything but miserable – there, Biddy! – Unless I can lead a very different sort of life from the life I lead now."

"That's a pity!" said Biddy, shaking her head with a sorrowful air.

I told her she was right, and I knew it was much to be regretted, but still it was not to be helped.

"If I could have settled down," I said to Biddy, plucking up the short grass, "and been but half as fond of the forge as I was when I was little, I know it would have been better for me. You and I and Joe would have wanted nothing then, and Joe and I would perhaps have gone partners when I was out of my time, and I might even have grown up to keep company with you, and we might have sat on this very bank on a fine

61

Sunday, quite different people. I should have been good enough for you; shouldn't I, Biddy?"

Biddy sighed as she looked at the ships sailing on, and answered, "Yes; I am not over-particular." It scarcely sounded flattering, but I knew she meant well.

"Instead of that," said I, plucking up more grass, "I am dissatisfied, and uncomfortable, and – what would it signify to me, being coarse and common, if nobody had told me so!"

Biddy turned her face suddenly towards mine.

"It was neither a very true nor a very polite thing to say," she remarked. "Who said it?"

I answered, "The beautiful young lady at Miss Havisham's, and she's more beautiful than anybody ever was, and I admire her dreadfully, and I want to be a gentleman on her account." Having made this lunatic confession, I began to throw my torn-up grass into the river.

"Do you want to be a gentleman, to spite her or to gain her over?" Biddy quietly asked me, after a pause.

"I don't know," I moodily answered.

"Because, if it is to spite her," Biddy pursued, "I should think – but you know best – that might be better and more independently done by caring nothing for her words. And if it is to gain her, I should think – but you know best – she was not worth gaining."

Exactly what I myself had thought, many times. But how could I, a poor dazed village lad, avoid that wonderful inconsistency into which the best and wisest of men fall every day?

"It may be all quite true," said I to Biddy, "but I admire her dreadfully."

Biddy was the wisest of girls, and she tried to reason no more with me. She put her hand, which was a comfortable hand though roughened by work, and patted my shoulder in a soothing way, while with my face upon my sleeve I cried a little – exactly as I had done in the brewery yard – and felt vaguely convinced that I was very much ill-used by somebody, or by everybody; I can't say which.

"I am glad of one thing," said Biddy, "that you have felt you could give me your confidence, Pip. And I am glad of another thing, and that is, that of course you know you may depend upon my keeping it and always so far deserving it." So, with a quiet sigh, Biddy rose from the bank, and said, with a fresh and pleasant change of voice, "Shall we walk a little further, or go home?"

"Biddy," I cried, getting up, putting my arm round her neck, and giving her a kiss, "I shall always tell you everything."

"Till you're a gentleman," said Biddy.

"You know I never shall be, so that's always."

"Ah!" said Biddy, quite in a whisper, as she looked away at the ships. And then repeated, with her former pleasant change; "shall we walk a little further, or go home?"

I said to Biddy we would walk a little further, and we did so, and the summer afternoon toned down into a beautiful summer evening. I wondered whether I was not more naturally situated, after all, to these circumstances, than playing beggar my neighbour by candlelight in the room with the stopped clocks, and being despised by Estella. I thought it would do me good if I could get her out of my head, with all the rest of those remembrances and fancies, and could go to work determined to make the best of it. The thing was I knew that if Estella were beside me at that moment instead of Biddy, she would make me miserable.

We talked a good deal, and all that Biddy said seemed right. Biddy was never insulting, or capricious, or Biddy today and somebody else tomorrow. How could it be, then, that I did not like her much the better of the two?

"Biddy," said I, when we were walking homeward, "I wish you could put me right."

"I wish I could!" said Biddy.

"If I could only get myself to fall in love with you – you don't mind my speaking so openly to such an old acquaintance?"

"Oh dear, not at all!" said Biddy. "Don't mind me."

"If I could, that would be the thing for me."

"But you never will, you see," said Biddy.

In my heart I believed her to be right; and yet I took it rather ill, too, that she should be so positive on the point.

Now, my mind was confused fifty thousand-fold, by having times when I was clear that Biddy was immeasurably better than Estella, and that the plain honest working life to which I was born, had nothing in it to be ashamed of. At those times, I would decide that my disaffection to dear old Joe was gone, and that I was growing up in a fair way to be

63

partners with Joe and to keep company with Biddy – when suddenly some confounding remembrance of the Havisham days would fall upon me, like a destructive missile, and scatter my wits again. Scattered wits take a long time picking up; and often, they would be dispersed in all directions by one stray thought, that perhaps Miss Havisham was going to make my fortune when my time was out.

If my time had run out, it would have left me still at the height of my perplexities, I dare say. It never did run out, however, but was brought to a premature end.

CHAPTER 17

It was in the fourth year of my apprenticeship to Joe, and it was a Saturday night. There was a group assembled round the fire at the Three Jolly Bargemen, attentive to Mr Wopsle as he read the newspaper aloud. I was there.

A highly popular murder had been committed, and Mr Wopsle was imbrued in blood to the eyebrows. He gloated over every abhorrent adjective in the description. He gave the medical testimony, in pointed imitation of our local practitioner. He enjoyed himself thoroughly, and we all enjoyed ourselves, and were delightfully comfortable. In this cosy state of mind we came to the verdict Wilful Murder.

Then I became aware of a strange gentleman leaning over the back of the settle opposite me, looking on. The gentleman, with an air of authority not to be disputed, and with a manner expressive of knowing something secret about every one of us that would effectually do for each individual if he chose to disclose it, left his seat, and came into the space between the two settles, where he stood, his left hand in his pocket, and biting the forefinger of his right.

"From information I have received," said he, looking round at us, "I have reason to believe there is a blacksmith among you, by name Joseph – or Joe – Gargery. Which is the man?"

"Here is the man," said Joe.

The strange gentleman beckoned him out of his place, and Joe went.

"You have an apprentice," pursued the stranger, "commonly known as Pip? Is he here?"

"I am here!" I cried.

The stranger did not know me, but I recognised him as the gentleman I had met on the stairs on my second visit to Miss Havisham. I had known him the moment I saw him looking over the settle. I remembered his large head, dark complexion, deep-set eyes, bushy black eyebrows, strong black dots of beard and whisker, and even the smell of scented soap on his great hand.

"I wish to have a private conference with you two," said he. "Perhaps we could go to your home. You can tell your friends afterwards if you wish; I have nothing to do with that."

We three then walked out of the Jolly Bargemen, and in a wondering silence walked home. While going along, the strange gentleman occasionally looked at me, and occasionally bit the side of his finger. As we neared home, Joe went on ahead to open the front door. Our conference was held in the state parlour.

The strange gentleman sat down at the table, drawing the candle to him, and looking over some entries in his pocket-book.

"My name," he said, "is Jaggers, and I am a lawyer in London. I am pretty well known. I have unusual business to transact with you, and I commence by explaining that it is not of my originating. If my advice had been asked, I should not have been here. It was not asked, and you see me here. I am the confidential agent of another."

"Now, Joseph Gargery, I am the bearer of an offer to relieve you of this young fellow your apprentice. You would not object to cancel his indentures, at his request and for his good? You would want nothing for so doing?"

"Lord forbid that I should want anything for not standing in Pip's way," said Joe, staring.

"The question is, would you want anything? Do you want anything?" returned Mr Jaggers.

"The answer is," returned Joe, sternly, "No."

I thought Mr Jaggers glanced at Joe, as if he considered him a fool for his disinterestedness. But I was too bewildered to be sure.

"Very well," said Mr Jaggers. "Now, I return to this young fellow. The communication I have to make is, that he has great expectations."

Joe and I gasped, and looked at one another.

"I am instructed to communicate to him," said Mr Jaggers, throwing his finger at me sideways, "that he will come into a handsome property. Further, that it is the desire of the present possessor of that property, that he be immediately removed from his present sphere of life and from this place, and be brought up as a gentleman – in a word, as a young fellow of great expectations."

My dream was out; my wild fancy surpassed by sober reality; Miss Havisham was going to make my fortune on a grand scale.

"Now, Mr Pip," pursued the lawyer, "I address the rest of what I have to say, to you. It is the request of the person from whom I take my instructions, that you always bear the name of Pip. You will have no objection, to your great expectations being encumbered with that easy condition. But if you have any objection, this is the time to mention it."

My heart beat so fast, that I could scarcely stammer I had no objection.

"I should think not! Now you are to understand, secondly, Mr Pip, that the name of your liberal benefactor remains a profound secret, until the person chooses to reveal it. It is the intention of the person to reveal it at first hand by word of mouth to yourself. When or where that may be carried out, I cannot say; no one can say. It may be years hence. Now, you must understand that you are most positively prohibited from making any inquiry. If you have a suspicion, keep that suspicion to yourself. The condition is laid down. Your acceptance and your observance of it are binding. That person is the person from whom you derive your expectations, and the secret is solely held by that person and by me."

Once more, I stammered that I had no objection.

"I should think not! Now, Mr Pip, I have done with stipulations. We come next, to mere details of arrangement. You must know that, although I have used the term "expectations" more than once, you are not endowed with expectations only. There is already lodged in my hands, a sum of money sufficient for your suitable education and maintenance. You will please consider me your guardian. I am paid for my services, or I shouldn't render them. You are to be better educated, in accordance with your altered position, and you will be alive to the importance and necessity of at once entering on that advantage."

I said I had always longed for it.

"Never mind what you have always longed for, Mr Pip," he retorted;

"Are you ready to be placed at once, under some proper tutor?"

I stammered yes.

"Good. Now, your inclinations are to be consulted. I don't think that wise, mind, but it's my trust. Have you ever heard of any tutor whom you would prefer to another?"

I shook my head. I knew none but Biddy.

"There is a certain tutor, of whom I have some knowledge, who I think may be suitable," said Mr Jaggers. "I don't recommend him, because I never recommend anybody. The gentleman I speak of is one Mr Matthew Pocket."

Ah! I caught at the name directly. Miss Havisham's relation. The Matthew whom Mr and Mrs Camilla had spoken of. The Matthew whose place was to be at Miss Havisham's head, when she lay dead, in her bride's dress on the bride's table.

"You know the name?" said Mr Jaggers, looking shrewdly at me, and then shutting up his eyes while he waited for my answer.

My answer was, that I had heard of the name.

"Oh!" said he. "You have heard of the name. But the question is, what do you say of it?"

I tried to say, that I was much obliged to him for his recommen-dation –

"No, my young friend!" he interrupted, shaking his great head. "Recollect yourself! It's very well done, but it won't do; you are too young to fix me with it. Recommendation is not the word, Mr Pip. Try another."

Correcting myself, I said that I was much obliged to him for his mention of Mr Matthew Pocket –

"That's more like it!" cried Mr Jaggers.

And (I added), I would gladly try that gentleman.

"Good. You had better try him in his own house. The way shall be prepared. You can see his son first, who is in London. When will you come to London?"

I said (glancing at the silent Joe), that I supposed I could come directly.

"First," said Mr Jaggers, "you should have some new clothes to come in, not working clothes. Say this day week. I shall leave you twenty guineas."

He counted them out on the table and pushed them over to me. He eyed Joe.

67

"Well, Joseph Gargery? You look dumbfounded?"

"I am!" said Joe, in a very decided manner.

"It was understood that you wanted nothing for yourself, remember?"

"It were understood," said Joe.

"But what," said Mr Jaggers, swinging his purse, "if it was in my instructions to make you a present, as compensation?"

"As compensation what for?" Joe demanded.

"For the loss of his services."

Joe laid his hand gently upon my shoulder. I have often thought him since, like the steam-hammer that can crush a man or pat an eggshell, in his combination of strength with gentleness. "Pip is that hearty welcome," said Joe, "to go free with his services, to honour and fortun', as no words can tell him. But if you think as money can make compensation to me for the loss of the little child – what come to the forge – and ever the best of friends! – "

O dear good Joe, whom I was so ready to leave and so unthankful to, I see you again, with your muscular blacksmith's arm before your eyes, and your broad chest heaving, and your voice dying away.

But I encouraged Joe at the time. I was lost in the mazes of my future fortunes, and could not retrace the by-paths we had trodden together. I begged Joe to be comforted, for (as he said) we had ever been the best of friends, and (as I said) we ever would be so. Joe said not another word.

"Well, Mr Pip, the sooner you leave – as you are to be a gentleman – the better. Let it stand for this day week, and you shall receive my printed address in the meantime. You can take a hackney-coach at the stagecoach office in London, and come straight to me. Understand, that I express no opinion, one way or other, on the trust I undertake. I am paid for undertaking it, and I do so. Now, understand that, finally. Understand that!"

Something came into my head, and I ran after him, as he was going down to the Jolly Bargemen where he had left a hired carriage.

"I beg your pardon, Mr Jaggers."

"Halloa!" said he, facing round, "what's the matter?"

"I wish to keep to your directions, Mr Jaggers, so I thought I had better ask. Would there be any objection to my taking leave of any one I know, about here, before I go away?"

"No," said he, looking as if he hardly understood me.

"Not in the village, but up-town?"

"No," said he. "No objection."

I thanked him and ran home again, and there I found that Joe had already locked the front door and was seated by the kitchen fire with a hand on each knee, gazing intently at the burning coals. I too sat down and nothing was said for a long time.

My sister was in her cushioned chair in her corner, and Biddy sat at her needlework before the fire.

At length I got out, "Joe, have you told Biddy?"

"No, Pip," returned Joe, still looking at the fire, and holding his knees, "I left it to yourself, Pip."

"I would rather you told, Joe."

"Pip's a gentleman of fortun' then," said Joe, "and God bless him in it!"

Biddy dropped her work, and looked at me. Joe held his knees and looked at me. I looked at both of them. After a pause, they both heartily congratulated me; but there was a certain touch of sadness in their congratulations that I rather resented.

I took it upon myself to impress Biddy (and through Biddy, Joe), to know nothing and say nothing about the maker of my fortune. It would all come out in good time, I observed, and in the meanwhile nothing was to be said, save that I had come into great expectations from a mysterious patron. Biddy nodded thoughtfully as she took up her work again, and said she would be very particular; and Joe, still detaining his knees, said, "Ay, ay, I'll be ekervally partickler, Pip;" and then they congratulated me again.

Infinite pains were then taken by Biddy to convey to my sister some idea of what had happened. To the best of my belief, those efforts entirely failed. She laughed and nodded her head a great many times, and even repeated after Biddy, the words "Pip" and "Property." But I doubt if they had more meaning in them than an election cry.

I never could have believed it, but as Joe and Biddy became more at their cheerful ease again, I became quite gloomy. Dissatisfied with my fortune, I could not be; but it is possible that I may have been, without quite knowing it, dissatisfied with myself.

Anyhow, I sat with my elbow on my knee and my face upon my hand, looking into the fire, as those two talked about my going away, and about what they should do without me, and all that. And whenever I caught one of them looking at me, though never so pleasantly (and they often looked at me – particularly Biddy), I felt offended: as if they were expressing some mistrust of me. Though Heaven knows they never did by word or sign.

"Saturday night," said I, when we sat at our supper of bread-and-cheese and beer. "Five more days, and then the day before the day! They'll soon go."

"Yes, Pip," observed Joe, whose voice sounded hollow in his beer mug. "They'll soon go."

"Soon, soon go," said Biddy.

"I have been thinking, Joe, that when I go down town on Monday, and order my new clothes, I shall tell the tailor that I'll try them on there, or have them sent to Mr Pumblechook's. It would be very disagreeable to be stared at by all the people here."

"Mr and Mrs Hubble might like to see you in your new genteel figure too, Pip," said Joe, industriously cutting his bread. "So might Wopsle. And the Jolly Bargemen might take it as a compliment."

"That's just what I don't want, Joe. They would make such a coarse and common business – that I couldn't bear myself."

"Ah, that indeed, Pip!" said Joe. "If you couldn't a-bear yourself – "

Biddy asked me here, as she sat holding my sister's plate, "Have you thought about when you'll show yourself to Mr Gargery, and your sister, and me? You will show yourself to us; won't you?"

"Biddy," I returned with some resentment, "you are so quick that it's difficult to keep up with you. If you had waited another moment, Biddy, you would have heard me say that I shall bring my clothes here in a bundle – most likely the evening before I leave."

Biddy said no more. Handsomely forgiving her, I soon exchanged an affectionate good-night with her and Joe, and went up to bed. When I got into my little room, I sat down and took a long look at it, as a mean little room that I should soon be parted from and raised above, forever.

The sun had been shining brightly all day on the roof of my attic, and the room was warm. As I opened the window and looked out, I saw Joe come slowly out at the dark door below, and take a turn or two in the air; and then Biddy came, and brought him his pipe. He never smoked so late, and it seemed that he wanted comforting, for some reason or other.

He presently stood at the door immediately beneath me, smoking his pipe, and Biddy stood there too, quietly talking to him, and I heard my name mentioned in an endearing tone by both of them more than once. I would not have listened for more, if I could have heard more: so, I drew away from the window, feeling it very sorrowful and strange that this first night of my bright fortunes should be the loneliest I had ever known.

Looking towards the open window, I saw light wreaths from Joe's pipe floating there, and I fancied it a blessing from Joe – pervading the air we shared together. I put my light out, and crept into bed; and it was an uneasy bed now, and I never slept the old sound sleep in it any more.

CHAPTER 18

Morning made a considerable difference in my general prospect of Life, and brightened it so much that it scarcely seemed the same. My worst fear in the intervening days was that something might happen to London, and that, when I got there, it would be either greatly deteriorated or clean gone.

Joe and Biddy were very sympathetic and pleasant when I spoke of our approaching separation; but only referred to it when I did. After breakfast, Joe brought out my indentures and we put them in the fire, and I felt free. With all the novelty of my emancipation on me, I went to church with Joe.

After an early dinner I strolled out alone, aiming to get done with the marshes. If I had thought before of my companionship with the fugitive, how the place now recalled the wretch, ragged and shivering, with his felon iron! My comfort was, that it happened a long time ago, and that he had doubtless been transported a long way off, and was dead to me, and might even be truly dead.

No more low wet grounds, no more dykes and sluices, no more of these grazing cattle – farewell, monotonous acquaintances of my childhood, henceforth I was for London and greatness! I made my exultant way to the old Battery, and, lying down there to consider whether Miss Havisham intended me for Estella, fell asleep.

When I awoke, I was much surprised to find Joe sitting beside me, smoking his pipe. He greeted me with a cheerful smile, and said: "As being the last time, Pip, I thought I'd foller."

"And Joe, I am very glad you did so. You may be sure, dear Joe, that I shall never forget you."

"No, no, Pip!" said Joe, in a comfortable tone, "I'm sure of that. Ay, ay, old chap! Bless you, it took a bit of time to get it well round, the change come so uncommon plump; didn't it?"

Somehow, I was not best pleased with Joe's being so mightily secure of me. I should have liked him to have betrayed emotion, or to have said, "It does you credit, Pip," or something of that sort. Therefore, I merely said that the tidings had indeed come suddenly, but that I had always wanted to be a gentleman.

"Have you though?" said Joe. "Astonishing!"

"It's a pity now, Joe," said I, "that you did not get on a little more, when we had our lessons here; isn't it?"

"Well, I don't know," returned Joe. "I'm so awful dull. I'm only master of my own trade. It were always a pity but it's no more of a pity now, than it was – this day twelvemonth?"

What I had meant was, that when I came into my property and was able to do something for Joe, it would have been much more agreeable if he had been better qualified for a rise in station. He was so perfectly innocent of my meaning, however, that I thought I would mention it to Biddy instead.

I therefore took Biddy into our little garden by the side of the lane, and, after saying that I should never forget her, said I had a favour to ask of her.

"And it is, Biddy," said I, "that you will miss no opportunity of helping Joe on, a little."

"How helping him on?" asked Biddy, steadily.

"Well! Joe is a dear good fellow – in fact, I think he is the dearest fellow that ever lived – but he is rather backward in some things. For instance, Biddy, in his learning and his manners."

I was looking at Biddy as I spoke, and although she opened her eyes very wide, she did not look at me.

"Oh, his manners! Won't his manners do, then?" asked Biddy, plucking a blackcurrant leaf.

"My dear Biddy, they do very well here – but if I were to remove Joe into a higher sphere, as I hope to do when I fully come into my property, they would hardly do him justice."

"And don't you think he knows that?" asked Biddy.

It was such a very provoking question (for it had never in the most distant manner occurred to me), that I said, snappishly, "What do you mean?"

Biddy, having rubbed the leaf to pieces between her hands, said, "Have you never considered that he may be proud?"

"Proud?" I repeated, with disdainful emphasis.

"Oh! There are many kinds of pride," said Biddy, looking full at me and shaking her head; "pride is not all of one kind – "

"Well? Why do you stop?" said I.

"Not all of one kind," resumed Biddy. "He may be too proud to let any one take him from a place that he is competent to fill, and fills well and with respect. To tell you the truth, I think he is."

"Now, Biddy," said I, "I am very sorry to see this in you. You are envious, Biddy. You are dissatisfied on account of my rise in fortune, and can't help showing it."

"If you have the heart to think so," returned Biddy, "say so."

"If you have the heart to be so, you mean, Biddy," said I, in a superior tone; "don't put it off upon me. I am very sorry to see it. I did intend to ask you to use any little opportunities you might have, of improving dear Joe. But after this, I ask nothing. It's a – it's a bad side of human nature."

"Whether you scold or approve of me," returned poor Biddy, "you may depend I shall always try to do all that lies in my power, here. And whatever opinion you take away of me, shall not alter how I remember you. Yet a gentleman should not be unjust neither," said Biddy, turning away her head.

I again repeated that it was a bad side of human nature and walked down the little path away from Biddy. Biddy went into the house, and I took a dejected stroll until supper-time; again feeling it very sorrowful that this, the second night of my bright fortunes, should be as lonely and unsatisfactory as the first.

But, morning once more brightened my view, and I extended my clemency to Biddy, and we dropped the subject. Putting on the best clothes I had, I went into town as early as I could hope to find the shops open, and presented myself before Mr Trabb, the tailor. I arranged for the new clothes to be delivered to Mr Pumblechook's.

Then I went to the hatter's, and the bootmaker's, and the hosier's. I also went to the coach-office and took my place for seven o'clock on Saturday

73

morning. It was not always necessary to explain that I had come into a handsome property; but whenever I said anything to that effect, the officiating tradesman ceased to have his attention diverted through the window by the High Street, and concentrated his mind upon me.

I had scant luggage to take with me to London, for little of what I possessed was adapted to my new station. But, I began packing that same afternoon, and wildly packed up things that I knew I should want next morning, in a fiction that there was not a moment to be lost.

So, Tuesday, Wednesday, and Thursday, passed; and on Friday morning I went to Mr Pumblechook's, to put on my new clothes and pay my visit to Miss Havisham. Mr Pumblechook's own room was given up to me to dress in. My clothes were rather a disappointment, of course. But after I had had my new suit on, some half an hour, and had postured before Mr Pumblechook's very limited dressing-glass, trying to see my legs, it seemed to fit me better. It being market morning at a neighbouring town some ten miles off, Mr Pumblechook was not at home. I had not told him exactly when I meant to leave, and was not likely to shake hands with him again before departing.

I went circuitously to Miss Havisham's by all the back ways, and rang at the bell. Sarah Pocket came to the gate, and positively reeled back when she saw me so changed.

"You?" said she. "Good gracious! What do you want?"

"I am going to London, Miss Pocket," said I, "and want to say good-bye to Miss Havisham."

I was not expected, for she left me locked in the yard, while she went to ask if I were to be admitted. After a very short delay, she returned and took me up, staring at me all the way.

Miss Havisham was taking exercise in the room with the long spread table, leaning on her crutch stick. The room was lighted as of yore, and at the sound of our entrance, she stopped and turned. She was then just abreast of the rotted bride-cake.

"Don't go, Sarah," she said. "Well, Pip?"

"I start for London, Miss Havisham, tomorrow," I was exceedingly careful what I said, "and I thought you would kindly not mind my taking leave of you."

"This is a gay figure, Pip," said she, making her crutch stick play round me.

"I have come into such good fortune since I saw you last, Miss Havisham," I murmured. "And I am so grateful for it!"

"Ay, ay!" said she, looking at the discomfited and envious Sarah, with delight. "I have seen Mr Jaggers. I have heard about it, Pip. So you go tomorrow? And you are adopted by a rich person?"

"Yes, Miss Havisham."

"Not named?"

"No, Miss Havisham."

"And Mr Jaggers is made your guardian?"

"Yes, Miss Havisham."

She delighted in Sarah Pocket's jealous dismay. "Well!" she went on, "you have a promising career before you. Be good – deserve it – and abide by Mr Jaggers's instructions." She looked at me, then at Sarah, and gave a cruel smile. "Good-bye, Pip! You will always keep the name of Pip, you know."

"Yes, Miss Havisham."

"Good-bye, Pip!"

She stretched out her hand, and I went down on my knee and put it to my lips. I had not considered how I should take leave of her; it came naturally to me at the moment, to do this. She looked at Sarah Pocket with triumph in her weird eyes, and so I left my fairy godmother, both her hands on her stick, standing in the midst of the dimly lighted room beside the rotten bride-cake hidden in cobwebs.

Sarah Pocket conducted me down, as if I were a ghost who must be seen out. She could not get over my appearance. I said, "Good-bye, Miss Pocket;" but she merely stared. Clear of the house, I returned to Pumblechook's, took off my new clothes, made them into a bundle, and went back home in my older dress, feeling – to speak the truth – much more at my ease.

And now, those six days had gone, and tomorrow looked me in the face. As the six evenings had dwindled away, to five, to four, to three, to two, I had become more and more appreciative of the society of Joe and Biddy. On this last evening, I dressed in my new clothes, for their delight, and sat in my splendour until bedtime. We had a hot supper on the occasion, graced by the inevitable roast fowl, and we had some flip to finish with. We were all very low, and none the higher for pretending to be in spirits.

I was to leave our village at five in the morning, carrying my little hand-portmanteau, and I had told Joe that I wished to walk away alone. I am afraid that this purpose originated in my sense of the contrast between myself and Joe, if we went to the coach together. I had pretended with myself that this was not the reason; but when I went up to my little room on this last night, I felt compelled to admit that it might be so. I wanted to go down and entreat Joe to walk with me in the morning. I did not.

All night there were coaches in my broken sleep, going to wrong places instead of to London, and having in the traces, now dogs, now cats, now pigs, now men – never horses.

Biddy was astir so early to get my breakfast, that I smelt the smoke of the kitchen fire when I started up thinking that it must be late. But long after that, I remained up there, repeatedly locking and unlocking my small portmanteau, until Biddy called to me that I was late.

I got up from the breakfast, saying, as if it had only just occurred to me, "Well! I suppose I must be off!" and then I kissed my sister who was laughing and nodding in her usual chair, and kissed Biddy, and threw my arms around Joe's neck. Then I took up my little portmanteau and walked out. The last I saw of them was dear old Joe waving his strong right arm above his head, crying huskily "Hooroar!" and Biddy putting her apron to her face.

I walked away at a good pace, thinking it was easier to go than I had supposed it would be. The village was very quiet.

When I was on the coach, and it was clear of the town, I deliberated whether I would not get down when we changed horses and walk back, to have another evening at home, and a better parting. We changed, and I had not made up my mind, when we changed again. It was now too late and too far to go back, and I went on.

THIS IS THE END OF THE FIRST STAGE OF PIP'S
EXPECTATIONS.

CHAPTER 19

The journey from our town to the metropolis was a journey of about five hours. It was a little past mid-day when we arrived at the Cross Keys, Wood Street, Cheapside, London.

I was scared by the immensity of London, and I did feel that it was rather ugly, crooked, narrow, and dirty.

Mr Jaggers had duly sent me his address; it was Little Britain, and he had written after it on his card, "just out of Smithfield, and close by the coach-office". A hackney-coachman took me to a gloomy street, leaving me at certain offices with an open door, whereon was painted *Mr Jaggers*.

I went into the front office with my little portmanteau in my hand and asked, Was Mr Jaggers at home?

"He is not," returned the clerk. "He is in Court at present. Am I addressing Mr Pip?"

I nodded.

"Mr Jaggers left word would you wait in his room? He couldn't say how long he might be, having a case on. But he won't be longer than he can help."

With those words, the clerk ushered me into an inner chamber at the back. Mr Jaggers's room was lighted by a skylight only, and was most dismal. There were not so many papers about, as I should have expected to see; and there were some odd objects about that I should not have expected to see – such as an old rusty pistol, a sword in a scabbard, several strange-looking boxes and packages, and two dreadful casts on a shelf, of faces peculiarly swollen, and twitchy about the nose. Mr Jaggers's own high-backed chair was of deadly black horse-hair, with rows of brass nails round it, like a coffin; and I fancied I could see how he leaned back in it, and bit his forefinger at the clients.

I sat down in the cliental chair opposite Mr Jaggers's chair, and became fascinated by the dismal atmosphere of the place. I wondered how many other clerks there were upstairs. I wondered about the history of all the odd litter about the room, and how it came there. I wondered whether the two swollen faces were of Mr Jaggers's family, and why he stuck them on that dusty perch, instead of giving them a place at home. Of course I had no experience of a London summer day, and my spirits may have been

77

oppressed by the hot exhausted air, and by the dust and grit that lay thick on everything. But I sat waiting in Mr Jaggers's close room, until I really could not bear the heat any more, and got up and went out.

When I told the clerk that I would take a turn in the air, he advised me to go round the corner and into Smithfield. So, I came into Smithfield; and the shameful place, being all a-smear with filth and fat and blood and foam, seemed to stick to me. So, I turned into a street where I saw the great black dome of Saint Paul's bulging at me from behind a grim stone building that a bystander said was Newgate Prison.

I dropped back into the office to ask if Mr Jaggers had come in yet, and I found he had not, and I strolled out again. This time, I made the tour of Little Britain. After a while my guardian appeared and he took me into his own room, and while he lunched, informed me of arrangements he had made for me. I was to go to "Barnard's Inn," to young Mr Pocket's rooms, where a bed had been sent in for my accommodation; I was to remain with young Mr Pocket until Monday, when I was to go with him to his father's house on a visit, that I might try how I liked it. Also, I was told what my allowance was to be – it was a very liberal one – and had handed to me from one of my guardian's drawers, the cards of certain tradesmen with whom I was to deal for all kinds of clothes, and such other things I could reasonably want. "You will find your credit good, Mr Pip," said my guardian, "but I shall by this means be able to check your bills, and to pull you up if I find you outrunning the constable. Of course you'll go wrong somehow, but that's no fault of mine."

After I had pondered a little over this encouraging sentiment, I asked Mr Jaggers if I could send for a coach? He said it was not worthwhile, I was so near my destination; Wemmick should walk round with me, if I pleased.

I found that Wemmick was the clerk in the next room. Another clerk was rung down from upstairs to take his place while he was out, and I accompanied him into the street, after shaking hands with my guardian.

CHAPTER 20

Casting my eyes on Mr Wemmick as we went along, to see what he was like in the light of day, I found him to be a dry man, rather short, with a square wooden face, whose expression seemed to have been imperfectly chipped out with a dull-edged chisel. I judged him to be a bachelor from the frayed condition of his linen, and he appeared to have sustained a good many bereavements; for he wore at least four mourning rings, besides a brooch representing a lady and a weeping willow at a tomb with an urn on it. He had glittering eyes – small, keen, and black – and thin wide mottled lips. He had had them, to the best of my belief, from forty to fifty years.

"So you were never in London before?" said Mr Wemmick.

"No," said I.

"I was new here once," said Mr Wemmick. "Rum to think it now!"

"You are well acquainted with it now?"

"Why, yes," said Mr Wemmick. "I know the moves of it."

"Is it a very wicked place?" I asked, more for the sake of speaking than for information.

"You may get cheated, robbed, and murdered, in London. But there are plenty of people anywhere, who'll do that for you."

"If there is bad blood between you and them," said I, to soften it off a little.

"Oh! I don't know about bad blood," returned Mr Wemmick. "They'll do it, if there's anything to be got by it."

"That makes it worse."

"You think so?" returned Mr Wemmick. "Much about the same, I should say."

He wore his hat on the back of his head, and looked straight before him.

"Do you know where Mr Matthew Pocket lives?" I asked Mr Wemmick.

"Yes," said he, nodding in the direction. "At Hammersmith, west of London."

"Is that far?"

"Well! Say five miles."

"Do you know him?"

"Why, you're a regular cross-examiner!" said Mr Wemmick, looking at me with an approving air. "Yes, I know him."

Moments later he said here we were at Barnard's Inn. I had supposed that establishment to be an hotel kept by Mr Barnard. But I now found Barnard to be a disembodied spirit, or a fiction, and his inn the dingiest collection of shabby buildings ever squeezed together.

We entered this haven through a wicket-gate, and entered a melancholy little square that looked to me like a flat burying-ground. I thought it had the most dismal trees in it, and the most dismal houses (in number half a dozen or so), that I had ever seen. I thought the windows of the sets of chambers into which those houses were divided, were in every stage of dilapidated blind and curtain, crippled flower-pot, cracked glass, dusty decay, and miserable makeshift; while To Let To Let To Let, glared at me from empty rooms.

I looked in dismay at Mr Wemmick. He led me into a corner and conducted me up a flight of stairs to a set of chambers on the top floor. *Mr Pocket, Jun.* was painted on the door, and there was a label on the letterbox, "Return shortly."

"He hardly thought you'd come so soon," Mr Wemmick explained. "You don't want me any more?"

"No, thank you," said I.

"As I keep the cash," Mr Wemmick observed, "we shall most likely meet pretty often. Good-day."

"Good-day."

I put out my hand, and Mr Wemmick at first looked at it as though I wanted something. Then he said, correcting himself, "To be sure! Yes. You're in the habit of shaking hands?"

I was rather confused, but said yes.

"I have got so out of it!" said Mr Wemmick. "Very glad, I'm sure, to make your acquaintance. Good-day!"

When we had shaken hands and he was gone, I opened the staircase window and had nearly beheaded myself, for the lines had rotted away, and it came down like the guillotine. Happily it was so quick that I had not put my head out. I was then content to take a foggy view of the Inn through the window's encrusting dirt, saying to myself that London was decidedly overrated.

Mr Pocket, Junior's, idea of Shortly was not mine, for I had nearly maddened myself with looking out for half an hour, before I heard footsteps on the stairs. Gradually there arose before me the hat, head, neckcloth, waistcoat, trousers, boots, of a member of society of about my own standing. He had a paper-bag under each arm and a pottle of strawberries in one hand, and was out of breath.

"Mr Pip?" said he.

"Mr Pocket?" said I.

"Dear me!" he exclaimed. "I am extremely sorry; but I knew there was a coach from your part of the country at midday, and I thought you would come by that one. The fact is, I have been out on your account – for I thought you might like a little fruit after dinner, and I went to Covent Garden Market to get it good."

For a reason that I had, I felt as if my eyes would start out of my head. I acknowledged his attention incoherently, and began to think this was a dream.

"Dear me!" said Mr Pocket, Junior. "This door sticks so!"

I begged him to allow me to hold the paper-bags of fruit while he wrestled with the door. He relinquished them with an agreeable smile. The door yielded so suddenly at last, that he staggered back upon me, and we both laughed. But still I felt as if this must be a dream.

"Pray come in," said Mr Pocket, Junior. "Allow me to lead the way. I am rather bare here, but I hope you'll be able to make out tolerably well till Monday. My father thought you would get on more agreeably through tomorrow with me than with him, and might like to take a walk about London. I shall be very happy to show London to you. As to our table, it will be supplied from our coffee house here, and (it is only right I should add) at your expense, such being Mr Jaggers's directions. The lodgings are by no means splendid, because I have my own bread to earn, and my father hasn't anything to give me, and I shouldn't be willing to take it, if he had.

"This is our sitting room – just such furniture and carpet as they could spare from home. This is my little bedroom; rather musty, but Barnard's is musty. This is your bedroom; the furniture's hired for the occasion, but I trust it will answer the purpose. The chambers are retired, and we shall be alone together, but we shan't fight, I dare say. But, dear me, I beg your pardon, you're still holding the fruit. Pray let me take these bags from you."

As I faced Mr Pocket, Junior, giving him the bags, One, Two, I saw the same amazed look in his eyes that I knew to be in mine, and he said, falling back: "Lord bless me, you're the prowling boy!"

"And you," said I, "are the pale young gentleman!"

CHAPTER 21

The pale young gentleman and I stood contemplating one another and then we both burst out laughing. "The idea of its being you!" said he.

"The idea of its being you!" said I. And then we contemplated one another afresh, and laughed again.

"Well!" said the pale young gentleman, reaching out his hand good-humouredly, "it's all over now, and I hope you'll forgive me for having knocked you about so."

I derived from this speech that Mr Herbert Pocket (for Herbert was his name) still rather muddled his intention with his execution. But I made a modest reply, and we shook hands warmly.

"You hadn't come into your good fortune at that time?" said Herbert Pocket.

"No," said I.

"No," he acquiesced. "I heard it had happened very lately. I was rather on the look-out for good-fortune then."

"Indeed?"

"Yes. Miss Havisham had sent for me, to see if she could take a fancy to me. But she couldn't – at all events, she didn't."

I thought it polite to remark that I was surprised to hear that.

"Bad taste," said Herbert, laughing, "but a fact. Yes, she sent for me on a trial visit, and if I had been successful, I suppose I should have been provided for; perhaps I should have been what-you-may-called it to Estella."

"What's that?" I asked, with sudden gravity.

He was arranging his fruit in plates while we talked, dividing his attention. "Affianced," he explained, still busy with the fruit. "Betrothed. Engaged. What's-his-named. Any word of that sort."

"How did you bear your disappointment?" I asked.

"Pooh!" said he, "I didn't care much for it. She's a Tartar."

"Miss Havisham?"

"I don't say no to that, but I meant Estella. That girl's hard and haughty and capricious to the last degree, and has been brought up by Miss Havisham to wreak revenge on all the male sex."

"What relation is she to Miss Havisham?"

"None," said he. "Only adopted."

"Why should she wreak revenge on all the male sex?"

"Lord, Mr Pip!" said he. "Don't you know?"

"No," said I.

"Dear me! It's quite a story, and shall be saved till dinner-time. Mr Jaggers is your guardian, I understand?" he went on.

"Yes."

"You know he is Miss Havisham's man of business and solicitor, and has her confidence when nobody else has?"

This was bringing me (I felt) towards dangerous ground. I answered with a constraint I made no attempt to disguise, that I had seen Mr Jaggers in Miss Havisham's house on the very day of our combat, but never at any other time, and that I believed he had no recollection of having ever seen me there.

"He was so obliging as to suggest my father for your tutor, and he called on my father to propose it. Of course he knew about my father from his connexion with Miss Havisham. My father is Miss Havisham's cousin; not that that implies familiar intercourse between them, for he is a bad courtier."

Herbert Pocket had a frank and easy way with him that was very taking. I had never seen any one then, and I have never seen any one since, who more strongly expressed to me, in every look and tone, a natural incapacity to do anything secret and mean. There was something wonderfully hopeful about his general air, and something that at the same time whispered to me he would never be very successful or rich. I don't know how this was. I became imbued with the notion on that first occasion before we sat down to dinner, but I cannot define by what means.

He was still a pale young gentleman. He had not a handsome face, but it was better than handsome: being extremely amiable and cheerful.

His figure was a little ungainly, as in the days when my knuckles had taken such liberties with it, but it looked as if it would always be light and young.

As he was so communicative, I felt that reserve on my part would be a bad return. I therefore told him my small story, laying stress on my being forbidden to inquire who my benefactor was. I further mentioned that as I had been brought up a blacksmith in a country place, and knew very little of the ways of politeness, I would take it as a great kindness in him if he would give me a hint whenever he saw me at a loss or going wrong.

"With pleasure," said he, "though I predict that you'll want very few hints. I dare say we shall be often together, and I should like to banish any needless restraint between us. Will you do me the favour to call me by my Christian name, Herbert?"

I thanked him, and said I would and told him that my Christian name was Philip.

"I don't take to Philip," said he, smiling, "for it sounds like a moral boy out of the spelling-book. I tell you what I should like. We are so harmonious, and you have been a blacksmith – would you mind it?"

"I shouldn't mind anything that you propose," I answered, "but I don't understand you."

"Would you mind me calling you Handel? There's a charming piece of music by Handel, called the Harmonious Blacksmith."

"I should like it very much."

"Then, my dear Handel," said he, turning round as the door opened, "here is the dinner, and I must beg of you to take the head of the table, because the dinner is of your providing."

This I would not hear of, so he took the top, and I faced him.

We had made some progress in the dinner, when I reminded Herbert of his promise to tell me about Miss Havisham.

"True," he replied. "Let me introduce the topic, Handel, by mentioning that in London it is not the custom to put the knife in the mouth – for fear of accidents – and that while the fork is reserved for that use, it is not put further in than necessary. Only it's as well to do as other people do. Also, the spoon is not generally used over-hand, but under."

He offered these friendly suggestions in such a lively way, that we both laughed and I scarcely blushed.

"Now," he pursued, "concerning Miss Havisham. Miss Havisham, you must know, was a spoilt child. Her mother died when she was a baby, and her father denied her nothing. Her father was a country gentleman down in your part of the world, and a brewer."

"Yet a gentleman may not keep a public house, may he?" said I.

"Not on any account," returned Herbert; "but a public house may keep a gentleman. Well! Mr Havisham was very rich and very proud. So was his daughter."

"Miss Havisham was an only child?" I hazarded.

"I am coming to that. No, she had a half-brother. Her father privately married again – his cook, I rather think."

"I thought he was proud," said I.

"My good Handel, so he was. He married his second wife privately, because he was proud, and in course of time she died. When she was dead, he first told his daughter what he had done, and then the son became a part of the family, residing in that house. As the son grew to a young man, he turned out riotous, extravagant, undutiful. At last his father disinherited him; but he softened when he was dying, and left him well off, though not nearly so well off as Miss Havisham. Miss Havisham was now an heiress, and was looked after as a great match. Her half-brother had now ample means again, but what with debts and what with new madness wasted them most fearfully again. There were stronger differences between him and her, than there had been between him and his father, and it is suspected that he cherished a deep and mortal grudge against her, as having influenced the father's anger. Now, I come to the cruel part of the story – merely breaking off, my dear Handel, to remark that a dinner-napkin will not go into a tumbler."

Why I was trying to pack mine into my tumbler, I am wholly unable to say. I thanked him and apologised, and again he said in the most cheerful manner, "Not at all, I am sure!" and resumed.

"There appeared upon the scene – say at the races, or anywhere else you like – a certain man, who made love to Miss Havisham. This happened five-and-twenty years ago (before you and I were, Handel), but I have heard my father mention that he was a showy-man. But that he was not to be mistaken for a gentleman, my father most strongly asserts. Well! This man pursued Miss Havisham closely, and professed to be devoted to her. I believe she had not shown much susceptibility before; but all the susceptibility she possessed, certainly came out then, and she passionately loved him. He practised on her affection so that he got great sums of money from her, and induced her to buy her brother out of a share in the brewery (which had been weakly left him by his father) at an immense price, on the plea that when he was her husband he must hold and manage it all. Your guardian was not at that time in Miss Havisham's councils, and she was too haughty and too much in love, to be advised by any one. Her relations were poor and scheming, with the exception of my father; he was poor certainly, but not jealous. The only independent one among them, he warned her that she was doing too much for this man, and was placing herself in his power. She angrily ordered my father from the house, in his presence, and my father has never seen her since."

I thought of her having said, "Matthew will come and see me at last when I am laid dead upon that table;" and I asked Herbert whether his father was so inveterate against her?

"It's not that," said he, "but she charged him, in front of her intended husband, with being disappointed in the hope of fawning upon her for his own advancement, and, if he were to go to her now, it would look true – even to him – and even to her. To return to the man and make an end of him. The marriage day was fixed, the wedding dresses were bought, the wedding tour was planned out, wedding guests were invited. The day came, but not the bridegroom. He wrote her a letter – "

"Which she received," I struck in, "when she was dressing for her marriage? At twenty minutes to nine?"

"At the hour and minute," said Herbert, nodding, "at which she afterwards stopped all the clocks. What was in it, further than that it most heartlessly broke the marriage off, I can't tell you, because I don't know. When she recovered from a bad illness that she had, she laid the whole place waste, as you have seen it, and she has never since looked upon the light of day."

"Is that all the story?" I asked, after considering it.

"All I know of it; and indeed I only know so much, through piecing it out for myself; for my father always avoids it, and, even when Miss Havisham invited me to go there, told me no more of it than it was absolutely requisite I should understand. But I have forgotten one thing. It has been supposed that the man acted throughout together with her half-brother; that it was a conspiracy between them; and that they shared the profits."

"I wonder he didn't marry her and get all the property," said I.

"He may have been married already, and her cruel mortification may have been a part of her half-brother's scheme," said Herbert. "Mind! I don't know that."

"What became of the two men?" I asked, after a moment.

"They fell into deeper shame and degradation – if there can be deeper – and ruin."

"Are they alive now?"

"I don't know."

"You said just now, that Estella was adopted. When?"

Herbert shrugged his shoulders. "There has always been an Estella, since I have heard of a Miss Havisham. I know no more. And now, Handel," said he, "there is open understanding between us. All that I know about Miss Havisham, you know."

"And all that I know," I retorted, "you know."

"I fully believe it. So there can be no difficulty between you and me. And as to the condition – namely, that you are not to inquire or discuss to whom you owe your advancement – you may be very sure that it will never be encroached upon, or even approached, by me, or by any one belonging to me."

In truth, he said this with so much delicacy, that I felt the subject done with, even though I should be under his father's roof for years to come. Yet he said it with so much meaning, too, that I felt he understood Miss Havisham to be my benefactress, as I understood the fact myself.

It had not occurred to me before, that he had led up to the theme for the purpose of clearing it out of our way. We were now very gay and sociable, and I asked him, in the course of conversation, what he was? He replied, "A capitalist – an Insurer of Ships." I suppose he saw me glancing about the room in search of some tokens of Shipping, or capital, for he added, "In the City."

I had grand ideas of the wealth and importance of Insurers of Ships in the City. But, again, there came upon me, for my relief, that odd impression that Herbert Pocket would never be very successful or rich.

"I shall not rest satisfied with merely employing my capital in insuring ships. I shall buy up some good Life Assurance shares, and cut into the Direction. I shall also do a little in the mining way. I think I shall trade," said he, leaning back in his chair, "to the East Indies, for silks, shawls, spices, dyes, drugs, and precious woods. It's an interesting trade."

"And the profits are large?" said I.

"Tremendous!" said he.

I wavered again, and began to think here were greater expectations than my own.

"I think I shall trade, also," said he, putting his thumbs in his waistcoat pockets, "to the West Indies, for sugar, tobacco, and rum. Also to Ceylon, specially for elephants' tusks."

Quite overpowered by the magnificence of these transactions, I asked him where the ships he insured mostly traded to at present?

"I haven't begun insuring yet," he replied. "I am looking about."

Somehow, that pursuit seemed more in keeping with Barnard's Inn.

"I am in a counting house, and looking about me."

"Is a counting house profitable?" I asked.

"To – do you mean to the young fellow who's in it?" he asked, in reply.

"Yes; to you."

"Why, n-no: not to me." He said this with the air of one carefully reckoning up and striking a balance. "Not directly profitable. That is, it doesn't pay me anything, and I have to – keep myself."

This certainly had not a profitable appearance.

"But the thing is," said Herbert Pocket, "that you look about you. That's the grand thing. You are in a counting house, and you look about you. Then the time comes when you see your opening. And you go in, and you swoop upon it and you make your capital, and then there you are! When you have once made your capital, you have nothing to do but employ it."

This was very like his way of conducting that encounter in the garden. His manner of bearing his poverty, too, exactly matched the way he took that defeat. It seemed to me that he took all blows now, with just the same air as he had taken mine then. It was evident that he had nothing around him but the simplest necessaries, for everything else turned out to have been sent in on my account from the coffee house or somewhere else.

Yet, having already made his fortune in his own mind, he was so unassuming with it that I felt quite grateful to him for not being puffed up. We got on famously. In the evening we went out for a walk in the streets, and went half-price to the Theatre; and next day we went to church at Westminster Abbey, and in the afternoon we walked in the Parks.

On a moderate computation, it seemed many months, that Sunday, since I had left Joe and Biddy.

On the Monday morning at a quarter before nine, Herbert went to the counting house to report himself – to look about him, too, I suppose – and I accompanied him. He was to come away in an hour or two to attend me to Hammersmith.

I waited about until it was noon, and when Herbert came, we went and had lunch at a celebrated house where I could not help noticing that there was much more gravy on the tablecloths and knives and waiters' clothes, than in the steaks. We then went back to Barnard's Inn and got my little portmanteau, and took coach for Hammersmith. We arrived there at two or three o'clock in the afternoon, and had very little way to walk to Mr Pocket's house. Lifting the latch of a gate, we passed direct into a little garden overlooking the river, where Mr Pocket's children were playing about.

Mrs Pocket was sitting on a garden chair under a tree, reading, and her two nursemaids, Flopson and Millers, were looking about them while the children played.

I counted that there were no fewer than six little Pockets present, in various stages. I had scarcely arrived at the total when a seventh was heard wailing dolefully from inside the house.

Millers retired into the house, and by degrees the child's wailing was hushed and stopped. Mrs Pocket read all the time, and I was curious to know what the book could be.

We were waiting, I supposed, for Mr Pocket to come out to us, so I had an opportunity of observing the remarkable family. When Flopson and Millers finally got the children into the house, like a little flock of sheep, and Mr Pocket came out of it to make my acquaintance, I was not much surprised to find that Mr Pocket was a gentleman with a rather perplexed expression, with his very grey hair disordered on his head, as if he didn't quite see his way to putting anything straight.

CHAPTER 22

Mr Pocket said he was glad to see me, and he hoped I was not sorry to see him. "For, I really am not," he added, with his son's smile, "an alarming personage." He was a young-looking man, in spite of his perplexities and his very grey hair and his manner was quite unaffected. When he had talked with me a little, he said to Mrs Pocket, rather anxiously, "Belinda, I hope you have welcomed Mr Pip?"

And she looked up from her book, and said, "Yes." She then smiled upon me absently, and asked me if I liked the taste of orange-flower water? As the question had no bearing on any foregone or subsequent transaction, I consider it to have been thrown out in general conversational condescension.

I found out within a few hours, and may mention at once, that Mrs Pocket was the only daughter of a certain quite accidental deceased Knight. I believe he had been knighted for storming the English grammar at the point of the pen, in a desperate address engrossed on vellum, on the occasion of the laying of the first stone of some building; and for handing some Royal Personage either the trowel or the mortar. He had therefore directed Mrs Pocket to be brought up from her cradle as one who must marry a title, and who was to be guarded from the acquisition of plebeian domestic knowledge.

So successful a watch was established over the young lady by this judicious parent, that she had grown up highly ornamental, but perfectly helpless and useless. With her character thus happily formed, in the first bloom of her youth she had encountered Mr Pocket: who was also in the first bloom of youth, and he and Mrs Pocket had married without the knowledge of the judicious parent. The judicious parent, having nothing to bestow but his blessing, had handsomely settled that upon them after a short struggle, and had informed Mr Pocket that his wife was "a treasure for a Prince." Mr Pocket had invested the Prince's treasure in the ways of the world ever since, and it was supposed to have brought him in but indifferent interest. Still, Mrs Pocket was in general the object of a queer sort of respectful pity, because she had not married a title; while Mr Pocket was the object of a queer sort of forgiving reproach, because he had never got one.

Mr Pocket took me into the house and showed me my room: which was a pleasant one, and so furnished as that I could use it with comfort for my own private sitting room.

He then knocked at the doors of two other similar rooms, and introduced me to Drummle and Startop. Drummle, an old-looking young man of a heavy order of architecture, was whistling. Startop, younger in years and appearance, was reading.

By degrees I learnt, chiefly from Herbert, that Mr Pocket had been educated at Harrow and at Cambridge, where he had distinguished himself; but that when he had had the happiness of marrying Mrs Pocket very early in life, he had impaired his prospects and taken up the calling of a Grinder. After grinding a number of dull blades – whose fathers, when influential, were always going to help him to preferment, but always forgot to do it when the blades had left the Grindstone – he had wearied of that poor work and had come to London. Here, after gradually failing in loftier hopes, he had "read" with divers who had lacked opportunities or neglected them, and had refurbished divers others for special occasions, and had turned his acquirements to the account of literary compilation and correction, and on such means, added to some very moderate private resources, still maintained the house I saw.

It came to my knowledge, through what passed between Mrs Pocket and Drummle while I was attentive to my knife and fork, spoon, glasses, and other instruments of self-destruction, that Drummle, Christian name Bentley, was actually the next heir but one to a baronetcy. It further appeared that the book I had seen Mrs Pocket reading in the garden, was all about titles, and that she knew the exact date at which her grandpapa would have come into the book, if he ever had come at all. Drummle didn't say much, but in his limited way (he struck me as a sulky kind of fellow) he spoke as one of the elect, and recognised Mrs Pocket as a woman and a sister.

After dinner the children were introduced. There were four little girls, and two little boys, besides the baby who might have been either, and the baby's next successor who was as yet neither.

In the evening there was rowing on the river. As Drummle and Startop had each a boat, I resolved to set up mine, and to cut them both out. I was pretty good at most exercises in which country-boys are adepts, but, as I was conscious of wanting elegance of style for the Thames – I at once placed myself under the tuition of the winner of a prize-wherry who plied at our stairs. This practical authority confused me, by saying I had the arm of a blacksmith. If he knew how nearly the compliment lost him his pupil, I doubt if he would have paid it.

CHAPTER 23

After two or three days, when I had established myself in my room and had gone backwards and forwards to London several times, and had ordered all I wanted of my tradesmen, Mr Pocket and I had a long talk together. He knew more of my intended career than I knew myself, having been told by Mr Jaggers that I was not designed for any profession, and that I should be well enough educated for my destiny if I could "hold my own" with the average of young men in prosperous circumstances. I acquiesced, of course, knowing nothing to the contrary.

He advised my attending certain places in London, for the acquisition of such mere rudiments as I wanted, and my investing him with the functions of explainer and director of all my studies. He hoped that with intelligent assistance I should meet with little to discourage me, and should soon be able to dispense with any aid but his. He placed himself on confidential terms with me in an admirable manner; and I may state at once that he was always so honourable in fulfilling his compact with me, that he made me honourable in fulfilling mine with him. If he had shown indifference as a master, I have no doubt I should have returned the compliment as a pupil; he gave me no such excuse, and each of us did the other justice.

When these points were settled, and so far carried out as that I had begun to work in earnest, it occurred to me that if I could retain my bedroom in Barnard's Inn, my life would be agreeably varied, while my manners would be none the worse for Herbert's society. Mr Pocket did not object to this arrangement, but urged that it must be submitted to my guardian. I felt that this delicacy arose out of the consideration that the plan would save Herbert some expense, so I went off to Little Britain and imparted my wish to Mr Jaggers.

"If I could buy the furniture now hired for me," said I, "and one or two other little things, I should be quite at home there."

"Go it!" said Mr Jaggers, with a short laugh. "I told you you'd get on. Well! How much do you want?"

I said I didn't know how much.

"Come!" retorted Mr Jaggers. "How much? Fifty pounds?"

"Oh, not nearly so much."

"Five pounds?" said Mr Jaggers.

This was such a great fall, that I said in discomfiture, "It is so difficult to fix a sum."

"Come!" said Mr Jaggers. "Let's get at it. Four times five; will that do?"

I said I thought that would do handsomely.

"Four times five will do handsomely, will it?" said Mr Jaggers, knitting his brows. "Now, what do you make of four times five?"

"I suppose you make it twenty pounds," said I, smiling.

"Wemmick!" said Mr Jaggers, opening his office door. "Take Mr Pip's written order, and pay him twenty pounds."

As Mr Jaggers happened to go out now, and as Wemmick was brisk and talkative, I said to Wemmick that I hardly knew what to make of Mr Jaggers's manner.

"Tell him that, and he'll take it as a compliment," answered Wemmick. He was at his desk, lunching – and crunching – on a dry hard biscuit; pieces of which he threw into his slit of a mouth, as if posting them.

"Always seems to me," said Wemmick, "as if he had set a man-trap and was watching it. Suddenly – click – you're caught!"

Without remarking that man-traps were not among the amenities of life, I said I supposed he was very skilful?

"Deep," said Wemmick, "as Australia," pointing with his pen at the office floor. "If there was anything deeper," he added, bringing his pen to paper, "he'd be it."

Then, I said I supposed he had a fine business, and Wemmick said, "Ca-pi-tal!" Then I asked if there were many clerks?

To which he replied: "We don't run much into clerks, because there's only one Jaggers, and people won't have him at second-hand. There are only four of us. Would you like to see 'em? You are one of us, as I may say."

I accepted the offer. When Mr Wemmick had put all the biscuit into the post, and had paid me my money from a cash-box in a safe, we went upstairs. The house was dark and shabby. In the front first floor, a clerk who looked something between a publican and a rat-catcher was attentively engaged with three or four people of shabby appearance.

"Getting evidence together," said Mr Wemmick, as we came out, "for the Bailey."

In the top room, a little flabby terrier of a clerk with dangling hair was similarly engaged with a man with weak eyes. In a back room, a high-shouldered man with a face-ache tied up in dirty flannel, was stooping over his work, making fair copies of notes, for Mr Jaggers's own use. This was the whole establishment. When we went downstairs again, Wemmick led me into my guardian's room, and said, "This you've seen already."

"Pray," said I, as the two odious casts caught my sight again, "whose likenesses are those?"

"These?" said Wemmick, getting upon a chair, and blowing the dust off the heads before bringing them down. "These are famous clients that got us a world of credit. This one murdered his master."

"Is it like him?" I asked, recoiling from the brute.

"Like him? It's himself, you know. The cast was made in Newgate, directly after he was taken down. You were particular fond of me, weren't you, Old Artful?" said Wemmick. He then touched his brooch representing the lady and the weeping willow at the tomb with the urn upon it, and saying, "Had it made for me, express!"

"Did that other creature come to the same end?" I asked. "He has the same look."

"You're right," said Wemmick; "it's the genuine look. Yes, he came to the same end. He forged wills, this blade did, if he didn't also put the supposed testators to sleep too. You were a gentlemanly Cove, though, and you said you could write Greek. Yah, Bounceable! What a liar you were!" Before putting his late friend on his shelf again, Wemmick touched the largest mourning ring and said, "Sent out to buy it for me, only the day before."

He went on to say, in a friendly manner: "If at any odd time when you have nothing better to do, you wouldn't mind coming over to see me at Walworth, I could offer you a bed, and I should consider it an honour."

I said I should be delighted to accept his hospitality.

"Thankee," said he; "then we'll consider that it's to come off, when convenient. Have you dined with Mr Jaggers yet?"

"Not yet."

"Well," said Wemmick, "he'll give you wine, and good wine. I'll give you punch, and not bad punch. And now I'll tell you something. When you go to dine with Mr Jaggers, look at his housekeeper."

"Shall I see something very uncommon?"

"Well," said Wemmick, "you'll see a wild beast tamed. Not so very uncommon, you'll tell me. I reply, that depends on the original wildness of the beast, and the amount of taming. It won't lower your opinion of Mr Jaggers's powers. Keep your eye on it."

I told him I would do so, with all the interest and curiosity that his preparation awakened.

CHAPTER 24

Bentley Drummle was a sulky fellow who did not take up an acquaintance in an agreeable spirit. Heavy in figure, movement, and comprehension – he was idle, proud, niggardly, reserved, and suspicious. He came of rich people down in Somersetshire, who had nursed this combination of qualities until they made the discovery that it was just of age and a blockhead. Thus, Bentley Drummle had come to Mr Pocket a head taller than that gentleman, and half a dozen heads thicker than most gentlemen.

Startop had been spoilt by a weak mother and kept at home when he ought to have been at school, but he was devotedly attached to her, and admired her beyond measure. He had a woman's delicacy of feature, and was, said Herbert to me, exactly like his mother. It was only natural that I should take to him much more kindly than to Drummle, and that, even in the earliest evenings of our boating, he and I should pull homeward abreast of one another, conversing from boat to boat, while Bentley Drummle came up in our wake alone. He would always creep inshore like some uncomfortable amphibious creature.

Herbert was my intimate companion and friend. I presented him with a share in my boat, which was the occasion of his often coming down to Hammersmith; and my possession of a share in his chambers often took me up to London. We used to walk between the two places at all hours.

When I had been in Mr Pocket's family a month or two, Mr and Mrs Camilla turned up. Camilla was Mr Pocket's sister. Georgiana, whom I had seen at Miss Havisham's on the same occasion, also turned up. She was a cousin. These people hated me with the hatred of cupidity and disappointment. As a matter of course, they fawned upon me in my prosperity with the basest meanness. Towards Mr Pocket, as a grown-up infant with no notion of his own interests, they showed the complacent forbearance I had heard them express. Mrs Pocket they held in contempt.

These were the surroundings among which I settled down, and applied myself to my education. I soon developed expensive habits, and began to spend an amount of money that within a few short months I should have thought almost fabulous. Between Mr Pocket and Herbert I got on fast; and, with one or the other always at my elbow to give me the start I wanted, and clear obstructions out of my road, I must have been as great a dolt as Drummle if I had done less.

I had not seen Mr Wemmick for some weeks, when I thought I would write to propose to go home with him on a certain evening. He replied that it would give him much pleasure, and that we should meet at the office at six o'clock. Thither I went, and there I found him.

"Did you think of walking down to Walworth?" said he.

"Certainly," said I, "if you approve."

"Very much," was Wemmick's reply, "for I have had my legs under the desk all day, and shall be glad to stretch them. Now, I'll tell you what I have got for supper, Mr Pip. I have got a stewed steak – which is of home preparation – and a cold roast fowl. You don't object to an aged parent, I hope?"

I really thought he spoke of the fowl, until he added, "Because I have an aged parent at my place." I then said what politeness required.

"So, you haven't dined with Mr Jaggers yet?" he pursued, as we walked along.

"Not yet."

"He told me so this afternoon when he heard you were coming. I expect you'll have an invitation tomorrow. He's going to ask your pals, too. Three of 'em; ain't there?"

Although I didn't usually count Drummle as one of my intimate associates, I answered, "Yes."

"Well, he's going to ask the whole gang, and whatever he gives you, he'll give you good. Don't look forward to variety, but you'll have excellence."

At first with such discourse, and afterwards with conversation of a more general nature, did Mr Wemmick and I beguile the time and the road, until we arrived in the district of Walworth.

It appeared to be a collection of back lanes, ditches, and little gardens. Wemmick's house was a little wooden cottage in the midst of plots of garden, and the top of it was cut out and painted like a battery mounted with guns.

"My own doing," said Wemmick. "Looks pretty; don't it?"

I highly commended it. I think it was the smallest house I ever saw; with the queerest gothic windows (by far the greater part of them sham), and a gothic door, almost too small to get in at.

"That's a real flagstaff, you see," said Wemmick, "and on Sundays I run up a real flag. Then look – after crossing this bridge, I hoist it up – so – and cut off communication."

The bridge was a plank, crossing a chasm about four feet wide and two deep. But it was very pleasant to see the pride with which he hoisted it up and made it fast; smiling as he did so.

"At nine o'clock every night, Greenwich time," said Wemmick, "the gun fires. There he is, you see! And when you hear him go, I think you'll say he's a Stinger."

The piece of ordnance referred to, was mounted in a separate fortress, constructed of lattice-work. It was protected from the weather by a contrivance in the nature of an umbrella.

"Then, at the back," said Wemmick, "out of sight, so as not to impede the idea of fortifications – there's a pig, and there are fowls and rabbits. I grow cucumbers; and you'll judge at supper what sort of a salad I can raise. So, sir," said Wemmick, smiling again, but seriously too, as he shook his head, "if you can suppose the little place besieged, it would hold out a devil of a time in point of provisions."

Then, he conducted me to a bower about a dozen yards off, but by such ingenious twists of path that it took quite a long time to get at; and in this retreat our glasses were already set forth. Our punch was cooling in an ornamental lake, on whose margin the bower was raised.

"I am my own engineer, and my own carpenter, and my own plumber, and my own gardener, and my own Jack of all Trades," said Wemmick, acknowledging my compliments. "Well; it brushes the Newgate cobwebs away, and pleases the Aged. You wouldn't mind being at once introduced to the Aged, would you?"

I expressed the readiness I felt, and we went into the castle. There, we found, sitting by a fire, a very old man in a flannel coat: clean, cheerful, comfortable, and well cared for, but intensely deaf.

"Well, aged parent," said Wemmick, shaking hands with him, "how am you?"

"All right, John; all right!" replied the old man.

"Here's Mr Pip, aged parent," said Wemmick, "and I wish you could hear his name. Nod away at him, Mr Pip; that's what he likes! "

"This is a fine place of my son's, sir," cried the old man, while I nodded as hard as I possibly could. "This spot and these beautiful works upon it ought to be kept together by the Nation, after my son's time, for the people's enjoyment."

"You're as proud of it as Punch; ain't you, Aged?" said Wemmick, contemplating the old man, with his hard face really softened; "there's a nod for you;" giving him a tremendous one; "you like that, don't you? If you're not tired, Mr Pip – will you tip him one more? You can't think how it pleases him."

I tipped him several more, and he was in great spirits. We left him feeding the fowls, and we sat down to our punch in the arbour; where Wemmick told me that it had taken him a good many years to bring the property up to its present pitch of perfection.

"Is it your own, Mr Wemmick?"

"O yes," said Wemmick, "I have got hold of it, a bit at a time. It's a freehold, by George!"

"Is it, indeed? I hope Mr Jaggers admires it?"

"Never seen it," said Wemmick. "Never heard of it. Never seen the Aged. Never heard of him. When I go into the office, I leave the Castle behind me, and when I come into the Castle, I leave the office behind me. If it's not disagreeable to you, you'll oblige me by doing the same. I don't wish it professionally spoken about."

Of course I felt my good faith involved in the observance of his request. The punch being very nice, we sat drinking and talking, until it was almost nine o'clock. "Getting near gun-fire," said Wemmick then; "it's the Aged's treat."

Proceeding into the Castle again, we found the Aged heating the poker, as a preliminary to the performance of this great nightly ceremony. Wemmick stood with his watch in his hand, until the moment was come for him to repair to the battery. He took it, and went out, and presently the Stinger went off with a Bang that shook the crazy little box of a cottage. Upon this, the Aged cried out exultingly, "He's fired! I heerd him!" and I nodded at the old gentleman.

Between then and supper, Wemmick showed me his collection of curiosities. They were mostly of a felonious character; comprising the pen with which a celebrated forgery had been committed, a distinguished razor or two, some locks of hair, and several manuscript confessions written under condemnation. They were all displayed in that chamber into which I had first entered, and which served, not only as general sitting room, but as kitchen too.

There was a neat little girl in attendance who looked after the Aged in the day. When she had laid the supper-cloth, the bridge was lowered, and she withdrew for the night. The supper was excellent and I spent the night in a little turret bedroom.

Wemmick was up early in the morning, and I am afraid I heard him cleaning my boots. After that, he fell to gardening, and I saw him from my gothic window pretending to employ the Aged, and nodding at him in a most devoted manner. Our breakfast was as good as the supper, and at half-past eight precisely we started for Little Britain. By degrees, Wemmick got dryer and harder as we went along, and his mouth tightened into a post-office again. At last, when we got to his place of business, he looked as unconscious of his Walworth property as if the Castle and drawbridge, arbour, lake and fountain and the Aged, had all been blown into space together by the last discharge of the Stinger.

CHAPTER 25

It fell out as Wemmick had told me it would. Mr Jaggers called me to him, and gave me the invitation for myself and my friends that Wemmick had warned me of. "No ceremony," he stipulated, "and no dinner dress, and say tomorrow. Come here, and I'll take you home with me."

I and my friends repaired to him at six o'clock next day and we walked westward. He was recognised ever and again by some face in the crowd of the streets, and whenever that happened he talked louder to me; but he never otherwise recognised anybody, or took notice that anybody recognised him.

He conducted us to Gerrard Street, Soho, to a house rather in want of painting, and with dirty windows. He unlocked the door, and we all went into a stone hall, bare, gloomy, and little used. So, up a dark brown staircase into a series of three dark brown rooms on the first floor. Dinner was laid in the best of these rooms; the second was his dressing room; the third, his bedroom. He told us that he held the whole house, but rarely used more than we saw. The table was comfortably laid and at the side of his chair was a capacious dumb-waiter, with a variety of bottles and decanters on it, and four dishes of fruit for dessert. I noticed throughout, that he kept everything under his own hand, and distributed everything himself.

There was a bookcase in the room; the books were about evidence, criminal law, criminal biography, trials, acts of parliament, and such things. The furniture was all very solid, with nothing merely ornamental to be seen. In a corner, was a little table of papers with a shaded lamp: so that he seemed to bring the office home with him in that respect too.

As he had scarcely seen my three companions until now, he stood on the hearthrug and took a searching look at them. To my surprise, he seemed mainly interested in Drummle.

"Pip," said he, moving me to the window, "I don't know one from the other. Who's the Spider?"

"The spider?" said I.

"The blotchy, sprawly, sulky fellow."

"That's Bentley Drummle," I replied; "the one with the delicate face is Startop."

Totally ignoring Startop, he returned, "Bentley Drummle is his name, is it? I like the look of that fellow."

He immediately began to talk to Drummle: not at all deterred by his reluctant replies, but apparently led on by it to screw discourse out of him. I was looking at them, when the housekeeper walked before me, with the first dish for the table.

She was a woman of about forty, I thought. Rather tall, of a lithe nimble figure, extremely pale, with large faded eyes, and a quantity of streaming hair.

She set the dish on, touched my guardian quietly on the arm with a finger to notify that dinner was ready, and vanished. We took our seats at the round table, and my guardian kept Drummle on one side of him, while Startop sat on the other. It was a noble dish of fish that the housekeeper had put on table, and we had a joint of equally choice mutton afterwards, and then an equally choice bird. Sauces, wines, all the accessories we wanted – and all of the best – were given out by our host. He dealt us clean plates and knives and forks, for each course, and dropped those just used into two baskets on the ground by his chair. No other attendant than the housekeeper appeared.

Taking particular notice of the housekeeper, both by her own striking appearance and by Wemmick's preparation, I observed that whenever she was in the room, she kept her eyes attentively on my guardian, and that she would remove her hands from any dish she put before him, hesitatingly, as if she dreaded his calling her back. He seemed aware of this.

Dinner went off gaily, and, although my guardian seemed to follow rather than originate subjects, I knew that he wrenched the weakest part of our dispositions out of us. I realised I was expressing my tendency to lavish expenditure, and to patronise Herbert, and to boast of my great prospects, before I quite knew that I had opened my lips. It was so with all of us, but with no one more than Drummle: the development of whose inclination to gird in a grudging and suspicious way at the rest, was screwed out of him before the fish was taken off.

It was not then, but with the cheese, that our conversation turned to rowing, and how Drummle was rallied for coming up slowly behind. Drummle then informed our host that he much preferred our room to our company, and that as to skill he was more than our master, and that as to strength he could scatter us like chaff. By some invisible agency, my guardian wound him up to a pitch little short of ferocity about this trifle; and he·fell to baring and spanning his arm to show how muscular it was, and we all fell to baring and spanning our arms in a ridiculous manner.

Now, the housekeeper was at that time clearing the table; my guardian suddenly clapped his large hand on the housekeeper's, like a trap, as she stretched across the table. We all stopped in our foolish contention.

"If you talk of strength," said Mr Jaggers, "I'll show you a wrist. Molly, let them see your wrist."

Her entrapped hand was on the table, but she had already put her other hand behind her waist. "Master," she said, in a low voice, with her eyes attentively and entreatingly fixed upon him. "Don't."

"I'll show you a wrist," repeated Mr Jaggers, with an immovable determination to show it. "Molly, let them see your wrist."

"Master," she again murmured. "Please!"

"Molly," said Mr Jaggers, not looking at her, but obstinately looking at the opposite side of the room, "let them see both your wrists. Show them. Come!"

He took her hand, and turned that wrist up on the table. She brought her other hand from behind her, and held the two out. The last wrist was deeply scarred across. When she held her hands out, she took her eyes from Mr Jaggers, and looked at each of us in succession.

"There's power here," said Mr Jaggers, coolly tracing out the sinews with his forefinger. "Very few men have the power of wrist that this woman has. I have had occasion to notice many hands; but I never saw stronger, man's or woman's, than these."

She continued to look at every one of us in regular succession as we sat. The moment he ceased speaking, she looked at him again. "That'll do, Molly," he said, giving her a slight nod; "you have been admired, and can go." She withdrew her hands and left the room, and Mr Jaggers filled his glass and passed round the wine.

"At half-past nine, gentlemen," said he, "we must break up. Pray make the best use of your time. I am glad to see you all. Mr Drummle, I drink to you."

If his object in singling out Drummle were to bring him out still more, it perfectly succeeded. In a sulky triumph, Drummle showed his morose depreciation of the rest of us, in a more and more offensive degree until he became downright intolerable.

"Gentlemen," said Mr Jaggers finally, deliberately putting down his glass, "I am exceedingly sorry to say that it's half-past nine."

On this hint we all rose to depart. Before we got to the street door, Startop was cheerily calling Drummle "old boy," as if nothing had happened. But the old boy would not even walk to Hammersmith on the same side of the way. Herbert and I were staying in town.

As the door was not yet shut, I thought I would leave Herbert a moment, and run upstairs again to speak to my guardian. I found him in his dressing room, already washing his hands of us.

I told him how sorry I was that anything disagreeable should have occurred, and that I hoped he would not blame me much.

"Pooh!" said he, sluicing his face, and speaking through the water-drops; "it's nothing, Pip. I like that Spider though."

"I am glad you like him, sir," said I; "but I don't."

"No, no," my guardian assented; "don't have too much to do with him. Keep as clear of him as you can. But I like the fellow, Pip; he is one of the true sort. Why, if I was a fortune-teller – but I am not a fortune-teller. You know what I am, don't you? Good-night, Pip."

"Good-night, sir."

About a month after that, the Spider's time with Mr Pocket was up, and, to the great relief of all, he went home to the family hole.

CHAPTER 26

I received a letter by the post one Monday morning, written by Biddy, telling me that Joe was coming to visit on the Tuesday. This appointment was therefore for next day. Let me confess exactly, with what feelings I looked forward to Joe's coming.

Not with pleasure, though I was bound to him by so many ties; no, it was with considerable disturbance. If I could have kept him away by paying money, I certainly would have paid. At least he was coming to Barnard's Inn, not to Hammersmith, and consequently would not meet Bentley Drummle. I had little objection to his being seen by Herbert or his father, for both of whom I had a respect; but I did not want him seen by Drummle, whom I held in contempt.

By this time, the rooms were vastly different from what I had found them, and I enjoyed the honour of occupying a few prominent pages in the books of a neighbouring upholsterer.

I came into town on the Monday night to be ready for Joe, and I got up early in the morning, and caused the sitting room and breakfast-table to assume their most splendid appearance. Unfortunately the morning was drizzly, and an angel could not have concealed the fact that Barnard was shedding sooty tears outside the window, like some weak giant of a Sweep.

As the time approached I should have liked to run away, but presently I heard Joe on the staircase. I knew it was Joe, by his clumsy manner of coming upstairs – his state boots being always too big for him. When at last he stopped outside our door, I could hear his finger tracing over the painted letters of my name. Finally he gave a faint single rap, and at last he came in.

"Joe, how are you, Joe?"

"Pip, how *air* you, Pip?"

With his good honest face all glowing and shining, and his hat put down on the floor between us, he caught both my hands and worked them straight up and down.

"Which you have that growed," said Joe, "and that swelled, and that gentle-folked;" Joe considered a little before he discovered this word; "as to be sure you are a honour to your king and country."

"And you, Joe, look wonderfully well."

"Thank God," said Joe, "And your sister, she's no worse than she were. And Biddy, she's ever right and ready. And all friends is no backerder, if not no forarder."

All this time, Joe was rolling his eyes round and round the room, and round and round the flowered pattern of my dressing gown.

Herbert had entered the room, so I presented Joe to Herbert.

"Do you take tea, or coffee, Mr Gargery?" asked Herbert, who always presided of a morning.

"Thankee, sir," said Joe, stiff from head to foot, "I'll take whichever is most agreeable to yourself."

"What do you say to coffee?"

"Thankee, sir," returned Joe, evidently dispirited by the proposal, "since you are so kind as make chice of coffee, I will not run contrairy to your own opinions. But don't you never find it a little 'eating?"

"Say tea then," said Herbert, pouring it out. "When did you come to town, Mr Gargery?"

"Were it yesterday afternoon?" said Joe, after coughing behind his hand. "No it were not. Yes it were – it were yesterday afternoon."

His shirt-collar and his coat-collar were perplexing to reflect upon – insoluble mysteries both. Why should a man suppose it necessary to be purified by suffering for his holiday clothes? While he ate, Joe fell into such unaccountable fits of meditation, with his fork midway between his plate and his mouth; his eyes attracted in such strange directions; was afflicted with such remarkable coughs; sat so far from the table, and dropped so much more than he ate, and pretended that he hadn't dropped it; that I was heartily glad when Herbert left us for the city.

I had neither the good sense nor the good feeling to know that this was all my fault, and that if I had been easier with Joe, Joe would have been easier with me. I felt impatient and out of temper with him; in which condition he heaped coals of fire on my head.

"Us two being now alone, sir," Joe began.

"Joe," I interrupted, pettishly, "how can you call me, sir?"

Joe looked at me for a single instant with something faintly like reproach. Utterly preposterous as his cravat was, and as his collars were, I was conscious of a sort of dignity in the look.

"Us two being now alone," resumed Joe, "and me having the intentions and abilities to stay not many minutes more, I will now conclude – leastways begin – to mention what have led to my having had the present honour. For was it not that my only wish were to be useful to you, I should not have had the honour of breaking wittles in the company and abode of gentlemen."

I was so unwilling to see the look again, that I made no remonstrance against this tone.

"Well, sir," pursued Joe, "I were at the Bargemen t'other night, Pip;" whenever he subsided into affection, he called me Pip, and whenever he relapsed into politeness he called me sir; "when there come up in his shay-cart, Pumblechook. He does annoy me sometimes by giving out as he ever had your infant companionation and were a playfellow to yourself."

"Nonsense. It was you, Joe."

"Which I fully believed it were, Pip," said Joe, slightly tossing his head, "though it signify little now, sir. Well, Pip; this same identical, come to me at the Bargemen and said, 'Joseph, Miss Havisham, she wish to speak to you.'"

"Miss Havisham, Joe?"

"'She wish,' were Pumblechook's word, 'to speak to you'." Joe sat and rolled his eyes at the ceiling.

"Yes, Joe? Go on, please."

"Next day, sir," said Joe, looking at me as if I were a long way off, "having cleaned myself, I go and I see Miss A. She said then as follering: 'Mr Gargery. You air in correspondence with Mr Pip?' Having had a letter from you, I were able to say 'I am'. 'Would you tell him, then,' said she, 'that Estella has come home and would be glad to see him'."

I felt my face fire up as I looked at Joe. I hope one remote cause of its firing may have been shame, that had I known his errand, I should have given him more encouragement.

"When I got home and asked Biddy to write the message to you, she says, 'I know he will be very glad to have it by word of mouth, it is holiday-time, you want to see him, go!' I have now concluded, sir," said Joe, rising from his chair, "and, Pip, I wish you ever well and ever prospering to a greater and a greater height."

"But you are not going now, Joe?"

"Yes I am," said Joe.

"But you are coming back to dinner, Joe?"

"No I am not," said Joe.

Our eyes met, and all the "Sir" melted out of that manly heart as he gave me his hand.

"Pip, dear old chap, life is made of ever so many partings welded together, as I may say, and one man's a blacksmith, and one's a whitesmith, and one's a goldsmith, and one's a coppersmith. Diwisions among such must come, and must be met as they come. If there's been any fault at all today, it's mine. You and me is not two figures to be together in London. It ain't that I am proud, but that I want to be right, so you shall never see me no more in these clothes. I'm wrong in these clothes and out of the forge, the kitchen, or off th' meshes. You won't find half so much fault in me if you think of me in my forge dress, with my hammer in my hand, or even my pipe. I'm awful dull, but I hope I've beat out something nigh the rights of this at last. And so God bless you, dear old Pip, old chap, God bless you!"

I had not been mistaken in my fancy that there was a simple dignity in him. He touched me gently on the forehead, and left. As soon as I had recovered myself sufficiently, I hurried after him but he was gone.

CHAPTER 27

It was clear that I must return home the next day, and in the first flow of repentance it was equally clear that I must stay at Joe's. But, when I had secured tomorrow's coach, and had been down to Mr Pocket's and back, I was not convinced on the last point, and began to invent reasons for putting up at the Blue Boar. I should be an inconvenience at Joe's; I was not expected; I should be too far from Miss Havisham's. All other swindlers upon earth are nothing to the self-swindlers, and with such pretences did I cheat myself.

Having settled that I must go to the Blue Boar, it was the afternoon coach I took, and, as winter had now come round, I would not arrive until two or three hours after dark. Our time of starting from the Cross Keys was two o'clock. I arrived on the ground with a quarter of an hour to spare.

At that time it was customary to carry convicts down to the dockyards by stage-coach. As I had often heard of them as outside passengers, and had more than once seen them on the high road dangling their ironed legs over the coach roof, I had no cause to be surprised when Herbert, meeting me in the yard, came up and told me there were two convicts going down with me. But I still faltered whenever I heard the word convict.

"You don't mind them, Handel?" said Herbert.

"Oh no!"

"It seemed as if you didn't like them?"

"I can't pretend that I do like them, and I suppose you don't particularly. But I don't mind them."

"See! There they are," said Herbert, "coming out of the Tap. What a degraded and vile sight it is!"

They had been treating their guard, I suppose, for they had a gaoler with them, and all three came out wiping their mouths on their hands. The two convicts were handcuffed together, and had irons on their legs. They wore the dress that I knew well. Their keeper had a brace of pistols, and carried a thick-knobbed bludgeon under his arm; but he was on good terms with them, and stood, with them beside him, looking on at the putting-to of the horses. One was taller and stouter than the other and I knew his half-closed eye at one glance. There stood the man whom I had seen on the settle at the Three Jolly Bargemen on a Saturday night, and who had brought me down with his invisible gun!

It was easy to make sure that as yet he knew me no more than if he had never seen me in his life.

But this was not the worst of it. It happened that the whole of the back of the coach had been taken by a family removing from London, and that there were no places for the two prisoners but on the seat in front, behind the coachman. Hereupon, a choleric gentleman, who had taken the fourth place on that seat, flew into a most violent passion, and said that it was a breach of contract to mix him up with such villainous company, and I don't know what else. At this time the coach was ready and the coachman impatient.

"Don't take it so much amiss, sir," pleaded the keeper to the angry passenger; "I'll sit next you myself. I'll put 'em on the outside of the row. They won't interfere with you, sir. You needn't know they're there."

"And don't blame me," growled the convict I had recognised. "I don't want to go. I am quite ready to stay behind. As fur as I am concerned any one's welcome to my place."

At length, it was voted that there was no help for the angry gentleman, and that he must either go, or remain behind. So, he got into his place, still complaining, and the keeper got into the place next him, and the convicts hauled themselves up, and the convict I had recognised sat behind me, breathing down my neck.

"Good-bye, Handel!" Herbert called out as we started. I gave thanks, that he had found another name for me than Pip.

It is impossible to express with what acuteness I felt the convict's breathing, not only on the back of my head, but all along my spine. The sensation was like being touched in the marrow with some pungent and searching acid, and it set my very teeth on edge.

The weather was miserably raw, and the two cursed the cold. It made

108

us all lethargic before we had gone far, and when we had left the Half-way House behind, we habitually dozed and shivered and were silent. I dozed off, considering the question whether I should restore a couple of pounds sterling to this creature before losing sight of him, and how it could best be done.

Cowering forward for warmth and to make me a screen against the wind, the convicts were closer to me than before. The very first words I heard them share were the words of my own thought, "Two one pound notes."

"How did he get 'em?" said the convict I had never seen.

"How should I know?" returned the other. "He had 'em stowed away somehows. Giv' him by friends, I expect."

"I wish," said the other, cursing the cold bitterly, "that I had 'em."

"Two one pound notes, or friends?"

"Two one pound notes. I'd sell all the friends I ever had, for one, and think it a blessed good bargain. Well? So he says – ?"

"So he says," resumed the convict I had recognised – "'You're a-going to be discharged?' Yes, I was. Would I find the boy that had fed him and kep his secret, and give him them two one pound notes? Yes, I would. And I did."

"More fool you," growled the other. "I'd have spent 'em in wittles and drink. He must have been a green one. Mean to say he know'd nothing of you?"

"Not a ha'porth. Different gangs and different ships. He was tried again for prison breaking, and got made a Lifer."

They had nothing left to say.

After overhearing this, I should assuredly have got down and been left in the solitude and darkness of the highway, but for feeling certain that the man had not recognised me. Indeed, I was not only older, but so differently dressed, that it was not at all likely he could have known me without accidental help. Still, the coincidence of our being together on the coach was sufficiently strange to fill me with a dread that some other coincidence might at any moment connect me, in his hearing, with my name. For this reason, I resolved to alight as soon as we touched the town, and put myself out of his hearing. This device I executed successfully. My little portmanteau was in the boot under my feet; I had but to turn a hinge to get it out: I threw it down before me, got down after it, and was left at the first lamp on the first stones of the town pavement.

I could not have said what I was afraid of, for my fear was vague, but there was great fear upon me – the revival for a few minutes of the terror of childhood.

The coffee-room at the Blue Boar was empty, and I had sat down to my dinner before the waiter knew me. As soon as he had apologised he asked me if he should send for Mr Pumblechook?

"No," said I, "certainly not."

The waiter appeared surprised, and took the earliest opportunity of putting a dirty old copy of a local newspaper before me. I took it up and read this paragraph:

"Our readers will learn, not altogether without interest, in reference to the recent romantic rise in fortune of a young artificer in iron of this neighbourhood, that the youth's earliest patron, companion, and friend, was a highly respected individual not entirely unconnected with the corn and seed trade, and whose eminently convenient and commodious business premises are situate within a hundred miles of the High Street. It is not wholly irrespective of our personal feelings that we record *him* as the Mentor of our young Telemachus, for it is good to know that our town produced the founder of the latter's fortunes. Does the thought-contracted brow of the local Sage or the lustrous eye of local Beauty inquire whose fortunes? We believe that Quentin Matsys was the *Blacksmith* of Antwerp. Verb. Sap.'

I am certain, that if in the days of my prosperity I had gone to the North Pole, I should have met somebody there, who would have told me that Pumblechook was my earliest patron and the founder of my fortunes.

CHAPTER 28

I was up early in the morning, too early to go to Miss Havisham's, so I wandered into the country on Miss Havisham's side of town – which was not Joe's side; I could go there tomorrow – thinking about my patroness, and painting brilliant pictures of her plans for me.

She had adopted Estella, she had as good as adopted me, and it could not fail to be her intention to bring us together. She wanted me to restore the desolate house, admit the sunshine into the dark rooms, set the clocks a-going and the cold hearths a-blazing, destroy the vermin – in short, do all the shining deeds of the young Knight of romance, and marry the Princess. But even though Estella had taken such strong possession of me, though my fancy and my hope were so set upon her, though her influence on my boyish life and character had been all-powerful, I did not, even that romantic morning, invest her with any attributes save those she possessed. I mention this in this place, of a fixed purpose, because it is the clue by which I am to be followed into my poor labyrinth. According to my experience, the conventional notion of a lover cannot be always true. The unqualified truth is, that when I loved Estella with the love of a man, I loved her simply because I found her irresistible. Once for all; I knew to my sorrow, often, if not always, that I loved her against reason, against promise, against peace, against hope, against happiness, against all discouragement that could be. Once for all; I loved her none the less because I knew it, and it had no more influence in restraining me, than if I had devoutly believed her to be human perfection.

I arrived at the gate at my old time. When I had rung at the bell with an unsteady hand, I turned my back upon the gate, while I tried to get my breath and keep the beating of my heart moderately quiet. I heard the side door open, and steps come across the courtyard; but I pretended not to hear, even when the gate swung on its rusty hinges.

I found Sarah Pocket: who appeared to have now become constitutionally green and yellow by reason of me.

"Oh!" said she. "You, is it, Mr Pip?"

"It is, Miss Pocket. I am glad to tell you that Mr Pocket and family are all well."

"Are they any wiser?" said Sarah, with a shake of the head; "they had better be wiser, than well. Ah, Matthew, Matthew! You know your way, sir?"

Tolerably, for I had gone up the staircase in the dark, many a time. I ascended it now and tapped in my old way at the door of Miss Havisham's room. "Pip's rap," I heard her say, immediately; "come in, Pip."

She was in the old dress, hands crossed on her stick, her chin resting on them, and her eyes on the fire. Sitting near her, with the white shoe that had never been worn in her hand, and her head bent as she looked at it, was an elegant lady whom I had never seen.

"Come in, Pip," Miss Havisham continued to mutter, without looking round or up; "come in, Pip, how do you do, Pip?"

She looked up at me suddenly, and repeated in a grimly playful manner, "Well?"

"I heard, Miss Havisham," said I, rather at a loss, "that you were so kind as to wish me to come and see you, and I came directly."

"Well?"

The other lady lifted up her eyes and looked archly at me, and then I saw that the eyes were Estella's eyes. But she had changed, was so much more beautiful, so much more womanly. I fancied, as I looked at her, that I slipped hopelessly back into the coarse and common boy again.

She gave me her hand. I stammered something about the pleasure I felt in seeing her again, and about having looked forward to it for a long, long time.

"Do you find her much changed, Pip?" asked Miss Havisham, striking her stick upon a chair, as a sign to me to sit down there.

"When I came in, Miss Havisham, I thought there was nothing of Estella in the face or figure; but now it all settles down so curiously into the old – "

"What? The old Estella?" Miss Havisham interrupted. "She was proud and insulting, and you wanted to leave her – remember?"

I said confusedly that that was long ago, and that I knew no better then. Estella smiled, and said she had no doubt of my having been quite right, and of her having been very disagreeable.

"Is he changed?" Miss Havisham asked her.

"Very much," said Estella, looking at me.

"Less coarse and common?" said Miss Havisham, playing with Estella's hair.

Estella laughed, and looked at the shoe in her hand, looked at me, and put the shoe down. She treated me as a boy still, but she lured me on.

We sat in the dreamy room among the old strange influences, and I learnt that she had just come home from France, and was going to London. Proud and wilful as of old, she had brought those qualities into such subjection to her beauty that it was impossible to separate them from her beauty. Truly it was impossible to dissociate her presence from all those wretched hankerings after money and gentility that had disturbed my boyhood – from all those ill-regulated aspirations that had first made me ashamed of home and Joe. In a word, it was impossible for me to separate her, in the past or in the present, from the innermost life of my life.

It was settled that I should stay there the rest of the day, and return to the hotel at night, and to London tomorrow. When we had conversed for a while, Miss Havisham sent us to walk in the neglected garden: on our coming in by-and-by, she said, I should wheel her about a little as in times of yore.

So, Estella and I went out into the garden – I, trembling in spirit and worshipping the very hem of her dress; she, quite composed and most decidedly not worshipping the hem of mine. As we drew near to the place of the fight, she stopped and said: "I must have been a singular little creature to watch that fight that day: but I did, and I enjoyed it very much."

"You rewarded me very much."

"Did I?" she replied, absently. "I remember objecting to your adversary, because I didn't like him being brought here to pester me with his company."

"He and I are great friends now."

"Are you? I remember – you read with his father? Since your change of fortune and prospects, you have changed your companions," said Estella.

"Naturally," said I.

"And necessarily," she added, in a haughty tone; "what was fit company for you once, would be quite unfit company for you now."

In my mind, I doubt whether I had any lingering intention left, of going to see Joe; but if I had, this observation put it to flight.

"You had no idea then of your impending good fortune?" said Estella.

"Not the least."

The air of completeness and superiority with which she walked at my side, and the air of youthfulness and submission with which I walked at hers, made a contrast that I strongly felt. The garden was too overgrown for walking in with ease, and after a round or two, we came into the brewery yard. I reminded her where she had come out of the house and given me my meat and drink, and she said, "I don't remember."

"Not remember that you made me cry?" said I.

"No," said she, and shook her head and looked about her. I verily believe that her not remembering and not minding in the least, made me cry again, inwardly – and that is the sharpest crying of all.

"You must know," said Estella, condescending to me as a brilliant and beautiful woman might, "that I have no heart – if that has anything to do with my memory."

I said something to the effect that I took the liberty of doubting that. That I knew better. That there could be no such beauty without it.

"Oh! No doubt I have a heart to be stabbed in or shot in," said Estella, "and, of course, if it ceased to beat I should cease to be. But you know what I mean. I have no softness there, no – sympathy – sentiment – nonsense."

What was it that was borne in upon my mind when she stood still and looked attentively at me? Anything that I had seen in Miss Havisham? No. In some of her looks and gestures there was a hint of Miss Havisham. And yet I could not trace this to Miss Havisham. I looked again, and though she was still looking at me, the suggestion was gone.

What was it?

"I am serious," said Estella, "if we are to be thrown much together, you had better believe it at once. No!" imperiously stopping me as I opened my lips. "I have not bestowed my tenderness anywhere. I have never had any such thing."

In another moment we were in the brewery, and she pointed to the high gallery. As my eyes followed her white hand, again the same dim suggestion that I could not possibly grasp, crossed me. My involuntary start occasioned her to lay her hand upon my arm. Instantly the ghost passed once more, and was gone.

What was it?

"Miss Havisham will soon be expecting you at your old post. Let us make one more round of the garden, and then go in. Come! You shall not shed tears for my cruelty today; you shall be my Page, and give me your shoulder."

Her handsome dress had trailed upon the ground. She held it in one hand now, and with the other lightly touched my shoulder as we walked. We walked round the ruined garden twice or thrice more, and it was all in bloom for me.

There was no discrepancy of years between us, to remove her far from me; we were of nearly the same age; but the air of inaccessibility that her beauty and her manner gave her, tormented me in the midst of my delight, and at the height of the assurance I felt that our patroness had chosen us for one another. Wretched boy!

At last we went back into the house, and there I heard, with surprise, that my guardian had come to see Miss Havisham on business, and would come back to dinner. The old wintry branches of chandeliers had been lighted while we were out, and Miss Havisham was in her chair and waiting for me.

It was like pushing the chair itself back into the past, when we began the old slow circuit round about the ashes of the bridal feast. But, in the funereal room, Estella looked more bright and beautiful than before, and I was under stronger enchantment.

The early dinner-hour drew close at hand, and Estella left us to prepare herself. We had stopped near the centre of the long table, and Miss Havisham rested a clenched hand upon the yellow cloth. As Estella looked back over her shoulder before going out, Miss Havisham kissed that hand to her, with a ravenous intensity that was quite dreadful.

Then, Estella being gone, she turned to me, and said in a whisper: "Is she beautiful, graceful, well-grown? Do you admire her?"

"Everybody must who sees her, Miss Havisham."

She drew an arm round my neck, and drew my head close down to hers as she sat in the chair. "Love her, love her! How does she use you?"

Before I could answer (if I could have answered such a question at all), she repeated, "Love her, love her! If she favours you, love her. If she wounds you, love her. If she tears your heart to pieces – and as it gets older and stronger, it will tear deeper – love her, love her!"

I could feel the muscles of the thin arm round my neck swell with the vehemence that possessed her.

"Hear me, Pip! I adopted her to be loved. I bred her and educated her, to be loved. I developed her into what she is, that she might be loved. Love her!"

She said the word often and she meant it; but if the often repeated word had been hate instead of love – it could not have sounded from her lips more like a curse.

"I'll tell you," said she, in the same hurried passionate whisper, "what real love is. It is blind devotion, unquestioning self-humiliation, utter submission, trust and belief against yourself and against the whole world, giving up your whole heart and soul to the smiter – as I did!"

She gave a wild cry and I caught her round the waist. For she rose up in the chair, in her shroud of a dress, and struck at the air.

All this passed in a few seconds. As I drew her down into her chair, I was conscious of a scent that I knew, and turning, saw my guardian in the room.

On meeting my eye, he said plainly, "Indeed? Singular!"

Miss Havisham had seen him as soon as I, and was (like everybody else) afraid of him. She made a strong attempt to compose herself, and stammered that he was as punctual as ever.

"As punctual as ever," he repeated, coming up to us. "(How do you do, Pip? Shall I give you a ride, Miss Havisham? Once round?) And so you are here, Pip?"

I told him when I had arrived, and how Miss Havisham had wished me to come and see Estella. To which he replied, "Ah! Very fine young lady!" Then he pushed Miss Havisham in her chair before him.

"Well, Pip! How often have you seen Miss Estella before?" said he, when he came to a stop.

"How often?"

"Ah! How many times? Ten thousand times?"

"Oh! Certainly not so many."

"Twice?"

"Jaggers," interposed Miss Havisham, much to my relief; "leave my Pip alone, and go with him to your dinner."

He complied, and we groped down the dark stairs together. While on our way to those detached apartments across the paved yard, he asked me how often I had seen Miss Havisham eat and drink.

I considered, and said, "Never."

"And never will, Pip," he retorted, with a frowning smile. "She has never allowed herself to be seen doing either, since she lived this present life of hers. She wanders about in the night, and then lays hands on such food as she takes."

"Pray, sir," said I, "may I ask you a question?"

"You may," said he, "and I may decline to answer it. Put your question."

"Estella's name. Is it Havisham or – ?"

"It is Havisham."

116

This brought us to the dinner table, where she and Sarah Pocket awaited us. Mr Jaggers presided, Estella sat opposite to him, I faced my green and yellow friend. We dined very well, and were waited on by a maid-servant whom I had never seen in all my comings and goings. After dinner, a bottle of choice old port was placed before my guardian, and the two ladies left us.

Mr Jaggers kept his very looks to himself, and scarcely directed his eyes to Estella's face once during dinner. When she spoke to him, he listened, and in due course answered, but never looked at her, that I could see. On the other hand, she often looked at him, with interest and curiosity, if not distrust, but his face never showed the least consciousness. Throughout dinner he took a dry delight in making Sarah Pocket greener and yellower, by often referring in conversation with me to my expectations.

And when he and I were left alone together, he sat quietly. Three or four times I feebly thought I would start conversation; but whenever he saw me going to ask him anything, he looked at me with his glass in his hand, rolling his wine about in his mouth, as if requesting me to take notice that he couldn't possibly answer.

Miss Pocket did not appear when we afterwards went up to Miss Havisham's room, and we four played at whist. In the interval, Miss Havisham, in a fantastic way, had put some of the most beautiful jewels from her dressing table into Estella's hair, and about her bosom and arms; and I saw even my guardian look at her and raise his eyebrows a little, when her loveliness was before him.

As we played, I suffered from the incompatibility between his cold presence and my feelings towards Estella. It was not that I knew I could never bear to speak to him about her, that I knew I could never bear to hear him creak his boots at her, that I knew I could never bear to see him wash his hands of her; it was, that my admiration should be within a foot or two of him – it was, that my feelings should be in the same place with him – that was the agonising circumstance.

We played until nine o'clock, and then we arranged that when Estella came to London I should be forewarned of her coming and should meet her at the coach. I then took leave of her, and touched her and left her.

My guardian lay at the Boar in the next room to mine. Far into the night, Miss Havisham's words, "Love her, love her!" sounded in my ears.

I adapted them for my own repetition, and said to my pillow, "I love her, I love her!" hundreds of times. Then, a burst of gratitude came upon me, that she should be destined for me, once the blacksmith's boy. Then I thought if she were by no means rapturously grateful for that destiny yet, when would she begin to be interested in me? When should I awaken the heart within her?

Ah me! I thought those were high and great emotions. But I never thought there was anything low and small in my keeping away from Joe, because I knew she would be contemptuous of him. It was but a day gone, and Joe had brought the tears into my eyes; they had soon dried, God forgive me! Soon dried.

CHAPTER 29

As we were going back together to London by the mid-day coach, this gave me an opportunity of saying that I wanted a walk, and that I would go on along the London-road while Mr Jaggers was occupied, if he would let the coachman know that I would get into my place when overtaken. I thus left the Blue Boar immediately after breakfast.

The coach, with Mr Jaggers inside, came up in due time, and I took my box-seat again, and arrived in London safe – but not sound, for my heart was gone. As soon as I arrived, I sent a penitential codfish and barrel of oysters to Joe (as reparation for not having gone myself), and then went on to Barnard's Inn.

I found Herbert dining on cold meat, and delighted to welcome me back. I felt that I must open my breast that very evening to my friend and chum.

Dinner done, and we sitting with our feet upon the fender, I said to Herbert, "My dear Herbert, I have something very particular to tell you."

"My dear Handel," he returned, "I shall esteem and respect your confidence."

"It concerns myself, Herbert," said I, "and one other person."

Herbert crossed his feet, looked at the fire with his head on one side, and then looked at me because I didn't go on.

"Herbert," said I, laying my hand upon his knee, "I love – I adore – Estella."

Instead of being transfixed, Herbert replied in an easy matter-of-course way, "Exactly. Well?"

"Well, Herbert? Is that all you say?"

"What next, I mean?" said Herbert. "Of course I know that."

"How do you know it?" said I.

"Why, from you."

"I never told you."

"Told me! You never say when you have your hair cut, but I know it has happened. You have always adored her, ever since I have known you. You brought your adoration and your portmanteau here, together. Told me! When you told me your own story, you told me plainly that you began adoring her the first time you saw her, when you were very young indeed."

"Very well, then," said I, "I have never left off adoring her. And she has come back, a most beautiful creature. And I saw her yesterday. And if I adored her before, I now doubly adore her."

"Lucky for you then, Handel," said Herbert, "that you are picked out for her. We may, I presume, say that there can be no doubt of that. Have you any idea yet, of Estella's views on the adoration question?"

I shook my head gloomily. "Oh! She is thousands of miles away from me."

"Patience, my dear Handel: time enough. But you have more to say?"

"I am ashamed to say it," I returned. "You call me a lucky fellow. Of course, I am. I was a blacksmith's boy but yesterday; I am – what shall I say I am – today?"

"Say, a good fellow, if you want a phrase," returned Herbert, clapping his hand on mine, "with impetuosity and hesitation, boldness and diffidence, action and dreaming, curiously mixed in him."

I stopped for a moment to consider whether there really was this mixture in my character.

"When I ask what I am to call myself today, Herbert," I went on, "I suggest what I have in my thoughts. You say I am lucky. I know I have done nothing to raise myself in life, and that Fortune alone has raised me, and that is lucky. And yet, when I think of Estella – then, my dear Herbert, I cannot tell you how dependent and uncertain I feel, and how exposed to hundreds of chances. On the constancy of one person (naming no person) all my expectations depend. And at the best, how indefinite, only to know

119

so vaguely what they are!" In saying this, I relieved my mind of what had always been there, more or less, though no doubt most since yesterday.

"Now, Handel," Herbert replied, in his gay hopeful way, "it seems to me that we are looking into our gift-horse's mouth with a magnifying-glass. Likewise, it seems that, concentrating on the examination, we altogether overlook one of the best points of the animal. Didn't you tell me that your guardian, Mr Jaggers, told you in the beginning, that you were not endowed with expectations only? And even if he had not told you so – though that is a very large If, I grant – could you believe that of all men in London, Mr Jaggers is the man to hold his present relations towards you unless he were sure of his ground?"

I could not deny that this was a strong point. I said it (as people often do so) like a rather reluctant concession to truth and justice; as if I wanted to deny it!

"I should think it was a strong point," said Herbert, "and I should think you would be puzzled to imagine a stronger; as to the rest, you must just bide your guardian's time, and he must bide his client's time. You'll be one-and-twenty before you know where you are, and then perhaps you'll get some further enlightenment. At all events, it must come at last."

"What a hopeful disposition you have!" said I, gratefully.

"I ought to have," said Herbert, "for I have not much else. I must acknowledge, by-the-by, that this good sense comes from my father. The only remark I ever heard him make on your story, was the final one: 'The thing is settled and done, or Mr Jaggers would not be in it.' And now before I say anything more about my father, or my father's son, and repay confidence with confidence, I want to make myself seriously disagreeable to you for a moment – positively repulsive."

"You won't succeed," said I.

"Oh yes I shall!" said he. "One, two, three, and now I am in for it. Handel, my good fellow;" though he spoke in this light tone, he was very much in earnest: "I have been thinking, that Estella surely cannot be a condition of your inheritance, if she was never referred to by your guardian. Am I right that he never referred to her, directly or indirectly, in any way? Never even hinted, for instance, that your patron might have views as to your marriage ultimately?"

"Never."

"Now, Handel, I am quite free from the flavour of sour grapes, upon

120

my soul and honour! Not being bound to her, can you not detach yourself from her? – I told you I should be disagreeable."

I turned my head aside, for, with a rush and a sweep, a feeling like that which had subdued me on the morning when I left the forge, smote upon my heart again. There was silence between us for a little while.

"Yes; but my dear Handel," Herbert went on, as if we had been talking instead of silent. "Think of her bringing-up, and think of Miss Havisham. Think of what she is herself (now I am repulsive and you abominate me). This may lead to miserable things."

"I know it, Herbert," said I, with my head still turned away, "but I can't help it."

"You can't detach yourself? You can't try, Handel?"

"No. Impossible!"

"Well!" said Herbert, getting up and stirring the fire; "I'll try to make myself agreeable again!"

So he went round the room, shaking curtains, tidying books, and then came back to his chair by the fire: where he sat down, nursing his left leg in both arms.

"I was going to say a word or two, Handel, concerning my father and my father's son. It is scarcely necessary to remark that my father's establishment is not particularly brilliant in its housekeeping."

"There is always plenty, Herbert," said I: to say something encouraging.

"Oh yes! and so the dustman says, I believe. But seriously, Handel, you know how it is, as well as I do. I suppose there was a time once when my father had not given matters up; but if ever there was, the time is gone. Has it been noticed, down in your part of the country, that the children of not exactly suitable marriages, are always most particularly anxious to be married?"

This was such a singular question, that I asked him in return, "Is it so?"

"I don't know," said Herbert, "I just want to know. My poor sister Charlotte who came after me and died before she was fourteen, was a striking example. Little Jane is the same. Little Alick in a frock has already made arrangements for his union with a suitable young person at Kew. And indeed, I think we are all engaged, except the baby."

"Then you are?" said I.

"I am," said Herbert; "but it's a secret."

121

I assured him of my keeping the secret. "May I ask the name?" I said.

"Name of Clara," said Herbert.

"Live in London?"

"Yes. But I should mention," said Herbert, who now seemed curiously crestfallen, "that she is rather below my mother's nonsensical family notions. Her father had to do with the victualling of passenger-ships. I think he was a species of purser."

"What is he now?" said I.

"An invalid," replied Herbert.

"Living on – ?"

"On the first floor," said Herbert. Which was not at all what I meant. "I have never seen him, for he keeps to his room. But I have heard him constantly. He makes a tremendous row – pegging at the floor with some frightful instrument." In looking at me and then laughing heartily, Herbert briefly recovered his usual lively manner.

"Don't you expect to see him?" said I.

"Oh yes, I constantly expect to see him," returned Herbert, "because I never hear him, without expecting him to come tumbling through the ceiling. But I don't know how long the rafters may hold."

When he had once more laughed heartily, he became meek again, and told me that the moment he began to realise Capital, it was his intention to marry this young lady. He added as a self-evident proposition, engendering low spirits, "But you can't marry, you know, while you're looking about you."

We contemplated the fire, and I thought what a difficult vision to realise this same Capital sometimes was. I therefore pledged myself to comfort and abet Herbert in the affair of his heart by all practicable and impracticable means.

CHAPTER 30

One day when I was busy with my books and Mr Pocket, I received a note by the post, the mere outside of which threw me into a great flutter; for, though I had never seen the handwriting, I divined whose hand it was. It had no set beginning, as Dear Mr Pip, or Dear Pip, or Dear Sir, or Dear Anything, but ran thus:

"I am to come to London the day after tomorrow by the mid-day coach. I believe it was settled you should meet me? At all events Miss Havisham has that impression, and I write in obedience to it. She sends you her regard.
Yours,
Estella."

If there had been time, I should probably have ordered several suits of clothes; but there was not, so I had to be content with those I had. My appetite vanished instantly, and I knew no peace until the day arrived. By then I was even worse, and was haunting the coach-office in Cheapside, before the coach had left the Blue Boar in our town. Even though I knew this, I still couldn't leave the coach-office longer than five minutes at a time. The wait seemed interminable, thoughts running through my head at how to greet her. Finally the wait was over and the coach came. I saw her face at the coach window and her hand waving to me. But what was the nameless shadow which again in that one instant had passed?

In her furred travelling-dress, Estella seemed more delicately beautiful than ever, even in my eyes. Her manner was more winning than she had cared to let it be to me before, and I thought I saw Miss Havisham's influence in the change.

We stood in the inn yard while she pointed out her luggage to me, and when it was all collected I remembered – having forgotten everything but herself in the meanwhile – that I knew nothing of her destination.

"I am going to Richmond," she told me. "The Richmond in Surrey, not in Yorkshire. The distance is ten miles. I am to have a carriage, and you are to take me. This is my purse, and you are to pay my charges out of it. Oh, you must take the purse! We have no choice, you and I, but to obey our instructions."

As she looked at me, I hoped there was an inner meaning in her words. She said them slightingly, but not with displeasure.

"A carriage will have to be ordered, Estella. Will you rest a little?"

"Yes, I am to rest here a little, and I am to drink some tea, and you are to take care of me the while."

"Where are you going to, at Richmond?" I asked Estella.

"I am going to live," said she, "at great expense, with a lady there who

123

has the power of taking me about, and introducing me. How do you thrive with Mr Pocket?" she suddenly asked, smiling delightfully.

"I live quite pleasantly there; at least – " It appeared to me that I was losing a chance.

"At least?" repeated Estella.

"As pleasantly as I could anywhere, away from you."

"You silly boy," said Estella, "how can you talk such nonsense? Your friend Mr Matthew, I believe, is superior to the rest of his family?"

"Very superior indeed. He is nobody's enemy– "

"Don't add but his own," interposed Estella, "for I hate that class of man. But he really is disinterested, and above small jealousy, I have heard?"

"I am sure I have every reason to say so."

"You would not say so of the rest of his people," said Estella, nodding at me, "for they beset Miss Havisham with reports and insinuations to your disadvantage. They watch you, misrepresent you, write letters about you (anonymous sometimes). You are the torment of their lives. You would scarcely believe the hatred those people feel for you."

"They do me no harm, I hope?"

Instead of answering, Estella burst out laughing. I looked at her in considerable perplexity. When she left off – and she had laughed with real enjoyment – I said, in my diffident way with her: "I hope I may suppose that you would not be amused if they did me harm."

"No, no you may be sure of that," said Estella. "I laugh because they fail. Oh, those people with Miss Havisham, and the tortures they undergo!" She laughed again, and even though it was genuine, it seemed too much for the occasion. I thought there must really be something more here than I knew; she saw the thought in my mind, and answered it.

"It is not easy for even you," said Estella, "to know what satisfaction it gives me to see those people thwarted, or how enjoyable it is when they are made ridiculous. For you were not brought up in that strange house from a mere baby. – I was. You did not gradually open your round childish eyes wider to the discovery of that impostor of a woman who calculates her stores of peace of mind for when she wakes up in the night. – I did."

It was no laughing matter with Estella now. I would not have been the cause of that look of hers, for all my expectations in a heap.

"Two things I can tell you," said Estella. "First, you may set your mind at rest that these people never will – in a hundred years – impair your ground with Miss Havisham. Second, I am beholden to you as the cause of their being so busy and so mean in vain, and there is my hand upon it."

As she gave it me playfully – for her darker mood had been but momentary – I held it and put it to my lips. "You ridiculous boy," she said, "will you never take warning? Or do you kiss my hand in the same spirit in which I once let you kiss my cheek?"

"What spirit was that?" said I.

"I must think a moment – a spirit of contempt for the fawners and plotters."

"If I say yes, may I kiss the cheek again?"

"You should have asked before you touched the hand. But, yes, if you like."

I leaned down, and her calm face was like a statue's. "Now," said Estella, gliding away the instant I touched her cheek, "you are to take me to Richmond."

Her reverting to this tone as if our association were forced upon us and we were mere puppets, gave me pain; but everything in our intercourse did give me pain. Whatever her tone with me happened to be, I could put no trust in it, and build no hope on it; and yet I went on against trust and against hope. Why repeat it a thousand times? So it always was.

We got into our post-coach and drove away, turning into Cheapside and rattling up past Newgate Prison.

"What place is that?" Estella asked me.

I told her. She looked at it, and drew in her head again, murmuring "Wretches!"

"Mr Jaggers," said I, "has the reputation of being more in the secrets of that dismal place than any man in London."

"He is more in the secrets of every place, I think," said Estella, in a low voice.

"You have seen him often, I suppose?"

"I have seen him at uncertain intervals, ever since I can remember. But I know him no better now, than I did then. What is your own experience of him? Do you advance with him?"

"Once habituated to his distrustful manner," said I, "I have done very well."

"Are you intimate?"

"I have dined with him at his private house."

"I fancy," said Estella, shrinking; "that must be a curious place."

"It is a curious place."

The subject changed, and it was principally about the route we were travelling, and about what parts of London lay on this side of it, and what on that. The great city was almost new to her, she told me, for she had never left Miss Havisham's neighbourhood until she had gone to France. I asked her if my guardian had any charge of her while she remained here? To that she emphatically said, "God forbid!" and no more.

It was impossible for me to avoid seeing that she cared to attract me; that she made herself winning. Yet this made me none the happier, for, even if she had not taken that tone of our being disposed of by others, I should have felt that she held my heart in her hand because she wilfully chose to do it, and not because it would have wrung any tenderness in her, to crush it and throw it away.

When passing through Hammersmith, I showed her where Mr Matthew Pocket lived, and said it was no great way from Richmond, and that I hoped I should see her sometimes.

"Oh yes, you are to see me; you are to come when you think proper; you are already mentioned to the family."

I inquired was it a large household she was going to be a member of?

"No; there are only two; mother and daughter. The mother is a lady of some station, though not averse to increasing her income."

"I wonder Miss Havisham could part with you again so soon."

"It is a part of Miss Havisham's plans for me, Pip," said Estella, with a sigh; "I am to write to her constantly and see her regularly, reporting how I go on – I and the jewels – for they are nearly all mine now."

It was the first time she had ever called me by my name. Of course she did so purposely, and knew that I should treasure it.

We came to Richmond all too soon, to a house by the Green; a staid old house, where hoops and powder and patches, embroidered coats, rolled stockings, ruffles, and swords, had had their court days many a time. Some ancient trees still stood before the house.

A bell with an old voice sounded gravely in the moonlight, and two cherry-coloured maids came fluttering out to receive Estella. The doorway soon absorbed her boxes, and she gave me her hand, and said good-night, and was absorbed likewise. I stood looking at the house, thinking how happy I should be if I lived there with her, knowing that I never was happy with her, but always miserable.

I got into the carriage to be taken back to Hammersmith, and I got out with a worse heartache. Mr Pocket was out lecturing; for he was a most delightful lecturer on domestic economy, and his treatises on the management of children and servants were considered the very best text-books on those themes.

Mr Pocket being justly celebrated for giving most excellent practical advice, I had some notion in my heartache of begging him to accept my confidence. But, happening to look at Mrs Pocket as she sat reading her book after prescribing Bed as a sovereign remedy for baby, I thought – Well – No, I wouldn't.

CHAPTER 31

I lived in a state of chronic uneasiness respecting my behaviour to Joe. I was not comfortable about Biddy. When I woke up in the night I used to think, with a weariness on my spirits, that I should have been happier and better if I had never seen Miss Havisham's face, and had risen to manhood content to be partners with Joe in the old forge. Many a time, when I sat alone looking at the fire, I thought, after all, there was no fire like the forge fire and the kitchen fire at home.

Yet Estella was inseparable from all my restlessness. That is to say, supposing I had had no expectations, and yet had had Estella to think of, I could not make out to my satisfaction that I should have done much better. Now, concerning the influence of my position on others, I was in no such difficulty, and so I perceived – though dimly enough perhaps – that above all it was not beneficial to Herbert. My lavish habits led his easy nature into expenses that he could not afford. I was not at all remorseful for having unwittingly set those other branches of the Pocket family to the poor arts they practised. But Herbert's was a very different case, and it often caused me a twinge to think that I had crowded his sparsely furnished chambers with incongruous upholstery work.

So now, as an infallible way of making little ease great ease, I began to contract a quantity of debt. Herbert soon followed. At Startop's suggestion, we put ourselves down for election into a club called The Finches of the Grove: the object of which institution seemed to be that the members should dine expensively once a fortnight.

The Finches spent their money foolishly (the Hotel we dined at was in Covent Garden), and the first Finch I saw was Bentley Drummle: at that time floundering about town in a cab of his own, and doing a great deal of damage to the posts at the street corners. But here I anticipate a little for I was not a Finch, and could not be, according to the sacred laws of the society, until I came of age.

In my confidence in my own resources, I would willingly have taken Herbert's expenses on myself; but Herbert was proud, and I could make no such proposal to him. So, he got into difficulties in every direction, and continued to look about him.

I was usually at Hammersmith about half the week, and when I was at Hammersmith I haunted Richmond. Herbert would often come to Hammersmith when I was there, and I think at those seasons his father would occasionally have some passing perception that the opening he was looking for, had not appeared yet. In the meantime Mr Pocket grew greyer, while Mrs Pocket tripped up the family with her footstool and read her book of dignities.

At certain times, depending on our humour, I would say to Herbert, as if it were a remarkable discovery: "My dear Herbert, we are getting on badly."

"My dear Handel," Herbert would say to me, in all sincerity, "those very words were on my lips, by a strange coincidence."

"Then, Herbert," I would respond, "let us look into our affairs."

We always derived profound satisfaction from making an appointment for this purpose.

We ordered something rather special for dinner, with a bottle of something similarly special, in order that our minds might be fortified for the occasion, and we might come well up to the mark. Dinner over, we produced pens, ink, and a goodly show of writing and blotting paper. There was something very comfortable in having plenty of stationery.

I would then take a sheet of paper, and write across the top, "Memorandum of Pip's debts". Herbert would do likewise, writing "Memorandum of Herbert's debts".

Each of us would then refer to a confused heap of papers at his side, which had been thrown into drawers, worn into holes in pockets, half-burnt in lighting candles, stuck for weeks in the looking-glass, and otherwise damaged.

When we had written a little while, I would ask Herbert how he got on? Herbert probably would have been scratching his head in a most rueful manner at the sight of his accumulating figures.

"They are mounting up, Handel," Herbert would say.

"Be firm, Herbert," I would retort, plying my own pen. "Look the thing in the face."

My determined manner would have its effect, and Herbert would fall to work again. After a time he would give up again, on the plea that he had not got Cobbs's bill, or Lobbs's, or Nobbs's, as the case might be.

"Then, Herbert, estimate in round numbers, and put it down."

"What a fellow of resource you are!" my friend would reply, with admiration. "Really your business powers are very remarkable."

I thought so too. When I had got all my responsibilities down upon my list, I compared each with the bill, and ticked it off. My self-approval when I ticked an entry was quite a luxurious sensation. When I had no more ticks to make, I folded all my bills up uniformly, docketed each on the back, and tied the whole into a symmetrical bundle. Then I did the same for Herbert (who modestly said he had not my administrative genius), and felt that I had brought his affairs into a focus for him.

We shut our outer door on these solemn occasions, in order that we might not be interrupted. One evening we heard a letter dropped through the slit in the said door, and fall on the ground. "It's for you, Handel," said Herbert, going out and coming back with it, "and I hope there is nothing the matter." This was in allusion to its heavy black seal and border.

The letter was signed "Trabb & Co.", and its contents were simply, that I was an honoured sir, and that they begged to inform me that Mrs J. Gargery had departed this life on Monday last, and that my attendance was requested at the internment on Monday next, at three o'clock in the afternoon.

CHAPTER 32

It was the first time that a grave had opened in my road of life. The figure of my sister in her chair by the kitchen fire haunted me night and day. She had seldom or never been in my thoughts of late, but I had now the strangest ideas that she was coming towards me in the street, or that she would presently knock at the door.

Whatever my fortunes might have been, I could scarcely have recalled my sister with much tenderness. But I suppose there is a shock of regret that may exist without much tenderness. Under its influence (and perhaps to make up for the want of the softer feeling) I was seized with a violent indignation against the assailant from whom she had suffered so much.

I wrote to Joe, to offer consolation, and to assure him that I should come to the funeral. I went down early in the morning, and alighted at the Blue Boar in good time to walk over to the forge.

It was fine summer weather again, and, as I walked along, the times when I was a little helpless creature, and my sister did not spare me, vividly returned.

At last I came within sight of the house, and saw that Trabb and Co. had taken possession. As I came up, one of the two black-dressed warders knocked at the door – implying that I was far too much exhausted by grief, to knock for myself.

Another warder opened the door, showing me into the parlour.

Poor dear Joe, entangled in a little black cloak tied in a large bow under his chin, was seated at the upper end of the room. When I bent down and said to him, "Dear Joe, how are you?" he said, "Pip, old chap, you know'd her when she were a fine figure of a – " and clasped my hand and said no more.

Biddy, looking very neat in her black dress, went quietly here and there, and was very helpful. When I had spoken to Biddy, I went and sat down near Joe, and there began to wonder in what part of the house it – she – my sister – was. The air of the parlour being faint with the smell of sweet cake, I looked about for the table of refreshments; it was scarcely visible in the gloom, but there was a cut-up plum-cake upon it, and there were cut-up oranges, and sandwiches, and biscuits, and two decanters that I had never seen used in all my life; one full of port, and one of sherry. Standing there was the servile Pumblechook in a black cloak and several yards of hatband, alternately stuffing himself, and making obsequious movements to catch my attention. The moment he succeeded, he came over to me (breathing sherry and crumbs), and said in a subdued voice, "May I, dear sir?" and did. I then descried Mr and Mrs Hubble. We were all to "follow," and were all being tied up separately (by Trabb) into ridiculous bundles.

"Which I meantersay, Pip," Joe whispered me, "as I would in preference have carried her to the church myself, along with three or four friendly ones wot come to it with willing harts and arms, but it were considered wot the neighbours would look down on such and would be of opinions as it were wanting in respect."

"Pocket-handkerchiefs out, all!" cried Mr Trabb at this point. "Pocket-handkerchiefs out! We are ready!"

So, we all put our pocket-handkerchiefs to our faces, as if our noses were bleeding, and filed out two and two; Joe and I; Biddy and Pumblechook; Mr and Mrs Hubble. The remains of my poor sister were by the kitchen door, and, it being a point of Undertaking ceremony that the six bearers must be stifled and blinded under a horrible black velvet housing with a white border, the whole looked like a blind monster with twelve human legs, shuffling and blundering along.

The neighbourhood, however, highly approved of these arrangements, and we were much admired as we went through the village. In this progress I was much annoyed by Pumblechook, who, being behind me, persisted all the way in arranging my streaming hatband, and smoothing my cloak. My thoughts were further distracted by the excessive pride of Mr and Mrs Hubble, at being members of so distinguished a procession.

And now, the range of marshes lay clear before us, with the sails of the ships on the river growing out of it; and we went into the churchyard, close to the graves of my unknown parents, Philip Pirrip, late of this parish, and Also Georgiana, Wife of the Above. And there, my sister was laid quietly in the earth while the larks sang high above it.

When we got back, Pumblechook had the hardihood to tell me that he wished my sister could have known I had done her so much honour, and to hint that she would have considered it reasonably purchased at the price of her death. After that, he drank the rest of the sherry, and Mr Hubble drank the port. Finally, he went away with Mr and Mrs Hubble –

to make an evening of it, I felt sure, and to tell the Jolly Bargemen that he was the founder of my fortunes and my earliest benefactor.

When they were all gone, Biddy, Joe, and I had a cold dinner together; but in the best parlour, not in the old kitchen, and Joe was so particular what he did with his knife and fork and the salt-cellar, that there was great restraint upon us. But after dinner, when he had his pipe, and when I had loitered with him about the forge, and then sat down together on the great block of stone outside, we got on better. Joe changed his clothes to make a compromise between his Sunday dress and working dress: now the dear fellow looked natural, and like the Man he was.

He was very pleased when I asked if I might sleep in my own little room, and I was pleased too; for I felt that I had done rather a great thing in making the request. When the evening shadows were closing in, I went into the garden with Biddy for a little talk.

"Biddy," said I, "I think you might have written to me about these sad matters."

"Do you, Mr Pip?" said Biddy. "I should have written if I had thought that."

"I don't mean to be unkind, Biddy, but you ought to have thought that."

"Should I, Mr Pip?"

She was so quiet, and had such a pretty way with her, that I did not like the thought of making her cry again. I therefore gave up that point.

"I suppose it will be difficult for you to remain here now, Biddy dear?"

"Oh! I can't do so, Mr Pip," said Biddy, in a tone of regret, but still of quiet conviction. "I have been speaking to Mrs Hubble, and I go to her tomorrow. I hope we shall be able to take care of Mr Gargery, together, until he settles down."

"How are you going to live, Biddy? If you want any mo– "

"How am I going to live?" repeated Biddy, striking in, with a momentary flush upon her face. "I am going to try to get the place of mistress in the new school here. I can be well recommended by all the neighbours, and I hope I can be industrious and patient, and teach myself while I teach others."

"I have not heard the particulars of my sister's death, Biddy."

"They are very slight, poor thing. She had been in one of her bad states for four days, when she came out of it in the evening, just at teatime, and said quite plainly, 'Joe'. As she had never said any word for a long while, I ran for Mr Gargery from the forge. She made signs that she wanted him to sit down close to her, and to put her arms round his neck. So I put them round his neck, and she laid her head down on his shoulder quite content and satisfied. She presently said 'Joe' again, and once 'Pardon', and once 'Pip'. And she never lifted her head again. An hour later we found she was gone."

Biddy cried; the darkening garden, and the stars that were coming out, were blurred in my own sight.

Moments later, she told me how Joe loved me, and how Joe never complained of anything – she didn't say, of me; she had no need; I knew what she meant – but ever did his duty in his way of life, with a strong hand, a quiet tongue, and a gentle heart.

"Indeed, it would be hard to say too much for him," said I; "and Biddy, we must often speak of these things, for of course I shall be often down here now. I am not going to leave poor Joe alone."

"Are you quite sure, then, that you *will* come to see him often?" asked Biddy, stopping in the narrow garden walk, and looking at me under the stars with a clear and honest eye.

"Oh dear me!" said I. "This really is a very bad side of human nature! Don't say any more, if you please, Biddy. This shocks me very much."

I kept Biddy at a distance during supper, and, when I went up to my room, took as stately a leave of her as I could, in my murmuring soul. As often as I was restless in the night, and that was every quarter of an hour, I reflected what an unkindness, what an injury, what an injustice, Biddy had done me.

Early in the morning I was out, and looking in, unseen, at one of the wooden windows of the forge. There I stood, for minutes, looking at Joe, already working with a glow of health and strength upon his face.

"Good-bye, dear Joe! – No, don't wipe it off – for God's sake, give me your blackened hand! – I shall be down soon, and often."

"Never too soon, sir," said Joe, "and never too often, Pip!"

Biddy waited at the kitchen door, with milk and a crust of bread. "Biddy," said I, when I gave her my hand at parting, "I am not angry, but I am hurt."

"No, don't be hurt," she pleaded quite pathetically; "let only me be hurt, if I have been ungenerous."

The mists were rising as I walked away. If they disclosed to me, as I suspect they did, that I should not come back, and that Biddy was quite right, all I can say is – they were quite right too.

133

CHAPTER 33

Herbert and I went from bad to worse, in the way of increasing our debts and looking into our affairs. Time went on, and I came of age – in fulfilment of Herbert's prediction, that I should do so before I knew where I was.

Herbert himself had come of age, eight months before me. As he had nothing else than his majority to come into, the event did not make a profound sensation in Barnard's Inn. But we had looked forward to my one-and-twentieth birthday, for we had both considered that my guardian would surely say something definite on that occasion.

I had ensured that everyone in Little Britain knew when my birthday was. On the day before I received a note from Wemmick, informing me that Mr Jaggers would be glad if I would call upon him at five in the afternoon. This convinced us that something great was to happen.

In the outer office Wemmick offered me his congratulations, and incidentally rubbed the side of his nose with a folded piece of tissue-paper that I liked the look of. But he said nothing, and motioned me with a nod into my guardian's room. It was November, and my guardian stood before his fire.

"Well, Pip," said he, "I must call you Mr Pip to-day. Congratulations, Mr Pip."

We shook hands and I thanked him.

"Take a chair, Mr Pip," said my guardian.

As I sat, and he remained standing, I felt at a disadvantage, which reminded me of when I had been put upon a tombstone.

"Now my young friend," my guardian began, as if I were a witness in the box, "I am going to have a word or two with you."

"If you please, sir."

"What do you suppose," said Mr Jaggers, "you are living at the rate of?"

"At the rate of, sir?"

"At," repeated Mr Jaggers, looking at the ceiling, "the – rate – of?" And then looked all round the room. Reluctantly, I confessed myself quite unable to answer the question. This reply seemed agreeable to Mr Jaggers, who said, "I thought so!"

134

"Now, I have asked a question, my friend," said Mr Jaggers. "Have you anything to ask?"

"It would be a great relief to ask you several questions, sir; but I remember your prohibition."

"Ask one," said Mr Jaggers.

"Is my benefactor to be made known to me today?"

"No. Ask another."

"Is that confidence to be imparted to me sòon?"

"Waive that, a moment," said Mr Jaggers, "and ask another."

I looked about me, but there appeared to be now no possible escape from the inquiry, "Have – I – anything to receive, sir?"

On that, Mr Jaggers said, triumphantly, "I thought we should come to it!" and called to Wemmick to give him that piece of paper. Wemmick brought it in.

"Now, Mr Pip," said Mr Jaggers, "attend, if you please. You have been drawing pretty freely; your name occurs pretty often in Wemmick's cash-book; but you are in debt, of course?"

"Yes, sir."

"I don't ask you what you owe, because you don't know; and if you did know, you wouldn't tell me," cried Mr Jaggers, waving his forefinger to stop me, as I made a show of protesting. "You'll excuse me, but I know better than you. Now, take this piece of paper. Unfold it and tell me what it is."

"This is a bank-note," said I, "for five hundred pounds."

"That is a bank-note," repeated Mr Jaggers, "for five hundred pounds. A very handsome sum of money too, I think. You consider it so?"

"How could I do otherwise!"

"Ah! But answer the question," said Mr Jaggers.

"Undoubtedly."

"You consider it, undoubtedly, a handsome sum of money. Now, that handsome sum of money, Pip, is your own. It is a present to you on this day. And on that handsome sum of money per annum, you are to live until the donor of the whole appears. That is to say, you now take your money affairs entirely into your own hands, and will draw from Wemmick one hundred and twenty-five pounds per quarter, until you are in communication with the fountain-head, and no longer with the mere agent. I execute my instructions, and I am paid for doing so. I think them injudicious, but I am not paid for giving any opinion on their merits."

After a pause, I hinted: "I had a question just now, Mr Jaggers, which you desired me to waive for a moment. May I ask it again?"

"What is it?" said he.

I knew he would never help me out; but it took me aback to have to shape the question afresh. "Is it likely," I said, after hesitating, "that my patron, the fountain-head you have spoken of, Mr Jaggers, will soon – " there I delicately stopped.

"Will soon what?" asked Mr Jaggers. "That's no question as it stands, you know."

"Will soon come to London," said I, after casting about for a precise form of words, "or summon me anywhere else?"

"Cast your mind back," replied Mr Jaggers, fixing me for the first time with his dark deep-set eyes, "what did I tell you when we met at your village, Pip?"

"You told me that it might be years hence when that person appeared."

"Just so," said Mr Jaggers; "that's my answer."

As we looked full at one another, I felt that I had less chance than ever of getting anything out of him.

"Do you suppose it will still be years hence, Mr Jaggers?"

Mr Jaggers shook his head. "Come!" he said, warming the backs of his legs, "I'll be plain with you, my friend Pip. That's a question I must not be asked. You'll understand that, better, when I tell you it's a question that might compromise me. I'll go a little further with you; I'll say something more."

He bent down low.

"When that person discloses," said Mr Jaggers, straightening again, "you and that person will settle your own affairs. When that person discloses, my part in this business will cease. When that person discloses, it will not be necessary for me to know anything about it. And that's all I have got to say."

From this last speech I felt that Miss Havisham, for some reason, had not told him as to her designing me for Estella; that he resented this, and felt a jealousy about it; or that he really did object to that scheme, and would have nothing to do with it. When I raised my eyes again, I found that he had been looking at me all the time, and was doing so still.

"If that is all you have to say, sir," I remarked, "there can be nothing left for me to say."

He nodded assent, and then asked me where I was going to dine? I replied at my own chambers, with Herbert. As a necessary sequence, I asked him if he would favour us with his company, and he promptly accepted the invitation. He insisted on walking home with me, but first he had a letter or two to write, so I said I would go into the outer office and talk to Wemmick.

The fact was, that with five hundred pounds in my pocket, a thought had come into my head which had been often there before; and it appeared to me that Wemmick was the person to talk with, concerning such thought.

He had already locked up his safe, and made preparations for going home.

"Mr Wemmick," said I, "I want to ask your opinion. I am very desirous to serve a friend."

Wemmick tightened his post-office and shook his head, as if dead against any fatal weakness of that sort.

"This friend," I pursued, "is trying to get on in commercial life, but has no money, and finds it difficult to make a beginning. Now, I want somehow to help him to a beginning."

"With money down?" said Wemmick.

"With some money down," I replied, remembering the bundle of papers at home; "and perhaps some anticipation of my expectations."

"Mr Pip," said Wemmick, "let's just run over, if you please, the names of the various bridges as high as Chelsea Reach. Let's see; there's London; Southwark; Blackfriars; Waterloo; Westminster and Vauxhall." He checked off each bridge in turn. "There's six, you see, to choose from."

"I don't understand," said I.

"Choose your bridge, Mr Pip," returned Wemmick, "and pitch your money into the Thames from your bridge, and you know the end of it. Serve a friend with it, and you may know the end of it too – but it's a less pleasant and profitable end."

I could have posted a newspaper in his mouth, he made it so wide after saying this.

"This is very discouraging," said I. "Then is it your opinion, that a man should never – "

" – Invest portable property in a friend?" said Wemmick. "He should not. Unless he wants to get rid of the friend – and then it becomes a question how much portable property it may be worth to get rid of him."

"And that," said I, "is your deliberate opinion, Mr Wemmick?"

"That," he returned, "is my deliberate opinion in this office."

"Ah!" said I, pressing him, for I thought I saw a loophole here; "but would that be your opinion at Walworth?"

"Mr Pip," he replied, with gravity, "Walworth is one place, and this office is another. My Walworth sentiments must be taken at Walworth; none but my official sentiments can be taken in this office."

"Very well," said I, much relieved, "then I shall look you up at Walworth, you may depend upon it."

"Mr Pip," he returned, "you will be welcome there, in a private and personal capacity."

We had held this conversation in a low voice, well knowing my guardian's ears to be sharp. As he now appeared in his doorway, towelling his hands, Wemmick got on his great-coat. We all three went into the street together, and Wemmick turned his way, and Mr Jaggers and I turned ours.

I could not help wishing more than once that evening, that Mr Jaggers had had an Aged in Gerrard Street. He was a thousand times better informed and cleverer than Wemmick, and yet I would a thousand times rather have had Wemmick to dinner. Mr Jaggers did not make only me intensely melancholy; after he was gone, Herbert said that he thought he must have committed a felony and forgotten the details of it, he felt so dejected and guilty.

CHAPTER 34

Deeming Sunday the best day for taking Mr Wemmick's Walworth sentiments, I devoted the following Sunday afternoon to a pilgrimage to the Castle. On arriving, I found the Union Jack flying and the drawbridge up; but undeterred, I rang at the gate, and was admitted in a most pacific manner by the Aged.

"My son, sir," said the old man, after securing the drawbridge, "rather had it in his mind that you might happen to drop in, and he left word that he would soon be home from his afternoon's walk. He is very regular in his walks, is my son. Very regular in everything, is my son."

I nodded at the old gentleman as Wemmick himself might have nodded, and we went in and sat down by the fireside.

I was startled by a sudden click in the wall, and the ghostly tumbling open of a little wooden flap with *John* upon it. The old man, following my eyes, cried with great triumph, "My son's come home!" and we both went out to the drawbridge.

It was worth any money to see Wemmick waving a salute to me from the other side of the moat, when we might have shaken hands across it with the greatest ease. Wemmick was accompanied by Miss Skiffins.

Miss Skiffins seemed to be a good sort of fellow, and showed a high regard for the Aged. She was a frequent visitor at the Castle.

While Miss Skiffins was taking off her bonnet, Wemmick invited me to take a walk with him round the property, and see how the island looked in winter-time. Thinking that he did this to give me an opportunity of taking his Walworth sentiments, I seized the opportunity as soon as we were out of the Castle.

Having thought of the matter with care, I approached my subject as if I had never hinted at it before. I informed Wemmick that I was anxious for Herbert Pocket, and I told him how we had first met. I glanced at Herbert's home, and at his character, and at his having no means but such as he was dependent on his father for: those, uncertain and unpunctual.

I alluded to the advantages I had derived from his society, and I confessed that I had ill repaid them, and that he might have done better without me and my expectations. Keeping Miss Havisham in the background, I hinted at the possibility of my having competed with him in his prospects, and at the certainty of his possessing a generous soul. For all these reasons, and because he was my companion and friend, and I had a great affection for him, I wished my own good fortune to help him, and therefore I sought advice from Wemmick's experience and knowledge, how I could best try to help Herbert to some present income – say of a hundred a year, to keep him in good hope and heart – and gradually to buy him on to some small partnership. I begged Wemmick, in conclusion, that my help must always be rendered without Herbert's knowledge or suspicion, and that there was no one else in the world with whom I could advise. I wound up by saying, "I can't help confiding in you, though I know it must be troublesome to you; but that is your fault, in having ever brought me here."

Wemmick was silent, and then said, "Well, Mr Pip, I must tell you one thing. This is devilish good of you."

"Say you'll help me to be good then," said I.

"Ecod," replied Wemmick, shaking his head, "that's not my trade."

"Nor is this your trading-place," said I.

"You are right," he returned. "Mr Pip, I'll put on my considering-cap, and I think all you want to do, may be gradually done. Skiffins (that's her brother) is an accountant and agent. I'll look him up and go to work for you."

"I thank you ten thousand times."

After a little further conversation to the same effect, we returned into the Castle where we found Miss Skiffins preparing tea. The responsible duty of making the toast was delegated to the Aged and he prepared such a haystack of buttered toast, that I could scarcely see him over it; while Miss Skiffins brewed a huge jorum of tea. I inferred from the methodical nature of Miss Skiffins's arrangements that she made tea there every Sunday night.

We ate the whole of the toast, and drank tea in proportion, and it was delightful to see how warm and greasy we all got after it. After a short pause for repose, Miss Skiffins – in the absence of the little servant who, it seemed, retired to the bosom of her family on Sunday afternoons – washed up the tea-things. Then she put on her gloves again, and we drew round the fire.

The Aged read the newspaper aloud, and as Wemmick and Miss Skiffins sat side by side, and I sat in a shadowy corner, I observed a slow and gradual elongation of Mr Wemmick's mouth, powerfully suggestive of his slowly and gradually stealing his arm round Miss Skiffins's waist. In course of time I saw his hand appear on the other side of Miss Skiffins; but at that moment Miss Skiffins neatly stopped him, unwound his arm again as if it were an article of dress, and with the greatest deliberation laid it on the table before her. Miss Skiffins's composure while she did this was one of the most remarkable sights I have ever seen.

At last, the Aged read himself into a light slumber. Wemmick then produced a little kettle, a tray of glasses, and a black bottle. With the aid of these appliances we all had something warm to drink: including the Aged, who was soon awake again. Miss Skiffins mixed, and I observed that she and Wemmick drank out of one glass. Of course I knew better than to offer to see Miss Skiffins home, and under the circumstances I thought I had best go first: which I did, taking a cordial leave of the Aged, and having passed a pleasant evening.

Before a week was out, I received a note from Wemmick, from Walworth, stating that he hoped he had made some advance in that matter appertaining to our private and personal capacities, and that he would be glad if I could come and see him again upon it. The upshot was, that we found a worthy young merchant or shipping-broker, not long established in business, who wanted intelligent help, and capital, and who in due course of time and receipt would want a partner. Between him and me, secret articles were signed of which Herbert was the subject, and I paid him half of my five hundred pounds, and engaged for sundry other payments: some, to fall due at certain dates out of my income: some, contingent on my coming into my property. Miss Skiffins's brother conducted the negotiation. Wemmick pervaded it throughout, but never appeared in it.

The whole business was so cleverly managed, that Herbert had not the least suspicion of my hand being in it. I never shall forget his radiant face when he came home one afternoon, and told me, how he had fallen in with one Clarriker (the young merchant), and of Clarriker's having shown an extraordinary inclination towards him, and of his belief that the opening had come at last. Day by day his hopes grew stronger and his face brighter, and I had the greatest difficulty in restraining my tears of triumph when I saw him so happy. At length, the thing was done, and he entered Clarriker's House, and talked to me for a whole evening in a flush of pleasure and success, and I did cry when I went to bed, to think that my expectations had done some good to somebody.

A great event in my life, the turning point of my life, now opens. But I must now give one chapter to Estella. It is not much to give to the theme that so long filled my heart.

CHAPTER 35

If that staid old house at Richmond should ever come to be haunted when I am dead, it will be haunted, surely, by my ghost. O the many, many nights and days my unquiet spirit haunted that house when Estella lived there! Let my body be where it would, my spirit was always wandering, wandering, wandering, about that house.

The lady with whom Estella was placed, Mrs Brandley by name, was a widow, with one daughter several years older than Estella. Little, if any, community of feeling existed between them and Estella, but that they were necessary to her, and she was necessary to them. Mrs Brandley had been a friend of Miss Havisham's before the time of her seclusion.

In Mrs Brandley's house and out of Mrs Brandley's house, I suffered every kind and degree of torture that Estella could cause me. The nature of my relations with her placed me on terms of familiarity but not on terms of favour. She used me to tease other admirers, and she turned the very familiarity between herself and me, to the account of putting a constant slight on my devotion to her. If I had been her secretary, steward, half-brother, poor relation – if I had been a younger brother of her appointed husband – I could not have seemed to myself, further from my hopes. The privilege of calling her by her name and hearing her call me by mine, became an aggravation of my trials; and while I think it likely that it almost maddened her other lovers, I know too certainly that it almost maddened me.

She had admirers without end. No doubt my jealousy made an admirer of all who went near her; but there were more than enough of them without that.

I saw her often at Richmond, I heard of her often in town; there were picnics, fête days, plays, operas, concerts, parties, all sorts of pleasures, through which I pursued her – and they were all miseries to me. I never had one hour's happiness in her society.

Throughout – and it seemed to me to last a long time – she habitually reverted to that tone which expressed that our association was forced upon us. There were other times when she would come to a sudden check, and would seem to pity me.

"Pip, Pip," she said one evening, when we sat apart at a darkening window of the house in Richmond; "will you never take warning?"

"Of what?"

"Of me."

"Not to be attracted by you, do you mean, Estella?"

"If you don't know what I mean, you are blind."

I should have replied that Love was commonly reputed blind, but for the reason that I always was restrained – and this was not the least of my miseries – knowing that she could not choose but obey Miss Havisham. My dread was, that this knowledge on her part laid me under a heavy disadvantage with her pride, and made me the subject of a rebellious struggle in her bosom.

"At any rate," said I, "you wrote to me to come to you, this time."

"That's true," said Estella, with a cold careless smile that always chilled me.

After looking at the twilight for a little while, she went on to say: "Miss Havisham wishes to have me for a day at Satis. You are to take me there, and bring me back, if you will. She would rather I did not travel alone. Can you take me?"

"Can I take you, Estella!"

"You can then? The day after tomorrow, if you please. You are to pay all charges out of my purse. You hear the condition of your going?"

"And must obey," said I.

This was all the preparation I received for that visit, or for others like it. We went down on the next day but one, and found her in the room where I had first beheld her. Needless to say there was no change in Satis House.

She was even more dreadfully fond of Estella than the last time I saw them together; there was something positively dreadful in the energy of her looks and embraces. She hung upon Estella's beauty, hung upon her words, hung upon her gestures, and sat mumbling her trembling fingers while she looked at her, as though devouring the beautiful creature she had reared.

She looked at me, with a searching glance that seemed to pry into my heart and probe its wounds. "How does she use you, Pip; how does she use you?" she asked me again. But, when we sat by her flickering fire at night, she was most weird; for then, keeping Estella's hand drawn through her arm and clutched in her own hand, she drew from Estella the names and conditions of the men whom she had fascinated; and as Miss

Havisham dwelt upon this roll, with the intensity of a mind mortally hurt and diseased, she looked at me, a very spectre.

I saw in this, that Estella was set to wreak Miss Havisham's revenge on men, and that she was not to be given to me until she had gratified it for a term. Sending her out to attract and torment, Miss Havisham sent her with the malicious assurance that she was beyond the reach of all admirers. I saw in this, that I, too, was tormented by a perversion of ingenuity, even while the prize was reserved for me. I saw in this, the reason for my being staved off so long, and the reason for my late guardian's declining to commit himself to the formal knowledge of such a scheme. In a word, I saw in this, Miss Havisham as I had her then and there before my eyes, and always had had her before my eyes; and I saw in this, the distinct shadow of the darkened and unhealthy house in which her life was hidden from the sun.

The candles that lighted that room of hers were placed in sconces on the wall, high off the ground, and they burnt with the steady dullness in air that is seldom renewed. As I looked round at the pale gloom, the stopped clock, the withered articles of bridal dress upon the table, and at her own awful figure, I saw in everything the construction that my mind had come to, repeated and thrown back to me. My thoughts passed into the great room across the landing where the table was spread, and I saw it written in the falls of the cobwebs, in the crawlings of the spiders on the cloth, in the tracks of the mice behind the panels, and in the gropings and pausings of the beetles on the floor.

On this visit some sharp words arose between Estella and Miss Havisham. It was the first time I had ever seen them opposed.

We were seated by the fire, as just now described, and Miss Havisham still had Estella's arm drawn through her own, and still clutched Estella's hand in hers, when Estella gradually began to detach herself. She had shown a proud impatience more than once before, and had rather endured that fierce affection than accepted or returned it.

"What!" said Miss Havisham, flashing her eyes upon her. "Are you tired of me?"

"Only a little tired of myself," replied Estella, disengaging her arm, and moving to the great chimney-piece.

"Speak the truth, you ingrate!" cried Miss Havisham, passionately striking her stick upon the floor; "you are tired of me."

Estella looked at her with perfect composure. Her beautiful face expressed a self-possessed indifference to the wild heat of the other that was almost cruel.

"You stock and stone!" exclaimed Miss Havisham. "You cold heart!"

"What?" said Estella, preserving her attitude of indifference; "do you reproach me for being cold? You?"

"Are you not?" was the fierce retort.

"You should know," said Estella. "I am what you have made me."

"O, look at her!" cried Miss Havisham, bitterly; "Look at her, so hard and thankless, on the hearth where she was reared! Where I have lavished years of tenderness upon her!"

"But what would you have? You have been very good to me, and I owe everything to you. What would you have?" asked Estella.

"Love," replied the other.

"You have it."

"I have not," said Miss Havisham.

"Mother by adoption," retorted Estella, never raising her voice as the other did, never yielding either to anger or tenderness, "I have said that I owe everything to you. All I possess is freely yours. All that you have given me, is at your command to have again. Beyond that, I have nothing. And if you ask me to give you what you never gave me, my gratitude and duty cannot do impossibilities."

"Did I never give her love!" cried Miss Havisham, turning to me. "Did I never give her a burning love, inseparable from jealousy at all times, while she speaks thus to me! Let her call me mad!"

"Why should I call you mad," returned Estella, "I, of all people? Who knows what set purposes you have, half as well as I do? Who knows what a steady memory you have, half as well as I do? I who have sat on the little stool that is even now beside you there, learning your lessons!"

"Soon forgotten!" moaned Miss Havisham.

"No, not forgotten," retorted Estella. "Not forgotten, but treasured up in my memory. When have you found me false to your teaching? When have you found me giving admission here," she touched her bosom with her hand, "to anything that you excluded? Be just to me."

"So proud!" moaned Miss Havisham, pushing away her grey hair.

"Who taught me to be proud?" returned Estella. "Who praised me when I learnt my lesson?"

"So hard!" moaned Miss Havisham.

"Who taught me to be hard?" returned Estella. "Who praised me when I learnt my lesson?"

"But to be proud and hard to me!" Miss Havisham quite shrieked, as she stretched out her arms.

Estella looked at her for a moment with a kind of calm wonder.

"I cannot think," she said, raising her eyes after a silence, "why you should be so unreasonable when I come to see you after a separation. I have never forgotten your wrongs and their causes. I have never been unfaithful to you or your schooling."

"Would it be weakness to return my love?" exclaimed Miss Havisham. "But yes, yes, she would call it so!"

"I begin to think," said Estella, in a musing way, "that I almost understand how this comes about. If you had brought up your adopted daughter wholly in the dark confinement of these rooms, and had never let her know that there was such a thing as the daylight by which she had never once seen your face – and then, had wanted her to understand the daylight and know all about it, you would have been disappointed and angry?"

Miss Havisham, with her head in her hands, sat making a low moaning, and swaying herself on her chair, but gave no answer.

"Or," said Estella, " – which is a nearer case – if you had taught her, from the start, with your utmost energy, that there was such a thing as daylight, but that it was her enemy and destroyer, and she must always turn against it, for it had blighted you and would else blight her; – if you had done this, and then, had wanted her to take naturally to the daylight and she could not do it, you would have been disappointed and angry?"

Miss Havisham sat listening but still made no answer.

"So," said Estella, "I must be taken as I have been made. The success is not mine, the failure is not mine, but the two together make me."

Miss Havisham had settled down upon the floor, among the faded bridal relics. I took advantage of the moment to leave the room, after beseeching Estella's attention to her, with a movement of my hand. When I left, Estella was yet standing by the great chimney-piece. Miss Havisham's grey hair was loose upon the ground, and was a miserable sight to see.

I walked in the starlight for an hour and more, about the court-yard, and about the ruined garden. When I at last returned to the room, I found Estella sitting at Miss Havisham's knee, taking up some stitches in one of those old articles of dress that were dropping to pieces. Afterwards, Estella and I played at cards, as of yore – only we were skilful now, and played French games – and so the evening wore away, and I went to bed.

I lay in that separate building across the court-yard. It was the first time I had ever slept in Satis House, and sleep refused to come. A thousand Miss Havishams haunted me. She was on this side of my pillow, on that, at the head of the bed, at the foot, behind the half-opened door of the dressing room, in the dressing room, in the room overhead, in the room beneath – everywhere. At last, when the night had crept to two o'clock, I felt that I must get up. I therefore dressed, and went out across the yard into the long stone passage, aiming for the outer court-yard. But I was no sooner in the passage than I extinguished my candle; for I saw Miss Havisham going along it in a ghostly manner, making a low cry. I followed her at a distance, and saw her go up the staircase. She carried a bare candle in her hand, probably taken from one of the sconces in her own room. Standing at the bottom of the staircase I heard her walking about up there, never ceasing the low cry. After a time, I tried to go back, but I could do neither until some streaks of day strayed in and showed me where to go.

Before we left next day, there was no revival of the difference between her and Estella, nor was it ever revived on any similar occasion; and there were four similar occasions, to the best of my remembrance. Nor did Miss Havisham's manner towards Estella in anywise change, except that I believed it to have something like fear infused among its former characteristics.

It is impossible to turn this leaf of my life, without putting Bentley Drummle's name upon it; or I would, very gladly.

On a certain occasion when the Finches were assembled, the presiding Finch called the Grove to order. Mr Drummle had not yet toasted a lady; which, according to our solemn constitution, it was the brute's turn to do that day. He leered in an ugly way at me, but as there was no love lost between us, that might easily be. What was my indignant surprise when he called upon the company to pledge him to "Estella!"

"Estella who?" said I.

"Never you mind," retorted Drummle.

"Estella of where?" said I. "You must say of where."

"Of Richmond, gentlemen," said Drummle, putting me out of the question, "and a peerless beauty."

Much he knew about peerless beauties, a mean miserable idiot! I whispered Herbert.

"I know that lady," said Herbert, across the table, when the toast had been honoured.

"Do you?" said Drummle.

"And so do I," I added, with a scarlet face.

"Do you?" said Drummle. "Oh, Lord!"

This was the only retort he was capable of making; but, I became highly incensed by it, and I immediately rose in my place and said that I could not but regard it as being like the honourable Finch's impudence to propose a lady of whom he knew nothing. Mr Drummle started up, demanding what I meant by that?

The debate grew lively. It was decided at last that if Mr Drummle would bring proof from the lady, confirming he had the honour of her acquaintance, Mr Pip must express his regret, as a gentleman and a Finch. Next day was appointed for the production, and next day Drummle appeared with a polite little avowal in Estella's hand, that she had had the honour of dancing with him several times. This left me no course but to regret my words. Drummle and I then sat snorting at one another for an hour.

I tell this lightly, but it was no light thing to me. For I cannot adequately express what pain it gave me to think that Estella should show any favour to a contemptible, clumsy, sulky booby, so very far below the average. No doubt I should have been miserable whomsoever she had favoured; but a worthier object would have caused me a different kind and degree of distress.

I soon found out that Drummle had begun to follow her closely, and that she allowed him to do it. Eventually he and I were crossing one another every day. He held on, in a dull persistent way, and Estella held him on; now with encouragement, now with discouragement, now almost flattering him, now openly despising him.

The Spider, as Mr Jaggers had called him, was used to lying in wait, however, and had the patience of his tribe. Added to that, he had a blockhead confidence in his money and in his family greatness. So, the

Spider doggedly watched Estella, often uncoiling himself and dropping at the nick of time.

At a certain Assembly Ball at Richmond where Estella had outshone all other beauties, this blundering Drummle so hung about her that I resolved to speak to her. When she was waiting for Mrs Brandley to take her home, and was sitting apart, ready to go, I was with her, for I almost always accompanied them to and from such places.

"Are you tired, Estella?"

"Rather, Pip. I have my letter to Satis House to write, before I go to sleep."

"Recounting tonight's triumph?" said I. "Estella, do look at that fellow in the corner yonder, who is looking over here at us."

"Why should I look at him?" returned Estella, with her eyes on me instead.

"Indeed, that is exactly the question I want to ask you," said I. "For he has been hovering about you all night."

"Moths, and all sorts of ugly creatures," replied Estella, with a glance towards him, "hover about a lighted candle. Can the candle help it?"

"No," I returned; "but cannot the Estella help it?"

"Well!" said she, laughing, after a moment, "perhaps. Yes. Anything you like."

"But, Estella, do hear me speak. It makes me wretched that you should encourage a man so generally despised as Drummle. You know he is despised, and is as ungainly within as without. A deficient, ill-tempered, lowering, stupid fellow."

"Well?" said she.

"You know he has nothing to recommend him but money, and a ridiculous roll of addle-headed predecessors; now, don't you?"

"Well?" said she again; and each time she said it, she opened her lovely eyes the wider. "Pip," she cast her glance over the room, "don't be foolish about its effect on you. It may have its effect on others, and may be meant to have. It's not worth discussing."

"Yes it is," said I, "because I cannot bear that people should say, 'she throws away her graces and attractions on a mere boor, the lowest in the crowd.'"

"I can bear it," said Estella.

"Oh! Don't be so proud, Estella, and so inflexible."

"Calls me proud and inflexible in this breath!" said Estella, opening her hands. "And in his last breath reproached me for stooping to a boor!"

"There is no doubt you do," said I, something hurriedly, "for you have given him looks and smiles this very night, such as you never give to – me."

"Do you want me then," said Estella, turning suddenly with a fixed, if not angry look, "to deceive and entrap you?"

"Do you deceive and entrap him, Estella?"

"Yes, and many others – all of them but you. Here is Mrs Brandley. I'll say no more."

And now that I have given the one chapter to the theme that so filled my heart, and so often made it ache and ache again, I pass to the event that had impended over me longer yet.

CHAPTER 36

I was three-and-twenty years of age. Not another word had I heard to enlighten me on the subject of my expectations, and my twenty-third birthday was a week gone. We now lived in the Temple. Our chambers were in Garden Court, down by the river.

Mr Pocket and I had for some time parted company as to our original relations, though we continued on the best terms. I had a taste for reading, and read regularly many hours a day. That matter of Herbert's was still progressing.

Business had taken Herbert to Marseilles. I was alone. Dispirited and anxious, long hoping that tomorrow or next week would clear my way, and long disappointed, I sadly missed the cheerful face and ready response of my friend.

It was wretched weather; stormy and wet; and mud, mud, mud, deep in all the streets. Day after day, a vast heavy veil had been driving over London from the East, and it drove still, as if in the East there were an Eternity of cloud and wind.

Alterations have been made in that part of the Temple since that time, and it is not so exposed to the river. We lived at the top of the last house, and the wind shook the house that night. The rain dashed against the windows, and I fancied myself in a storm-beaten lighthouse. Occasionally, smoke rolled back down the chimney, as though afraid to go out into such a night. The lamps in the court were blown out, and the lamps on the bridges and the shore were shuddering.

I aimed to read until eleven o'clock. As I shut my book, Saint Paul's struck that hour. Then I heard a footstep on the stair.

I listened again, and heard the footstep stumble in coming on. The staircase-lights were blown out, so I took up my reading-lamp and went out to the stair-head. Whoever was below had stopped on seeing my lamp.

"There is some one down there, is there not?" I called out, looking down.

"Yes," said a voice from the darkness beneath.

"What floor do you want?"

"The top. Mr Pip."

"That is my name. – There is nothing the matter?"

"Nothing the matter," returned the voice. And the man came on.

He came slowly within the light of my lamp. It was a shaded lamp, to shine upon a book; so that he was in it for a mere instant, and then out of it. In the instant, I saw a face strange to me, but looking as though touched and pleased by the sight of me.

I made out that he was substantially dressed, but roughly; like a voyager by sea. He had long iron-grey hair, and was about sixty. He was a muscular man, browned and hardened by exposure to weather. As he ascended the last stair or two, and the light of my lamp included us both, I saw, with a stupid kind of amazement, that he was holding out both his hands to me.

"Pray what is your business?" I asked him.

"My business?" he repeated, pausing. "Ah! Yes. I will explain my business, by your leave."

"Do you wish to come in?"

"Yes," he replied; "I wish to come in, Master."

The question was inhospitably asked, for I resented the bright recognition that still shone in his face. I resented it, because it implied that he expected me to respond to it. But I took him back into the room, and asked him as civilly as I could to explain himself.

He looked about him with the strangest air – an air of wondering

151

pleasure, as if he had some part in what he admired. He pulled off a rough outer coat, and his hat. Then I saw that his head was furrowed and bald, with long iron-grey hair that grew only on its sides. Next moment he once more held out both his hands to me.

"What do you mean?" said I, half suspecting him to be mad.

He stopped, and slowly rubbed his right hand over his head. "It's disappointing to a man," he said, in a coarse broken voice, "arter having looked for'ard so distant, and come so fur; but you're not to blame for that – neither on us is to blame for that. I'll speak in half a minute. Give me half a minute, please."

He sat down on a chair before the fire, and covered his forehead. I looked at him attentively, and recoiled a little; but I did not know him.

"There's no one nigh," said he, looking over his shoulder; "is there?"

"Why do you, a stranger in my rooms at this time of the night, ask that question?" said I.

"You're a game one," he returned, shaking his head at me with a deliberate affection; "I'm glad you've grow'd up, a game one! But don't catch hold of me. You'd be sorry arterwards to have done it."

I knew him! I could not recall a single feature, but I knew him! If the wind and the rain had driven away the intervening years, had swept us to the churchyard where we first met, I could not have known my convict more clearly. No need to take a file from his pocket and show it to me; no need to hug himself with both his arms, and take a shivering turn across the room, looking back at me for recognition

He came back to where I stood, and again held out both his hands. Not knowing what to do – for I had lost my self-possession – I reluctantly gave him my hands. He grasped them, raised them to his lips, kissed them, and still held them.

"You acted noble, my boy," said he. "Noble, Pip! And I have never forgot it!"

He looked as if he was going to embrace me, and I laid a hand upon his breast.

"Stay!" said I. "If you are grateful for what I did as a child, I hope you have shown your gratitude by mending your way of life. If you are here to thank me, it was not necessary. Still, however you have found me out, there must be something good in the feeling that has brought you here, and I will not repulse you; but surely you must understand that – I – "

The words died away on my tongue.

"You was a-saying," he observed, after a moment of silence, "what, surely must I understand?"

"That I cannot wish to renew that chance meeting, under these different circumstances. I am glad to believe you have repented and recovered yourself. I am glad that, thinking I deserve to be thanked, you have come to thank me. But our ways are different ways, none the less. You are wet, and you look weary. Will you drink something before you go?"

"I think," he answered, "that I will drink afore I go."

There was a tray ready on a side-table. I made him some hot rum-and-water. I tried to keep my hand steady while I did so, but his look at me made my hand very difficult to master. When at last I gave the glass to him, I saw with amazement that his eyes were full of tears.

"I hope," said I, hurriedly filling a glass for myself, and drawing a chair to the table, "that you will not think I spoke harshly to you just now. I had no intention of doing it. I wish you well, and happy!"

As I put my glass to my lips, he stretched out his hand. I gave him mine, and then he drank, and drew his sleeve across his eyes and forehead.

"How are you living?" I asked him.

"I've been a sheep-farmer, stock-breeder, other trades besides, away in the new world," said he. "Many a thousand mile of stormy water away."

"I hope you have done well?"

"I've done wonderfully well."

"I am glad to hear it."

"I hope to hear you say so, my dear boy."

Without stopping to try to understand those words, I mentioned a point that had just come into my mind.

"Have you ever seen a messenger you once sent to me," I inquired, "since he undertook that trust?"

"Never set eyes upon him. I warn't likely to it."

"He came faithfully, bringing me the two one-pound notes. I was a poor boy then, as you know, and they were a little fortune. But, like you, I have done well since, and you must let me pay them back. You can put them to some other poor boy's use." I took out my purse.

He watched me as I separated two one-pound notes from the contents of my purse. I handed them over to him. Still watching me, he laid them

153

one upon the other, folded them long-wise, set fire to them at the lamp, and dropped the ashes into the tray.

"May I make so bold," he said then, with a smile that was like a frown, "as ask you how you have done well, since you and me was out on them lone shivering marshes?"

"How?"

"Ah!"

He went and stood beside the fire, his heavy brown hand on the mantelshelf. He put a foot up to the bars, and the wet boot began to steam; but he looked steadily at me. It was only now that I began to tremble.

When my lips had parted, and had shaped some soundless words, I forced myself to say (though unclearly), that I had been chosen to succeed to some property.

"Might a mere warmint ask what property?" said he.

I faltered, "I don't know."

"Might a mere warmint ask whose property?" said he.

I faltered again, "I don't know."

"Could I make a guess, I wonder," said the Convict, "at your income since you come of age! As to the first figure now. Five?"

My heart thumped furiously and I rose out of my chair, looking wildly at him.

"There ought to have been some guardian," he went on, "whiles you was a minor. Some lawyer, maybe. As to the first letter of that lawyer's name now. Would it be J?"

All the truth of my position came flashing on me; and its disappointments, dangers, disgraces, consequences of all kinds – I – was borne down by them and had to struggle for every breath I drew.

"Put it," he resumed, "that the employer of that lawyer who might be Jaggers – put it that he had come over sea to land at Portsmouth, and had wanted to come to you. 'However you have found me out,' you says. Well! However did I find you out? Why, I wrote to a person in London, for your address. That person? Why, Wemmick."

I could not have spoken one word, even to save my life. I stood, and seemed to be suffocating – looking wildly at him, until I grasped at the chair, when the room began to surge and turn. He caught me, drew me to the sofa, and bent on one knee before me: bringing the face that I now well remembered, and that I shuddered at, very near to mine.

154

"Yes, Pip, dear boy, I've made a gentleman on you! It's me wot has done it! I swore that time, sure as ever I earned a guinea, that guinea should go to you. I swore arterwards, sure as ever I spec'lated and got rich, you should get rich. I lived rough, that you should live smooth; I worked hard, that you should be above work. Do I tell it, fur you to feel a obligation? Not a bit. I tell it, fur you to know as that there hunted dunghill dog wot you kep life in, got his head so high that he could make a gentleman – and, Pip, you're him!"

The dread I had of the man, the repugnance with which I shrank from him, could not have been exceeded if he had been some terrible beast.

"Lookee here, Pip. I'm your second father. You're my son – more to me nor any son. I've put away money, only for you to spend. When I was a hired-out shepherd in a solitary hut, not seeing no faces but faces of sheep till I half forgot wot men's and women's faces wos like, I see yourn. I see you there a many times, as plain as ever I see you on them misty marshes. 'Lord strike me dead!' I says each time – and I goes out in the air to say it under the open heavens – 'but wot, if I gets liberty and money, I'll make that boy a gentleman!' And I done it. Why, look at you, dear boy! Look at these here lodgings o'yourn, fit for a lord! A lord? Ah! You shall show money with lords for wagers, and beat 'em!"

In his heat and triumph, and knowing that I had been nearly fainting, he did not remark on my reception of all this. It was the one grain of relief I had.

"Lookee here!" he went on, taking my watch out of my pocket, and turning towards him a ring on my finger, while I recoiled from his touch, "a gold 'un and a beauty: that's a gentleman's! A diamond all set round with rubies; that's a gentleman's! Look at your linen and your clothes; fine and beautiful! And your books too," turning his eyes round the room, "mounting up, on their shelves, by hundreds! And you read 'em; don't you? Ha, ha, ha! You shall read 'em to me, dear boy!"

Again he took both my hands and put them to his lips, while my blood ran cold within me.

"Don't you mind talking, Pip," said he, after again drawing his sleeve over his eyes and forehead; "you can't do better nor keep quiet, dear boy. You ain't looked slowly forward to this as I have; you wosn't prepared for this, as I wos. But didn't you never think it might be me?"

"O no, no," I returned, "Never, never!"

155

"Well, you see it wos me, and single-handed. Never a soul in it but my own self and Mr Jaggers."

"Was there no one else?" I asked.

"No," said he, with a glance of surprise: "who else should there be? And, dear boy, how good looking you have growed! There's bright eyes somewheres – eh? – wot you love the thoughts on?"

O Estella, Estella!

"They shall be yourn, dear boy, if money can buy 'em. Not that a gentleman like you can't win 'em off of his own game; but money shall back you! Let me finish wot I was a-telling you, dear boy. From that there hiring-out, I got money left me by my master and got my liberty and went for myself. In every single thing I went for, I went for you. It all prospered wonderful. It was the money left me, and the gains of the first few year wot I sent home to Mr Jaggers – all for you – when he first come arter you, agreeable to my letter."

O, that he had never come! That he had left me at the forge – far from contented, yet, by comparison, happy!

"And then, dear boy, it was a recompense to me, to know in secret that I was making a gentleman. When one of 'em colonists says to another, 'He was a convict, a few year ago, and is a ignorant common fellow now, for all he's lucky,' what do I say? I says to myself, 'If I ain't a gentleman, I'm the owner of such. All on you owns stock and land; which on you owns a brought-up London gentleman?' This way I kep myself a-going. And I knew one day I would come and see my boy, and make myself known to him, on his own ground."

He laid his hand on my shoulder. I shuddered at the thought that for anything I knew, his hand might be stained with blood.

"It warn't easy, Pip, for me to leave them parts, nor yet it warn't safe. But I held to it, and the harder it was, the stronger I held, for I was determined. At last I done it!"

I tried to collect my thoughts, but I was stunned.

"Where will you put me?" he asked, presently. "I must be put somewheres, dear boy."

"To sleep?" said I.

"Yes. And to sleep long and sound," he answered; "for I've been sea-tossed and sea-washed, months and months."

"My friend and companion," said I, rising from the sofa, "is absent; you must have his room."

"He won't come back tomorrow; will he?"

"No," said I, answering almost mechanically, in spite of my utmost efforts; "not tomorrow."

"Because, lookee here, dear boy," he said, dropping his voice, "caution is necessary."

"How do you mean? Caution?"

"By G–, it's Death!"

"What's death?"

"I was sent for life. It's death to come back. I should of a certainty be hanged if took."

This wretched man, after loading me with his gold and silver chains for years, had risked his life to come to me, and I held it there in my keeping! If I had loved him instead of abhorring him, it could have been no worse. On the contrary, it would have been better, for his preservation would then have naturally and tenderly addressed my heart.

My first care was to close the shutters, so that no light might be seen from without, and then to close and make fast the doors. He stood at the table drinking rum and eating biscuit; and I saw my convict on the marshes at his meal again.

I prepared Herbert's room, and then asked him if he would go to bed? He said yes, but asked me for some of my "gentleman's linen" to put on in the morning. I brought it out, and laid it ready for him, and my blood again ran cold when he again took me by both hands to give me good-night.

I got away from him, and sat down by the fire, afraid to go to bed. For an hour or more, I remained too stunned to think; and then I began fully to know how wrecked I was, and how the ship in which I had sailed was gone to pieces.

Miss Havisham's intentions towards me, all a mere dream; Estella not designed for me; I only suffered in Satis House as a convenience, a sting for the greedy relations; those were the first smarts I had. But, sharpest and deepest pain of all – it was for the convict, guilty of I knew not what crimes, that I had deserted Joe.

I would not have gone back to Joe now, simply, I suppose, because my sense of my own worthless conduct to him was greater than every consideration. I could never, never, undo what I had done.

I took a candle to look at my dreadful burden.

He was asleep, and quietly too, though he had a pistol lying on the pillow. I softly removed the key to the outside of his door, and turned it on him before I again sat down by the fire. Gradually I slipped from the chair and lay on the floor. When I awoke, the clocks of the eastward churches were striking five, the candles were out, the fire was dead, and the wind and rain intensified the thick black darkness.

THIS IS THE END OF THE SECOND STAGE OF PIP'S EXPECTATIONS.

CHAPTER 37

The impossibility of keeping my visitor concealed in the chambers was self-evident. It could not be done, and the attempt to do it would inevitably engender suspicion. I was looked after by an inflammatory old female, and to keep a room secret from her would be to invite curiosity and exaggeration. Not to get up a mystery with her, I resolved to announce in the morning that my uncle had unexpectedly come from the country.

This course I decided on while I was yet groping about in the darkness for a light. Not finding means, I had to go to the adjacent Lodge and get the watchman there to come with his lantern. Now, in groping my way down the black staircase I fell over something, and that something was a man crouching in a corner.

As the man made no answer when I asked him what he did there, I ran to the Lodge and urged the watchman to come quickly, telling him of the incident on the way back. We examined the staircase from the bottom to the top and found no one there. It then occurred to me that the man might have slipped into my rooms; so, lighting my candle at the watchman's, I examined them carefully, including the room in which my dreaded guest lay asleep. All was quiet.

It troubled me that there should have been a lurker on the stairs, on that night of all nights, and I asked the watchman, whether he had admitted at his gate any gentleman who had been dining out? Yes, he said; three. One lived in Fountain Court, and the other two lived in the Lane, and he had seen them all go home.

"The night being so bad, sir," said the watchman, "uncommon few have come in at my gate. Besides them three gentlemen, I don't call to mind another since about eleven o'clock, when a stranger asked for you."

"My uncle," I muttered. "Yes."

"You saw him, sir?"

"Oh yes."

"Likewise the person with him?"

"Person with him!" I repeated.

"I judged the person to be with him," returned the watchman. "He stopped when your visitor stopped to ask me, and took this way when your visitor took this way."

159

"What sort of person?"

The watchman had not particularly noticed; he should say a working person; to the best of his belief, he had a dust-coloured kind of clothes on, under a dark coat. The watchman made more light of the matter than I did, not having my reason for attaching weight to it.

My mind was much troubled by these two circumstances taken together.

I lighted my fire, and fell into a doze before it. I seemed to have been dozing a whole night when the clocks struck six. As there was full an hour and a half between me and daylight, I dozed again.

I was greatly dejected and distressed, but in an incoherent wholesale sort of way. As to forming any plan for the future, I could as soon have formed an elephant. When I opened the shutters and looked out at the wet wild morning; when I walked from room to room; when I sat down again shivering, before the fire; I thought how miserable I was, but hardly knew why or how long, or on what day of the week I made the reflection, or even who I was that made it.

By-and-by, his door opened. I could not bring myself to bear the sight of him, and I thought he had a worse look by daylight.

"I do not even know," said I, speaking low as he took his seat at the table, "by what name to call you. I have given out that you are my uncle."

"That's it, dear boy! Call me uncle."

"What is your real name?" I asked him in a whisper.

"Magwitch," he answered, "chrisen'd Abel. But on board ship I assumed the name of Provis."

"When you came into the Temple last night – " said I, pausing to wonder whether that could really have been last night.

"Yes, dear boy?"

"When you asked the watchman the way here, had you anyone with you?"

"With me? No, dear boy."

"But there was some one there?"

"I didn't take particular notice," he said, dubiously, "not knowing the ways of the place. But I think there was a person, too, come in alonger me."

"Are you known in London?"

"I hope not!" said he, giving his neck a jerk with his forefinger that made me turn hot and sick.

"Were you known in London, once?"

"Not over and above, dear boy. I was in the provinces mostly."

"Were you – tried – in London?"

"Which time?" said he, with a sharp look.

"The last time."

He nodded. "First know'd Mr Jaggers that way. Jaggers was for me." He added, "And what I done is worked out and paid for!" and fell to at his breakfast.

He ate in a ravenous way that was very disagreeable, and all his actions were uncouth, noisy, and greedy. If I had begun with any appetite, he would have taken it away, and I should have sat much as I did – repelled from him by an insurmountable aversion, and gloomily looking at the cloth.

"I'm a heavy grubber, dear boy," he said, as a polite kind of apology when he made an end of his meal, "but I always was."

He then went through his favourite action of holding out both his hands for mine.

"And this," said he, dandling my hands up and down in his; "is the gentleman what I made! The real genuine One! It does me good fur to look at you, Pip."

I released my hands as soon as I could, and found that I was beginning slowly to settle down to the contemplation of my condition. What I was chained to, and how heavily, became intelligible to me, as I heard his hoarse voice, and sat looking up at his furrowed bald head, with its iron grey hair at the sides.

"I mustn't see my gentleman a-footing it in the mire of the streets; there mustn't be no mud on his boots. My gentleman must have horses, Pip! Shall colonists have their horses and not my London gentleman? No, no. We'll show 'em another pair of shoes than that, Pip; won't us?"

He took out a great thick pocket-book, bursting with papers, and tossed it on the table.

"There's something worth spending in that there book, dear boy. It's yourn. All I've got ain't mine; it's yourn. Don't you be afeerd on it. There's more where that come from. I've come to the old country fur to see my gentleman spend his money like a gentleman. That'll be my pleasure. And blast you all!" he wound up, looking round the room and snapping his fingers, "blast you every one, I'll show a better gentleman than the whole kit on you put together!"

"Stop!" said I, almost in a frenzy of fear and dislike, "I want to speak to you. I want to know how you are to be kept out of danger, how long you are going to stay, what projects you have."

"Well, dear boy, the danger ain't so great. There's Jaggers, and there's Wemmick, and there's you. Who else is there to inform?"

"Is there no chance person who might identify you in the street?" said I.

"Well," he returned, "there ain't many. I don't intend to advertise myself in the newspapers. Still, lookee here, Pip. If the danger had been fifty times as great, I should ha' come to see you, mind you."

"And how long do you remain?"

"How long?" said he, dropping his jaw as he stared at me. "I'm not a-going back. I've come for good."

"Where are you to live?" said I. "What is to be done with you? Where will you be safe?"

"Dear boy," he returned, "there's disguising wigs can be bought, and there's spectacles and black clothes. Others has done it safe afore, and what others has done afore, others can do agen. As to the where and how of living, dear boy, give me your own opinions on it."

"You take it smoothly now," said I, "but you were very serious last night, when you swore it was Death."

"And so I swear it is Death," said he, putting his pipe back in his mouth, "by the rope, in the open street not fur from this, and it's serious that you should fully understand it to be so. Here I am. To go back now, 'ud be as bad as to stand ground – worse. Besides, Pip, I'm here, because I've meant it by you, years and years And now let me have a look at my gentleman agen."

Once more, he took me by both hands and surveyed me with an air of admiring proprietorship.

It appeared to me that I could do no better than secure him some quiet lodging hard by, where he might move to when Herbert returned: whom I expected in two or three days. That the secret must be confided to Herbert, together with the immense relief I should derive from sharing it with him, was plain to me. But it was by no means so plain to Mr Provis (I resolved to call him by that name), who reserved his consent until he had seen him and formed a favourable judgement of him. "And even then, dear boy," said he, pulling a greasy little clasped black Testament out of his pocket, "we'll have him on his oath."

We next discussed what dress he should wear. He had in his own mind sketched a dress for himself that was something between a dean and a dentist. With considerable difficulty, I won him over to dressing more like a prosperous farmer; and we arranged that he should cut his hair close.

I did not get out to complete these precautions until two or three in the afternoon. He was to remain shut up in the chambers while I was gone, and was on no account to open the door.

There was a respectable lodging-house in Essex Street, the back of which was almost within hail of my windows. I was fortunate enough to secure the second floor for my uncle, Mr Provis. I then went from shop to shop, making such purchases as were necessary to change his appearance. I then returned, on my own account, to Little Britain. Mr Jaggers was at his desk, but seeing me enter, got up immediately and stood before his fire.

"Now, Pip," said he, "be careful."

"I will, sir," I returned. For, coming along I had thought well of what I was going to say.

"Don't commit yourself," said Mr Jaggers, "and don't commit any one. You understand – any one. Don't tell me anything: I am not curious."

I realised that he knew the man was come.

"I merely want, Mr Jaggers," said I, "to assure myself that what I have been told is true. May I verify it?"

Mr Jaggers nodded. "But did you say 'told' or 'informed'?" he asked me, with his head on one side. "Told would seem to imply verbal communication. You can't have verbal communication with a man in New South Wales, you know."

"I will say, informed, Mr Jaggers."

"Good."

"I have been informed by a person named Abel Magwitch that he is the benefactor so long unknown to me."

"That is the man," said Mr Jaggers, " – in New South Wales."

"I am not so unreasonable, sir, as to think you at all responsible for my wrong conclusions; but I always supposed it was Miss Havisham."

"As you say, Pip," returned Mr Jaggers, "I am not at all responsible for that."

"And yet it looked so like it, sir," I pleaded with a downcast heart.

"Not a particle of evidence, Pip," said Mr Jaggers, shaking his head. "Take nothing on its looks; take everything on evidence."

"I have no more to say," said I, with a sigh, after a moment's silence. "I have verified my information, and there's an end."

"And Magwitch – in New South Wales – having at last disclosed himself," said Mr Jaggers, "you will comprehend, Pip, how I have always adhered to the strict line of fact. You are quite aware of that?"

"Quite, sir."

"I communicated to Magwitch – in New South Wales – the caution that he must not expect me ever to deviate from the strict line of fact. I also communicated to him, as he appeared to have obscurely hinted in his letter at some distant idea he had of seeing you in England here, that I must hear no more of that. He was expatriated for the term of his natural life; and that his presenting himself in this country would render him liable to the extreme penalty of the law," said Mr Jaggers, looking hard at me.

"No doubt," said I.

"I have been informed by Wemmick," pursued Mr Jaggers, "that he has received a letter from Portsmouth, from a colonist by the name of Purvis, or – "

"Provis," I suggested.

"Perhaps you know it's Provis?"

"Yes," said I.

"You know it's Provis. A letter, asking for your address, on behalf of Magwitch. Wemmick sent him the particulars, I understand. Probably it is through Provis that you have received the explanation of Magwitch – in New South Wales?"

"It came through Provis," I replied.

"Good-day, Pip," said Mr Jaggers, offering his hand; "glad to have seen you. In writing by post to Magwitch – in New South Wales – or in communicating with him through Provis, please mention that the particulars and vouchers of our long account shall be sent to you, together with the balance; for there is still a balance remaining. Good-day, Pip!"

We shook hands, and he looked hard at me as long as he could see me. I turned at the door, and he was still looking hard at me.

Wemmick was out, and though he had been at his desk he could have done nothing for me. I went straight back to the Temple, where I found the terrible Provis drinking rum-and-water in safety.

Next day the clothes I had ordered all arrived, and he put them on. Whatever he put on became him less. To my thinking, there was something that made it hopeless to attempt to disguise him. The more I dressed him and the better I dressed him, the more he looked like the slouching fugitive on the marshes.

The influences of his solitary hut-life were still upon him, and gave him a savage air that no dress could tame. In all his ways of sitting and standing, and eating and drinking – of taking out his great horn-handled jack-knife and wiping it on his legs and cutting his food – of chopping a wedge off his bread, and soaking up with it the last fragments of gravy round and round his plate, as if to make the most of an allowance – in these ways and a thousand others, there was Prisoner, Felon, Bondsman, plain as plain could be.

Words cannot tell what a sense I had of the dreadful mystery that he was to me. When he fell asleep of an evening, with his knotted hands clenching the sides of the easy-chair, and his bald head tattooed with deep wrinkles falling forward on his breast, I would sit and look at him, wondering what he had done. Every hour so increased my abhorrence of him that I even think I might have run away, notwithstanding all he had done for me, and the risk he ran, but for the knowledge that Herbert must soon come back. When he was not asleep, or playing a complicated kind of patience with a ragged pack of cards of his own – a game that I never saw before or since, and in which he recorded his winnings by sticking his jack-knife into the table – when he was not engaged in either of these pursuits, he would ask me to read to him.

This is written of, I know, as if it had lasted a year. It lasted about five days. Expecting Herbert all the time, I dared not go out, except when I took Provis for an airing after dark. At length, one evening when dinner was over and I had dropped into a slumber quite worn out, I was roused by the welcome footstep on the staircase. Provis, who had been asleep too, staggered up at the noise I made, and in an instant I saw his jack-knife shining in his hand.

"Quiet! It's Herbert!" I said; and Herbert came bursting in, with the airy freshness of six hundred miles of France upon him.

165

"Handel, my dear fellow, how are you, and again how are you? I seem to have been gone a twelvemonth! Why, you have grown quite thin and pale! Handel, my – Halloa! I beg your pardon."

He was stopped in his shaking hands with me, by seeing Provis, who regarding him with a fixed attention, was slowly putting up his jack-knife, and groping in another pocket for something else.

"Herbert, my dear friend," said I, shutting the double doors, while Herbert stood staring and wondering, "something very strange has happened. This is – a visitor of mine."

"It's all right, dear boy!" said Provis coming forward, with his little black book, and then addressing Herbert. "Take it in your right hand. Lord strike you dead on the spot, if ever you split in any way sumever! Kiss it!"

"Do as he wishes," I said to Herbert. So, Herbert, looking at me with a friendly amazement, complied, and Provis immediately shaking hands with him, said, "Now you're on your oath!"

CHAPTER 38

In vain should I attempt to describe the astonishment and disquiet of Herbert, when we three sat down before the fire, and I recounted the whole of the secret. Enough, that I saw my own feelings reflected in Herbert's face, not least among them, my repugnance towards the man who had done so much for me.

What would alone have set a division between that man and us, if there had been no other dividing circumstance, was his triumph in my story. He simply had no perception of the possibility of my finding any fault with my good fortune. His boast that he had made me a gentleman, and that we must both be very proud of it, was a conclusion quite established in his own mind.

"Though, lookee here, Pip's comrade," he said to Herbert, "I know very well that once since I come back – for half a minute – I've been low. But don't you fret yourself on that score. Dear boy, and Pip's comrade, you two may count upon me always having a gen-teel muzzle on.

Muzzled I have been since that half a minute when I was betrayed into lowness, muzzled I am now, muzzled I will stay."

Herbert said, "Certainly," but looked as if there were no specific consolation in this, and remained perplexed and dismayed. We were anxious for him to go to his lodging, to leave us together, but he sat late. It was midnight before I took him round and saw him safely in at his own dark door. When it closed, I felt the first moment of relief I had known since his arrival.

Remembering the man on the stairs, I always looked about me in taking my guest out after dark, and in bringing him back; and I looked about me now. The few people passing, passed on their several ways, and the street was empty when I turned back into the Temple. Nobody had come out at the gate with us, nobody went in at the gate with me.

Herbert received me with open arms, and I had never felt before, so blessedly, what it is to have a friend. When he had spoken some words of sympathy and encouragement, we sat to consider what should be done?

Herbert unconsciously took the chair that Provis had used, but next moment started out of it, and took another. He had no need to say, after that, that he had conceived an aversion for my patron, neither had I occasion to confess my own. That was understood without words.

"What," said I to Herbert, when he was safe in another chair, "is to be done?"

"My poor dear Handel," he replied, holding his head, "I am too stunned to think."

"So was I, Herbert, when he arrived. Still, something must be done. He is intent upon various new expenses – horses, and carriages. He must be stopped somehow."

"You mean that you can't accept – "

"How can I?" I interposed. "Think of him! Look at him!"

An involuntary shudder passed over both of us.

"Yet I am afraid the dreadful truth is, Herbert, that he is strongly attached to me. Was there ever such a fate!"

"My poor dear Handel," Herbert repeated.

"Then," said I, "after all, stopping short here, never taking another penny from him, think what I owe him already! Then again: I am heavily in debt – I have now no expectations – and I have been bred to no calling – I am fit for nothing."

Herbert remonstrated. "Don't say fit for nothing."

"What am I fit for? I know only one thing and that is, to go for a soldier. And I might have already gone, my dear Herbert, but I needed your friendship and affection."

I naturally broke down there: and Herbert, of course, beyond seizing a warm grip of my hand, pretended not to know it.

"Anyhow, my dear Handel," said he presently, "soldiering won't do. If you were to renounce this patronage and these favours, you could never repay what you have already had if you went soldiering! Besides, it's absurd. You would be infinitely better in Clarriker's house, small as it is. I am working up towards a partnership, you know."

Poor fellow! He little suspected with whose money.

"But there is another question," said Herbert. "This is an ignorant determined man, who has long had one fixed idea. More than that, he seems to me to be a man of a desperate and fierce character."

"I know he is," I returned. "Let me tell you what evidence I have seen of it." And I told him of the encounter with the other convict.

"See, then," said Herbert; "He comes here at the peril of his life, for the realisation of his fixed idea. In the moment of realisation, after all his toil and waiting, you cut the ground from under his feet, destroy his idea, and make his gains worthless to him. What might he do, under the disappointment?"

"I have seen it, Herbert, and dreamed of it, ever since the fatal night of his arrival. I fear he will put himself in the way of being taken."

"Then you may rely upon it," said Herbert, "that is his power over you as long as he remains in England, and that would be his reckless course if you forsook him."

I was horrified at this idea, and it had weighed upon me from the first, as I knew I would regard myself, in some sort, as his murderer. I said to Herbert, meanwhile, that even if Provis were recognised and taken, in spite of himself, I should be wretched as the cause, however innocently. I was so wretched in having him near me, and I would far rather have worked at the forge all the days of my life than ever have come to this!

But there was no ignoring the question – What was to be done?

"The first and the main thing," said Herbert, "is to get him out of England. You will have to go with him, and then he may go."

"But get him where I will, could I prevent his returning?"

"My good Handel, with Newgate in the next street, there is a far greater hazard in your breaking your mind to him and making him reckless. Better a pretext to get him away – that other convict or something in his life."

"There, again!" said I, stopping before Herbert, with my open hands held out towards him.

"I know nothing of his life. It has almost made me mad to sit here and see him before me, so bound up with my fortunes and misfortunes, and yet so unknown, except as the miserable wretch who terrified me two days in my childhood!"

Herbert got up, and linking his arm in mine, we slowly walked to and fro, studying the carpet.

"Handel," said Herbert, stopping, "you feel convinced that you can take no further benefits from him?"

"Surely you would, too, if you were in my place?"

"And you must break with him?"

"Herbert, can you ask me?"

"And you have that tenderness for the life he has risked on your account, that you must save him, if possible, from throwing it away. Then you must get him out of England before you stir a finger to extricate yourself. That done, extricate yourself, in Heaven's name, and we'll see it out together, dear old boy."

It was a comfort to shake hands upon it, and walk up and down again, with only that done.

"Now, Herbert," said I, "to gain some knowledge of his history I must ask him point-blank."

"Yes. Ask him," said Herbert, "when we sit at breakfast."

With this plan, we went to bed. I had the wildest dreams concerning him, and woke unrefreshed.

He came round at the appointed time, took out his jack-knife, and sat down to his meal. He was full of plans 'for his gentleman's coming out strong', and urged me to begin speedily upon the pocket-book.

He advised me to look at once for a 'fashionable crib' near Hyde Park, in which he could have 'a shake-down'.

"After you were gone last night," I began, "I told my friend of the struggle with that other man on the marshes, you remember?"

"Remember!" said he. "I think so!"

"Tell us something about that man – and about you. It is strange to know no more about either, and particularly you."

"Well!" he said, after consideration. "You're on your oath, you know, Pip's comrade? Wotever I done, is worked out and paid for."

"So be it."

He spread a hand on each knee, and looked angrily at the fire for a few silent moments, looked round at us and said what follows.

CHAPTER 39

"Dear boy and Pip's comrade. I am not a-going to tell you my life, like a song or a story-book. I'll put it at once into a mouthful of English. In jail and out of jail, in jail and out of jail. There, you got it. That's my life pretty much, 'til when I got shipped off, arter Pip stood my friend.

"I've been done everything to, pretty well – except hanged. I've been locked up. I've been carted here and there, and put out of this and that town, and stuck in the stocks, and whipped and worried and drove. I've no notion where I was born. I first become aware of myself, down in Essex, a-thieving turnips for my living. Summun had run away from me – a tinker – and he'd took the fire with him, and left me wery cold.

"I know'd my name to be Magwitch, chrisen'd Abel. How did I know? Much as I know'd the birds' names in the hedges to be chaffinch or thrush.

"When I was a ragged little creetur I got the name of being hardened. 'This is a terrible hardened one,' they says to prison wisitors, picking out me. 'May be said to live in jails, this boy.' Then they looked at me, and I looked at them, and they give me tracts what I couldn't read, and made me speeches what I couldn't understand. They always went on agen me about the Devil. But what the Devil was I to do? I must put something into my stomach, mustn't I?

"Tramping, begging, thieving, working sometimes when I could – a bit of a poacher, a labourer, a waggoner, a haymaker, a hawker, a bit of most things that don't pay and lead to trouble. I got to be a man. A deserting soldier learnt me to read; and a travelling Giant what signed his name at a penny a time learnt me to write.

"At Epsom races, over twenty years ago, I met a man whose skull I'd crack wi' this poker, if I'd got it on this hob. His right name was Compeyson; and that's the man, dear boy, what you see me a-pounding in the ditch.

"This Compeyson had been to a public boarding-school and had learning. He was a smooth one to talk, with the makings of a gentleman. He was good-looking too. It was the night afore the great race, when I found him on the heath, in a booth. Him and some more was a-sitting among the tables when I went in, and the landlord, who knew me, called him out, 'I think this is a man that might suit you,' – meaning I was.

"Compeyson, he looks at me and I look at him. He has a watch and a chain and a ring and a handsome suit of clothes.

"'To judge from appearances, you're out of luck,' says Compeyson to me.

"'Yes, master, and I've never been in it much.'

"'Luck changes,' says Compeyson; 'perhaps yours is going to change.'

"I says, 'I hope it may be so. There's room.'

"'What can you do?' says Compeyson.

"'Eat and drink,' I says; 'if you'll find the materials.'

"Compeyson laughed, giv' me five shillings, and appointed me for next night. Same place.

"I went to Compeyson next night, and he took me on as his man and pardner. And what was his business? Swindling, handwriting forging, stolen bank-note passing, and such-like. Any trap Compeyson could set with his head, and keep his own legs out of, and get the profits from and let another man in for, was his business. He'd no more heart than a iron file, he was as cold as death, with the head of the Devil.

"There was another with Compeyson, called Arthur. He was in a Decline, and was a shadow to look at. Him and Compeyson had been in a bad thing with a rich lady some years afore, and they'd made a pot of money; but Compeyson betted and gamed, and he'd have run through the king's taxes. So, Arthur was a-dying, and a-dying poor, and Compeyson's wife (who Compeyson kicked mostly) was a-having pity on him when she could, and Compeyson was a-having pity on nothing and nobody.

"I might a-took warning by Arthur, but I didn't. So I begun wi' Compeyson, and a poor tool I was in his hands. Arthur lived at the top of Compeyson's house and Compeyson kept careful account agen him for

171

board and lodging, in case he should ever get better to work it out. The second or third time as ever I see him, Arthur come a-tearing down into Compeyson's parlour late at night, in only a flannel gown, and he says to Compeyson's wife, 'Sally, she really is upstairs alonger me, now, and I can't get rid of her. She's all in white,' he says, 'wi' white flowers in her hair, and she's awful mad, and she's got a shroud, and she says she'll put it on me at five in the morning.'

"Says Compeyson: 'Why, you fool, don't you know she's got a living body? And how should she be up there, without coming through the door, and up the stairs?'

"'I don't know how she's there,' says Arthur, shivering dreadful with the horrors, 'but she's standing at the foot of the bed, awful mad. And over where her heart's broke – you broke it! – there's drops of blood.'

"Compeyson was always a coward. 'Go up alonger this drivelling sick man,' he says to his wife, 'and Magwitch, lend her a hand.' But he never went himself.

"We took him up to bed agen, and he raved most dreadful. 'Why look at her!' he cries out. 'She's a-shaking the shroud at me! Don't you see her? Ain't it awful to see her so mad?' Next, he cries, 'She'll put it on me, and then I'm done for! Take it away from her!' And then he catched hold of us, and kep on a-talking to her, and answering of her, till I half believed I see her myself.

"Compeyson's wife, being used to him, give him some liquor to get the horrors off, and by-and-by he quieted. 'Oh, she's gone! Has her keeper been for her?' he says. 'Yes,' says Compeyson's wife. 'Did you tell him to lock her in?' 'Yes.' 'And to take that ugly thing away from her?' 'Yes, all right.' 'You're a good creetur,' he says, 'don't leave me, and thank you!'

"He rested pretty quiet till just before five, and then he starts up with a scream, 'Here she is! She's got the shroud again. She's coming out of the corner. She's coming to the bed. Hold me, both on you – don't let her touch me with it. Hah! She missed that time. Don't let her lift me to get it round me. She's lifting me. Keep me down!' Then he lifted himself up hard, and was dead.

"Compeyson took it as a good riddance for both sides. Him and me was soon busy, and first he swore me (being ever artful) on my own book – this here little black book, dear boy, what I swore your comrade on.

"I'll simply say to you both, that that man got me into such nets as made me his slave. I was always in debt to him, always a-working, always a-getting into danger. He was younger than me, but he was crafty, and he'd got learning. My Missis as I had the hard time wi' – Stop though! I ain't brought her in – "

He looked about him in a confused way, as if he had lost his place; and he turned to the fire, and spread his hands broader on his knees.

"There ain't no need to go into it," he said, looking round once more. "The time wi' Compeyson was as hard a time as ever I had. Did I tell you as I was tried, alone, for misdemeanour, while with Compeyson?"

I answered, No.

"Well!" he said, "I was, and got convicted. At last, me and Compeyson was both committed for felony – on a charge of putting stolen notes in circulation. Compeyson says to me, 'separate defences, no communication', and that was all. And I was so miserable poor, that I sold everything I had, afore I could get Jaggers.

"When we was put in the dock, I noticed what a gentleman Compeyson looked, wi' his black clothes and his white pocket-handkercher, and what a common sort of a wretch I looked. When the prosecution opened and the evidence was put short, I noticed how heavy it all bore on me, and how light on him. When evidence was giv' in the box, I noticed how it was always me that the money had been paid to, always me that had seemed to work the thing and get the profit. But, when the defence come on, it's plain; his counsellor says, 'My lord and gentlemen, here afore you, are two persons as your eyes can separate wide; one, the younger, well brought up; one, the elder, ill brought up; the younger, seldom if ever seen in these transactions, and only suspected; t'other, the elder, always seen in 'em and always wi' his guilt brought home. Can you doubt which is the guilty one?' And such-like. And when it come to character, warn't it Compeyson as had been to the school, with schoolfellows in this position and in that, and warn't he know'd by witnesses in such clubs and societies, and nowt to his disadvantage? And warn't it me as had been tried afore, and was know'd up hill and down dale in Bridewells and Lock-Ups? And when it come to speech-making, warn't it Compeyson who spoke to 'em wi' his face dropping every now and then into his white pocket-handkercher – and warn't it me as could only say, 'Gentlemen, this man at my side is a most precious rascal'? And when the verdict come, Compeyson was recommended to mercy on account of good

173

character and bad company, and giving information agen me, and warn't it me as got never a word but Guilty? And when I says to Compeyson, 'Once out of this court, I'll smash that face of yourn!' it's Compeyson as prays to be protected, and gets two turnkeys stood betwixt us? And when we're sentenced, he gets seven year, and me fourteen, and ain't it him as the Judge is sorry for, because he might a done so well, and ain't it me the Judge says is a old offender of wiolent passion, likely to come to worse?"

He had worked himself into a state of great excitement, but he checked it, took two or three short breaths, and swallowed as often.

He wiped his face and head and neck and hands, before he could go on.

"We was in the same prison-ship, but I couldn't get at him for long, though I tried. At last I come behind him and got him to turn and got a smashing one at him, but I was seen and seized. The black-hole of that ship warn't strong. I escaped to the shore, and I was a hiding among the graves there when I first see my boy!"

He regarded me with a look of affection that made him almost abhorrent to me again, though I had felt great pity for him.

"My boy giv' to understand as Compeyson had escaped, I half believe, in his terror, to get quit of me, not knowing I had got ashore. I hunted him down. I smashed his face. 'And now,' says I, 'I'll drag you back.' And I'd have swum off, towing him by the hair, if it had come to that, and I'd a got him aboard without the soldiers.

"Of course he'd much the best of it – his character was so good. He had escaped, terrified by me and my murderous intentions; and his punishment was light. I was put in irons, brought to trial again, and sent for life. I didn't stop for life, dear boy and Pip's comrade, being here."

"Is he dead?" I asked, after a silence.

"Is who dead, dear boy?"

"Compeyson."

"He hopes I am, if he's alive, you may be sure," with a fierce look. "I never heerd no more of him."

Herbert had been writing in the cover of a book. He softly pushed it over to me, as Provis stood gazing at the fire, and I read: "Young Havisham's name was Arthur. Compeyson is the man who professed to be Miss Havisham's lover."

I shut the book and nodded slightly to Herbert, and put the book by but neither of us said anything.

CHAPTER 40

His narrative gave form and purpose to a fear that was already there. If Compeyson were alive and should discover his return, I could hardly doubt the consequence. That Compeyson stood in mortal fear of him, no one could know better than I; and that the man described, would hardly hesitate to get rid of a feared enemy by becoming an informer was scarcely to be imagined.

Never had I breathed, and never would I breathe – or so I resolved – a word of Estella to Provis. But I said to Herbert that before I could go abroad, I must see both Estella and Miss Havisham. This was decided after Provis told us his story. I resolved to go out to Richmond next day, and I went.

On my presenting myself at Mrs Brandley's, I was told that Estella had gone into the country, to Satis House, as usual. Not as usual, I said, for she had never yet gone there without me; when was she coming back? Her maid believed she was only coming back for a little while. I could make nothing of this, and I went home again in complete discomfiture.

Another consultation with Herbert after Provis had gone home led us to decide that nothing should be said about going abroad until I came back from Miss Havisham's. In the meantime, Herbert and I were to consider separately whether we should pretend to be afraid that he was under suspicious observation; or whether I, who had never yet been abroad, should propose an expedition. We both knew that I had but to propose anything, and he would consent.

Next day I was mean enough to pretend that I had promised to see Joe. Provis was to be careful while I was gone, and Herbert was to take the charge of him. I would be away one night.

Having thus cleared the way for my expedition to Miss Havisham's, I set off by the early morning coach before it was yet light. When we drove up to the Blue Boar after a drizzly ride, whom should I see come out under the gateway, toothpick in hand, to look at the coach, but Bentley Drummle!

As he pretended not to see me, I pretended not to see him. It was a very lame pretence on both sides. It was poisonous to me to see him in the town, for I very well knew why he had come there.

Pretending to read a smeary newspaper, I sat at my table while he stood before the fire. After a while I got up, determined to have my share of the fire. I had to put my hand behind his legs for the poker, but still pretended not to know him.

"Is this a cut?" said Mr Drummle.

"Oh!" said I, poker in hand; "it's you, is it? I was wondering who it was, who kept the fire off."

With that, I poked tremendously, and having done so, planted myself side by side with Mr Drummle.

"You have just come down?" said Mr Drummle, edging me a little away with his shoulder.

"Yes," said I, edging him a little away with my shoulder.

"Beastly place," said Drummle. "Your part of the country, I think?"

"Yes," I assented. "I am told it's very like your Shropshire."

"Not in the least like it," said Drummle, looking at his boots. I looked at mine, and then Mr Drummle looked at my boots, and I looked at his.

"Have you been here long?" I asked, determined not to yield an inch of the fire.

"Long enough to be tired of it," returned Drummle, pretending to yawn, but equally determined.

"Do you stay here long?"

"Can't say," answered Mr Drummle. "Do you?"

"Can't say," said I.

Drummle called the waiter.

"Is that horse of mine ready?"

"Brought round to the door, sir."

"Look here. The lady won't ride today; the weather won't do."

"Very good, sir."

"And I don't dine, because I'm dining at the lady's."

"Very good, sir."

Then, Drummle glanced at me, with an insolent triumph that cut me to the heart.

Neither of us would move from the fire. The waiter had served my breakfast, and now he felt my fast cooling teapot with the palm of his hand, looked imploringly at me, and went out. Drummle, careful not to move, took a cigar from his pocket and bit the end off. Choking and boiling as I was, I felt that we could go no further, without introducing

Estella's name, which I could not endure to hear him utter. I therefore looked stonily at the opposite wall and forced myself to silence. How long we might have stayed there it is impossible to say, but for the entrance of three farmers – led by the waiter, I think – who came into the coffee-room rubbing their hands, and before whom, as they charged at the fire, we had to give way.

I saw him through the window, mounting his horse in his blundering brutal manner. I thought he was gone, when he came back, calling for a light for his cigar. A man in dust-coloured dress appeared – I could not have said from where – and as Drummle leaned down from the saddle and lighted his cigar and laughed, the slouching shoulders of this man, whose back was to me, reminded me of Orlick.

Not caring too much at the time whether it were he or no, I washed the weather and the journey from my face and hands, and went out to the memorable old house that it would have been so much the better for me never to have entered, never to have seen.

CHAPTER 41

In the room where the dressing-table stood, I found Miss Havisham and Estella; Miss Havisham seated on a settee near the fire, and Estella, knitting, on a cushion at her feet. They both saw an alteration in me. I derived that, from the look they interchanged.

"And what wind," said Miss Havisham, "blows you here, Pip?"

I saw that she was rather confused. Estella paused a moment in her knitting to look at me. I fancied that I read in the action of her fingers that she perceived I had discovered my real benefactor.

"Miss Havisham," said I; "I went to Richmond yesterday, to speak to Estella; and finding that some wind had blown her here, I followed."

Miss Havisham motioned me to the chair by the dressing-table. With all that ruin at my feet and about me, it seemed a natural place for me.

"What I had to say to Estella, Miss Havisham, I will say before you, presently. It will not surprise you, it will not displease you. I am as unhappy as you can ever have meant me to be."

Miss Havisham continued to look at me. I could see that Estella attended to what I said: but she did not look up.

"I have found out who my patron is. It is not a fortunate discovery, and is not likely ever to enrich me in reputation, station, fortune, anything. I must say no more on this. It is not my secret, but another's."

As I was silent for a while, Miss Havisham repeated, "It is not your secret, but another's. Well?"

"When you first had me brought here, Miss Havisham; when I belonged to the village over yonder, that I wish I never left; I suppose I did really come here, as a kind of servant, to gratify a want, and to be paid for it?"

"Ay, Pip," replied Miss Havisham, nodding her head; "you did."

"And that Mr Jaggers – "

"Mr Jaggers," said Miss Havisham, firmly, "had nothing to do with it. His being my lawyer, and his being the lawyer of your patron, is a coincidence."

Any one could tell that there was no evasion so far.

"But when I fell into the mistake I have so long remained in, you led me on?" said I.

"Yes," she returned, again nodding.

"Was that kind?"

"Who am I," cried Miss Havisham, so suddenly that Estella glanced up at her in surprise, "for God's sake, that I should be kind?"

It was weak of me to complain so, and I had not meant to. I told her so.

"Well!" she said. "What else?"

"I was liberally paid," I said, to soothe her, "in being apprenticed. I have asked these questions for my own information. But perhaps, in humouring my mistake, Miss Havisham, you punished – your self-seeking relations?"

"I did. They took it so! So did you. You all made your own snares. I never made them."

Waiting until she was quiet again – for this, too, was expressed in a wild and sudden way – I went on.

"I have been constantly with one family of your relations, Miss Havisham, since I went to London. I know they were as honestly under my delusion as I myself. And I should be false and base if I did not tell you, whether you like it or no, and whether you believe it or no, that you deeply wrong both Mr Matthew Pocket and his son Herbert, if you think them other than generous, upright and incapable of anything designing or mean."

"They are your friends," said Miss Havisham.

"They made themselves my friends," said I, "when they thought I had superseded them; and when Sarah Pocket, Miss Georgiana, and Mistress Camilla, were not my friends."

This contrasting of them with the rest seemed to do them good with her. She looked at me for a little while, and then said quietly:

"What do you want for them?"

"Only," said I, "that you would not confuse them with the others. They may be of the same blood, but, believe me, they are not of the same nature."

Still looking at me, Miss Havisham repeated: "What do you want for them?"

"I am not so cunning, you see," I replied, conscious I reddened a little, "that I could hide from you that I do want something. Miss Havisham, if you would spare the money to do my friend Herbert a lasting service in life, but which could be done without his knowledge, I could show you how."

"Why without his knowledge?" she asked, regarding me more attentively.

"Because," said I, "I began the service myself, over two years ago, without his knowledge, and I don't want to be betrayed. Why I am unable to finish it, I cannot explain. It is a part of the secret which is another person's and not mine."

She gradually turned to the fire. After watching it for what appeared to be a very long time, she looked towards me again. All this time, Estella knitted on.

"What else?"

"Estella," said I, turning to her, trying to command my trembling voice, "you know I love you, and that I have loved you long and dearly. I should have said this sooner, but for my long mistake. It induced me to hope that Miss Havisham meant us for one another."

Looking at me, her face unmoved, and with her fingers still going, Estella shook her head.

"I know," said I, in answer to that action; "I have no hope that I shall

179

ever call you mine, Estella. I know not what may become of me – how poor I may be, or where I may go. Still, I love you. I have loved you since I first saw you in this house."

She shook her head again.

"It would have been cruel in Miss Havisham, horribly cruel, to practise on the susceptibility of a poor boy, and to torture me through all these years, if she had reflected on what she did. But I think she did not. I think that in the endurance of her own trial, she forgot mine, Estella."

I saw Miss Havisham put her hand to her heart, as she sat looking by turns at Estella and at me.

"It seems," said Estella, very calmly, "that there are feelings I am unable to comprehend. When you say you love me, I know what you mean, as a form of words; but nothing more. You touch nothing in my heart. I don't care for what you say at all. I have tried to warn you of this, have I not?"

I said miserably, "Yes."

"Yes. But you thought I did not mean it."

"I thought and hoped you could not mean it."

"It is in my nature," she returned. And then she added, with a stress upon the words, "It is in the nature formed within me. I make a great difference between you and all other people when I say so much. I can do no more."

"Is it not true," said I, "that Bentley Drummle is in town here, pursuing you?"

"It is quite true," she replied, referring to him with the indifference of utter contempt.

"That you encourage him, and that he dines with you today?"

She seemed a little surprised, but again replied, "Quite true."

"You cannot love him, Estella!"

Her fingers stopped for the first time, "what have I told you? Do you still think, in spite of it, that I do not mean what I say?"

"You would never marry him, Estella?"

She looked towards Miss Havisham, considering, and then said, "Why not tell you the truth? I am going to be married to him."

I dropped my face to my hands, but controlled myself better than I could have expected, considering my agony at hearing those words. When I looked up, I noticed a ghastly look upon Miss Havisham's face.

"Estella, dearest Estella, do not let Miss Havisham lead you into this fatal step. Put me aside for ever – you have done – but choose someone better than Drummle. Miss Havisham gives you to him, to slight and injure the many far better men who admire you, and the few who truly love you. Among those few, there may be one who loves you as dearly, though not as long, as I. Take him, and I can bear it better, for your sake!"

"I am going," she said again, in a gentler voice, "to be married to him soon. Why do you use the name of my adopted mother? It is my own act."

"Your own act, Estella, to fling yourself away upon a brute?"

"On whom should I fling myself away?" she retorted. "Should I fling myself away upon the man who would be glad that I took nothing to him? There! It is done. I shall do well enough, and so will my husband. And Miss Havisham would have had me wait, and not marry yet; but I am tired of the life I have led, which has very few charms for me, and I am willing enough to change it. Say no more. We shall never understand each other."

"Such a mean brute, such a stupid brute!" I urged in despair.

"Don't be afraid of my being a blessing to him," said Estella; "I shall not be that. Here is my hand. Do we part on this, you visionary boy – or man?"

"O Estella!" I answered, as my bitter tears fell fast on her hand – I could not restrain them; "how could I see you Drummle's wife?"

"Nonsense," she returned. "This will pass in no time."

"Never, Estella!"

"I will be gone from your thoughts in a week."

"Estella! You are part of myself. Estella, to the last hour of my life, you will remain part of my character, part of the little good in me, part of the evil. But in this separation I associate you only with the good, and I will faithfully hold you to that always, for you must have done me far more good than harm. O God bless you, God forgive you!"

I got these broken words out. I held her hand to my lips some lingering moments, and so I left her. But ever afterwards, I remembered that while Estella looked at me with incredulous wonder, the figure of Miss Havisham, her hand still covering her heart, seemed just a ghastly stare of pity and remorse.

All done, all gone! Even the light of day seemed darker when I went out the gate. For a while I hid myself among some lanes and by-paths, and then struck off to walk all the way to London. For I knew I could not go back to the inn and see Drummle there; that I could not bear to sit upon the coach and be spoken to.

It was past midnight when I crossed London Bridge. My readiest access to the Temple was by the riverside, through Whitefriars. I very rarely came in at that gate, and I was muddy and weary, so the night porter examined me with much attention as he held the gate open for me to pass in. I mentioned my name.

"I have a note, sir. The messenger asked that you read it by my lantern."

Much surprised, I took the note. It was directed to Philip Pip, Esquire, with the instruction, "*Please read this, here*." I opened it, and by the watchman's light read in Wemmick's writing: "*Don't go home*."

CHAPTER 42

Turning away as soon as I had read the warning, I made my way to Fleet Street, and there got a late hackney chariot and drove to the Hummums Hotel in Covent Garden, where a bed was available any hour of the night. When I reached my bed, and lay there footsore, weary, and wretched, I found that I could not close my eyes.

There was an inhospitable smell in the room, of cold soot and hot dust. But why I was not to go home, and what had happened there and when I should go home, and whether Provis was safe at home, were questions occupying my mind. I thought of Estella, and how we had parted that day forever, and I recalled all the circumstances of our parting, and all her looks, and the action of her fingers while she knitted.

I had left directions that I was to be called at seven; for it was plain that I must see Wemmick before seeing any one else, and therefore I was at the Castle by eight o'clock. The little servant happening to be entering with two hot rolls, I crossed the drawbridge in her company, and so came without announcement into the presence of Wemmick.

"Halloa, Mr Pip!" said Wemmick. "You came home, then?"

"Yes," I returned; "but I didn't go home."

"That's all right," said he, rubbing his hands. "I'll go round the gates and destroy the notes. It's a good rule never to leave documentary evidence if you can help it, because you don't know when it may be put in."

I thanked him for his friendship and caution, and our discourse proceeded in a low tone.

"Now, Mr Pip, you know," said Wemmick, "you and I understand one another. We are in our private and personal capacities, and we have been engaged in a confidential transaction before today. Official sentiments are one thing. We are extra official."

I cordially assented.

"I accidentally heard, yesterday morning," said Wemmick, "that a certain person not altogether of uncolonial pursuits, and not unpossessed of portable property – I don't know who it may really be – we won't name this person – "

"Not necessary," said I.

" – had made some little stir in a certain part of the world where a good many people go, not always for their own inclinations, and not quite at their own expense – "

I watched his face.

" – by disappearing from such place. From which," said Wemmick, "I also heard that you at your chambers had been watched, and might be watched again."

"By whom?" said I.

"I wouldn't go into that," said Wemmick, evasively, "it might clash with official responsibilities."

"This watching of me at my chambers (which I have once had reason to suspect)," I said to Wemmick, "is inseparable from the person to whom you have hinted?"

Wemmick looked very serious. "I couldn't undertake to say it was at first. But it either is, or will be, or is in danger of being."

I saw that he was restrained by fealty to Little Britain from saying as much as he could, and I knew how far out of his way he went to say what he did. I did not press him. After a while I told him that I would like to ask a question, subject to his answering or not, as he deemed right. He paused in his breakfast, and crossed his arms.

"You have heard of a man of bad character, Compeyson?"

He answered with a nod.

"Is he living?"

183

Another nod.

"Is he in London?"

He gave me one more nod, compressed the post-office exceedingly, gave one last nod, and went on with his breakfast.

"Now," said Wemmick, "after hearing what I heard; I went to Garden Court to find you; not finding you, I went to Clarriker's to find Mr Herbert."

"And him you found?" said I.

"And him I found. Without going into detail, I gave him to understand that if he knew of anybody – Tom, Jack, or Richard – being about the chambers, or in the immediate neighbourhood, he should get this person out of the way while you were out of the way."

"He would be greatly puzzled what to do?"

"He was puzzled what to do; not least, because I told him it was not safe to try to get this person too far away at present. Mr Pip, I'll tell you something. There is no safer place than a city once you are in it. Don't break cover too soon. Wait till things slacken, before you try the open, even for foreign air."

I thanked him for his advice, and asked what Herbert had done?

"Mr Herbert," said Wemmick, "struck out a plan. He mentioned to me as a secret, that he is courting a young lady who has a bedridden Pa, who lies a-bed in a bow-window where he can see the ships sail up and down the river. You know the young lady?"

"Not personally," said I.

"The house with the bow-window," said Wemmick, "being by the river-side, between Limehouse and Greenwich, has a furnished upper floor to let. Mr Herbert put it to me, what did I think of that as a temporary tenement for our friend? Now, I thought very well of it for three reasons. Firstly. It's altogether out of all your beats. Secondly. Without going near it yourself, you could always hear of his safety through Mr Herbert. Thirdly. After a while and when it might be prudent, if you should want to slip him on board a foreign packet-boat, there he is – ready."

I thanked Wemmick again and again, and begged him to proceed.

"Well, sir! By nine o'clock last night Mr Herbert had housed our man successfully. At the old lodgings it was understood that he was summoned to Dover. Now, another great advantage of all this is, that it was done without you – you were ever so many miles off and quite otherwise engaged. This diverts suspicion and for that reason I recommended that you should not go home. It brings in more confusion, and you want confusion."

Wemmick had finished breakfast and began to get his coat on.

"And now, Mr Pip," said he, "I have probably done the most I can do; but if I can ever do more – from a Walworth point of view – I shall be glad to do it. Here's the address. There can be no harm in your going here tonight and seeing that all is well, before you go home. But after you have gone home, don't go back there. You are very welcome, I am sure, Mr Pip,"

I shook his hand.

"Let me finally impress one important point upon you." He laid his hands upon my shoulders: "This evening it is best to lay hold of his portable property. You don't know what may happen to him. Don't let anything happen to the portable property."

Quite despairing of making my mind clear to Wemmick on this point, I didn't try.

"Time's up," said Wemmick, "and I must be off. If you can do so, I would stay here 'til dark. A perfectly quiet day with the Aged would do you good."

I accepted the invitation.

"Good-bye, Aged Parent!" Wemmick called cheerily.

"All right, John!" piped the old man from within.

I soon fell asleep before Wemmick's fire, and the Aged and I enjoyed one another's society by falling asleep before it more or less all day. We had loin of pork for dinner, and greens grown on the estate. When it was quite dark, I left the Aged preparing the fire for toast; and I inferred from his glances at the two little doors in the wall, that Miss Skiffins was expected.

CHAPTER 43

Eight o'clock had struck before I reached air scented by the chips and shavings of the long-shore boatbuilders. I found Chinks's Basin and Mill Pond Bank.

Selecting a house with a wooden front and three storeys of bow-window, I knocked, and a pleasant looking elderly woman responded. Herbert instantly appeared and led me into the parlour. It was odd to see his very familiar face quite at home in that very unfamiliar room.

"All is well, Handel," he said, "and he is quite satisfied, though eager to see you. My dear girl is with her father; and if you'll wait till she comes down, I'll make you known to her, and then we'll go upstairs."

"Mrs Whimple," said Herbert, "is the best of housewives, and I do not know what my Clara would do without her motherly help. For Clara has no relation in the world but old Gruffandgrim."

"Surely that's not his name, Herbert?"

"No," said Herbert, "that's my name for him. His name is Mr Barley. But what a blessing it is for me, to love a girl who has no relations, and who need never bother herself, or anybody else, about her family!"

Herbert now reminded me that he first knew Miss Clara Barley when she was completing her education at Hammersmith.

As we were thus conversing in a low tone, the door opened, and a very pretty, slight, dark-eyed girl of twenty or so, came in with a basket in her hand: whom Herbert tenderly relieved of the basket, and presented blushing as "Clara." She really was a most charming girl.

I was looking at her with admiration, when suddenly the growl above us swelled into a roar. Upon this Clara said to Herbert, "Papa wants me, darling!" and ran away.

"What do you suppose he wants now, Handel?" said Herbert.

"I don't know," said I. "Something to drink?"

"That's it!" cried Herbert. "He keeps his grog ready-mixed in a little tub on the table. Wait a moment, and you'll hear Clara lift him up to take some. – There he goes!" Another roar, with a prolonged shake at the end. "Now," said Herbert, as it was succeeded by silence, "he's drinking. Now," said Herbert, as the growl resounded in the beam once more, "he's down again on his back!"

Clara returned soon afterwards, and Herbert accompanied me upstairs to see our charge.

In his rooms at the top of the house, which were fresh and airy, I found Provis comfortably settled. He expressed no alarm, and seemed to feel none that was worth mentioning.

The day's rest had given me time for reflection, and I determined to say nothing to him of Compeyson. For all I knew, his animosity towards the man might just lead to his seeking him out and rushing on his own destruction. Therefore, when Herbert and I sat down with him by his fire, I firstly asked him whether he relied on Wemmick's judgement?

"Ay, ay, dear boy!" he answered, with a grave nod, "Jaggers knows."

"Then, I have talked with Wemmick," said I, "and have come to tell you what caution and advice he gave me."

This I did accurately, without mentioning Compeyson; and I told him how Wemmick had heard that he was under some suspicion, and that my chambers had been watched; how Wemmick had recommended my keeping away from him; and what Wemmick had said about getting him abroad. I added, that of course, when the time came, I should go with him. What was to follow that, I did not touch upon; neither indeed was I at all clear or comfortable about it in my own mind. As to altering my way of living, by enlarging my expenses, I put it to him whether in our present unsettled and difficult circumstances, it would not be simply ridiculous, if it were no worse?

He could not deny this, and was very reasonable throughout. His coming back was a venture, he said. He would do nothing to make it a desperate venture, and he had very little fear of his safety with such good help.

Herbert, who had been pondering, here said that something had occurred to him following Wemmick's suggestion. "We are both good watermen, Handel, and could take him down the river ourselves when the time comes. No boat would then be hired for the purpose. But don't you think it a good idea to have a boat at the Temple stairs, and get in the habit of rowing up and down the river? Who will then notice or mind? Twenty or fifty times later, and there is nothing special in your doing it the twenty-first or fifty-first."

I liked this scheme, and Provis was quite elated by it. We agreed the idea and also that Provis should never recognise us if we rowed past Mill Pond Bank. But we further agreed that he should pull down his blind in the window looking east, whenever he saw us and all was right.

Everything arranged, I rose to go; remarking to Herbert that he and I had better not go home together. "I don't like to leave you here," I said to Provis, "though you are so much safer here than near me. Good-bye!"

187

"Dear boy," he answered, clasping my hands, "I don't know when we may meet again. Good-night!"

"Good-night! Herbert will go regularly between us, and when the time comes I shall be ready. Good-night!"

We left him on the landing outside his door, holding a light over the stair-rail to light us downstairs.

When we got to the foot of the stairs, I asked Herbert whether he still used the name Provis. He replied that the lodger was now Mr Campbell, and also explained Mr Campbell had been consigned to him, Herbert.

I returned to the Temple, and all was quiet. The windows of Provis's rooms were dark and still. I walked past the fountain twice or thrice, but I was quite alone.

Next day I bought the boat, and it was taken to the Temple stairs, where I could reach her within a minute or two. Then I began to train and practise: sometimes alone, sometimes with Herbert. I was often out in cold, rain, and sleet, but nobody took much note of me after a few times. At first, I kept above Blackfriars Bridge; but as the hours of the tide changed, I took towards London Bridge. The first time I passed Mill Pond Bank, we saw the blind towards the east come down. Herbert was rarely there less than three times in a week, and he never told me anything alarming. Still, I knew that there was cause for alarm, and I could not get rid of the notion of being watched.

CHAPTER 44

Some weeks passed bringing no change. No sign came from Wemmick.

My worldly affairs began to wear a gloomy appearance, and I was pressed for money by creditors. I converted some easily spared jewellery into cash. But I knew it would be wrong to take more money from my patron in my present state of uncertainty. Therefore, I sent him the unopened pocket-book, and felt a grim kind of satisfaction in not having profited by his generosity since his revelation of himself.

As the time wore on, an impression settled heavily upon me that Estella was married. Fearful of having it confirmed, I avoided the newspapers, and begged Herbert (to whom I had confided the circumstances of our last interview) never to speak of her to me.

It was an unhappy life that I lived, and its one dominant anxiety never disappeared from my view. Still, no new cause for fear arose. I would listen, with dread, for Herbert's returning step at night, lest it should be fleeter than ordinary, winged with evil news; but for all that, the round of things went on. I rowed about in my boat, and waited as I best could.

There were states of the tide when, having been down the river, I could not get back; then, I left my boat at a wharf near the Custom House, to be brought afterwards to the Temple stairs. This served to make me and my boat a common incident among the waterside people there.

One afternoon, late in February, I came ashore at dusk. I had been as far as Greenwich with the ebb tide, and had turned with the tide. It had become foggy as the sun dropped, and I had had to feel my way back among the shipping pretty carefully. Both in going and returning, I had seen the signal in his window – all well.

As it was a raw evening and I was cold, I thought I would comfort myself with dinner at once; and then afterwards go to the play and to see Mr Wopsle who had abandoned life in our own town for a life on the stage. After sitting through various scenes of Mr Wopsle dressed in more and more bizarre outfits, the night's entertainment was over. I met him by the stage door a short while later.

"How do you do?" said I, shaking hands with him as we turned down the street together. "I saw that you saw me."

"Saw you, Mr Pip!" he returned. "Yes, of course I saw you. But who else was there? It is the strangest thing, and yet I could swear to him."

Becoming alarmed, I entreated Mr Wopsle to explain his meaning.

"Whether I should have noticed him at first but for your being there," said Mr Wopsle, going on in the same lost way, "I can't be positive; yet I think I should."

Involuntarily I looked round me, as I was accustomed to look round me when I went home; for his words gave me a chill.

"Oh! He can't be in sight," said Mr Wopsle. "He went out, before I went off, I saw him go."

I glanced at him as we walked on together, but said nothing.

"I had a ridiculous fancy that he must be with you, Mr Pip, till I saw that you were quite unaware of him, sitting behind you there, like a ghost."

189

My former chill crept over me again. Of course, I was perfectly sure and safe that Provis had not been there.

"You remember in old times a certain Christmas Day, when you were quite a child, and I dined at Gargery's, and some soldiers came to the door to get a pair of handcuffs mended?"

"I remember it very well."

"And there was a chase after two convicts?"

"I remember it all very well."

"And you remember that we came up with the two in a ditch, and that there was a scuffle between them?"

"I see it all before me."

"Then, Mr Pip, one of those two prisoners sat behind you tonight. I saw him over your shoulder."

"Steady!" I thought. I asked him then, "Which of the two was it?"

"The one who had been mauled," he answered readily, "and I'll swear I saw him."

"This is very curious!" said I, as if it meant nothing to me. "Very curious indeed!"

I cannot exaggerate the disquiet into which this conversation threw me, or the terror I felt at Compeyson's having been behind me, "like a ghost."

It was between twelve and one o'clock when I reached the Temple, and the gates were shut. No one was near me when I went in and went home.

Herbert had come in, and we held a very serious council by the fire. But there was nothing to be done, saving to communicate to Wemmick and to remind him that we waited for his hint. As I thought that I might compromise him if I went too often to the Castle, I made this communication by letter. Herbert and I agreed that we could do nothing else but be very cautious. And we were very cautious indeed and I for my part never went near Chinks's Basin, except when I rowed by, and then I only looked at Mill Pond Bank as I looked at anything else.

CHAPTER 45

About a week later, I had again left my boat below Bridge; and, undecided where to dine, I had strolled up into Cheapside. I was strolling along when a large hand was laid upon my shoulder, by some one overtaking me. It was Mr Jaggers's hand, and he passed it through my arm.

"As we are going in the same direction, Pip, we may walk together. Where are you bound for?"

"For the Temple, I think," said I.

"Then," said Mr Jaggers, "come and dine with me."

I was going to excuse myself, when he added, "Wemmick's coming." So I changed my excuse into an acceptance.

We went to Gerrard Street, all three together, in a hackney coach. As soon as we got there, dinner was served. Although I would not have referred to Wemmick's Walworth sentiments, it would have been nice to catch his eye now and then in a friendly way. But it was not to be done. He turned his eyes on Mr Jaggers whenever he raised them from the table, and was as dry and distant to me as if there were twin Wemmicks and this was the wrong one.

"Did you send that note of Miss Havisham's to Mr Pip, Wemmick?" Mr Jaggers asked, soon after we began dinner.

"No, sir," returned Wemmick; "it was going by post, when you brought Mr Pip into the office. Here it is." He handed it to his principal, instead of to me.

"It's a note of two lines, Pip," said Mr Jaggers, handing it on, "sent to me by Miss Havisham, as she was not sure of your address. She wants to see you on a little matter of business you mentioned to her. You'll go down?"

"Yes," said I, casting my eyes over the note.

"When do you think of going down?"

"I have an impending engagement," said I, glancing at Wemmick, "that renders me rather uncertain of my time. At once, I think."

"If Mr Pip has the intention of going at once," said Wemmick to Mr Jaggers, "he needn't write an answer, you know."

Receiving this as an intimation that it was best not to delay, I settled that I would go tomorrow. Wemmick drank a glass of wine and looked with a grimly satisfied air at Mr Jaggers, but not at me.

"So, Pip! Our friend the Spider," said Mr Jaggers, "has played his cards. He has won the pool."

It was as much as I could do to assent.

"Hah! He is a promising fellow, but he may not have it all his own way. The stronger will win in the end. If he should turn to, and beat her – "

"Surely," I interrupted, with burning heart, "you do not seriously think he would do that, Mr Jaggers?"

"I am merely putting a case. If he should turn to and beat her, he may possibly get the strength on his side; if it becomes a question of intellect, he certainly will not. A fellow like our friend the Spider either beats, or cringes. Ask Wemmick his opinion."

"Either beats or cringes," said Wemmick, not at all addressing himself to me.

"So, here's to Mrs Bentley Drummle," said Mr Jaggers, taking a decanter of wine and filling for each of us and himself, "and may the question of supremacy be settled to the lady's satisfaction! Now, Molly, Molly, how slow you are today!"

She was putting a dish upon the table. As she withdrew her hands, she fell back a step or two, nervously muttering. A certain action of her fingers as she spoke arrested my attention.

"What's the matter?" said Mr Jaggers.

"Nothing. Only the subject we were speaking of," said I, "was rather painful to me."

The action of her fingers was like the action of knitting. She stood, not understanding whether to go, or whether he had more to say to her. Her look was very intent. Surely, I had seen exactly such eyes and such hands, on a memorable occasion very lately!

He dismissed her, and she glided out of the room. But she remained before me, as if she were still there. I looked at those hands, those eyes, that flowing hair; and I compared them with other hands, other eyes, other hair that I knew of, and with what they might be after twenty years of a brutal husband and a stormy life. I looked again at those hands and eyes of the housekeeper, and I felt absolutely certain that this woman was Estella's mother.

Mr Jaggers had seen me with Estella, and would not have missed the sentiments I had been at no pains to conceal. He nodded when I said the subject was painful to me, put round the wine again, and went on with his dinner.

Only twice more did the housekeeper reappear, and then her stay in the room was very short, and Mr Jaggers was sharp with her. But her hands were Estella's hands, and her eyes were Estella's eyes.

It was a dull evening, for Wemmick, with his eyes on his chief, sat in a state of perpetual readiness for cross-examination. Again I felt I dined with the wrong twin.

We took our leave early, and left together. Even while we groped for our hats, I felt that the right twin was on his way back; and we had not gone far down Gerrard Street in the Walworth direction before I found that I was with the right twin, and that the wrong twin had evaporated.

"Well!" said Wemmick, "that's over! He's a wonderful man; but I feel that I have to screw myself up when I dine with him – and I dine more comfortably unscrewed. Wouldn't say it to anybody but yourself. I know what is said between us, goes no further."

I asked him if he had ever seen Miss Havisham's adopted daughter, Mrs Bentley Drummle? He said no.

"Wemmick," said I, "do you remember telling me before I first went to Mr Jaggers's home, to notice that housekeeper?"

"Did I?" he replied. "Ah, I dare say I did."

"A wild beast tamed, you called her. How did Mr Jaggers tame her, Wemmick?"

"That's his secret. She has been with him many a long year."

"I wish you would tell me her story. I feel I need to know it. You know that what we say goes no further."

"Well!" Wemmick replied, "I don't know all her story. But what I know, I'll tell you. We are in our private and personal capacities, of course."

"Of course."

"A score or so of years ago, she was tried at the Old Bailey for murder, and was acquitted. She was a very handsome young woman, and I believe had some gipsy blood in her. Mr Jaggers was for her, and worked the case in a way quite astonishing. It was a desperate case. The murdered person was a woman, a good ten years older, larger, and stronger. It was a case of jealousy over her husband. The murdered woman was found dead in a barn near Hounslow Heath. There had been a violent struggle. She was bruised and scratched, and had been held by the throat and choked. Now, on the improbabilities of this woman having been able to do it, Mr Jaggers principally rested his case.

"Well, sir!" Wemmick went on; "it happened that this woman was artfully dressed so that she looked much slighter than she really was. She was also under strong suspicion of having, at about the time of the murder, frantically destroyed her child by this man – some three years old – to revenge herself upon him. But Mr Jaggers was altogether too many for the Jury, and they had to give in."

"Has she been in his service ever since?"

"Yes; but not only that," said Wemmick. "She went into his service immediately after her acquittal, tamed as she is now."

"Do you remember the sex of the child?"

"Said to have been a girl."

We exchanged a cordial Good Night, and I went home, with new matter for my thoughts.

CHAPTER 46

Putting Miss Havisham's note in my pocket, as proof of her invitation for so soon reappearing at Satis House, I went down again by the coach next day.

The best light of the day was gone when I passed along the quiet echoing courts behind the High Street. The cathedral chimes had a sad and remote sound to me, as I hurried on avoiding observation; and the rooks, as they hovered about the grey tower, seemed to call to me that the place was changed, and that Estella was gone out of it forever.

An elderly woman whom I had seen before opened the gate. I took the lighted candle and ascended the staircase alone. Miss Havisham was in the larger room across the landing. I saw her sitting in a ragged chair, lost in the contemplation of the ashy fire.

I stood, touching the old chimneypiece, where she could see me when she raised her eyes. There was an air of utter loneliness upon her. As I stood thinking how in the progress of time I too had come to be a part of the wrecked fortunes of that house, her eyes rested on me. She stared, and said in a low voice, "Is it real?"

"It is I, Pip. Mr Jaggers gave me your note yesterday, and I lost no time."

"Thank you. Thank you."

I brought another ragged chair to the hearth and sat down, noting a new expression on her face, as if she were afraid of me.

"I want," she said, "to pursue that subject you mentioned to me when you were last here, and to show you that I am not all stone."

I said some reassuring words, and she stretched out a shaking hand, as though to touch me; but she recalled it again before I understood the action, or knew how to receive it.

"You said, speaking for your friend, that you could tell me how to do something useful and good. Something that you would like done, is it not?"

"Something that I would like done very much."

"What is it?"

I began explaining to her that secret history of the partnership. I told her how I had hoped to complete the transaction out of my means, but how in this I was disappointed. That part of the subject (I reminded her) involved the weighty secrets of another.

"So!" said she, assenting with her head, but not looking at me. "And how much money is wanting to complete the purchase?"

I was rather afraid of stating it, for it sounded a large sum. "Nine hundred pounds."

"If I give you the money for this purpose, will you keep my secret as you have kept your own?"

"Quite as faithfully."

"And your mind will be more at rest?"

"Much more at rest."

"Are you very unhappy now?"

She asked this question in a tone of sympathy. I could not reply, for my voice failed me. She put her left arm across the head of her stick, and softly laid her forehead on it.

"I am far from happy, Miss Havisham, and I have other causes of disquiet. They are the secrets I have previously mentioned."

After a little while, she looked at the fire again.

"Can I only serve you, Pip, by serving your friend? Regarding that as done, is there nothing I can do for you yourself?"

"Nothing. I thank you for the question. But, there is nothing."

She presently rose from her seat, and looked about for the means of writing. There were none, so she took from her pocket a yellow set of ivory tablets, mounted in tarnished gold, and wrote upon them with a pencil.

"You are still on friendly terms with Mr Jaggers?"

"Quite. I dined with him yesterday."

"This is an authority to him to pay you that money."

"Thank you, Miss Havisham."

She read me what she had written, and it was evidently intended to absolve me from any suspicion of profiting from the money. She put the pencil in my hand.

"My name is on the first leaf. If you can ever write under that, 'I forgive her', even long after my broken heart is dust – pray do it!"

"O Miss Havisham," said I, "I can do it now. I want forgiveness and direction far too much, to be bitter with you."

She turned to me again, and, to my amazement, dropped on her knees at my feet; with her folded hands raised to me. To see her thus gave me a shock. I entreated her to rise, and got my arms about her to help her up; but she hung her head over my hands and wept. I had never seen her weep, and, hoping that the relief might do her good, I did not speak. She now was down upon the ground.

"O!" she cried, despairingly. "What have I done?"

"If you mean, to injure me – very little. I should have loved her under any circumstances. – Is she married?"

"Yes."

I needn't have asked, the desolate house had told me so.

"What have I done?" She wrung her hands and cried over and over again. "What have I done?"

I knew not how to comfort her. That she had done a grievous thing in taking an impressionable child to mould into the form that her wild resentment, spurned affection, and wounded pride, found vengeance in, I knew full well. But that, in shutting out the light of day, she had shut out infinitely more; that, in seclusion, she had secluded herself from a thousand healing influences; that, her mind, brooding alone, had grown

196

diseased, I knew equally well. And could I look upon her without compassion, seeing her punishment in the ruin she was?

"Until you spoke to her the other day, and I saw in you a looking-glass that showed me what I once felt myself, I did not know what I had done. What have I done?" And so again, twenty, fifty times over.

"Miss Havisham," I said, when her cry had died away, "dismiss me from your mind and conscience. But Estella is a different case, and if you can ever undo what you have done amiss it will be better to do that."

"Yes, I know it. But, Pip – my Dear!" There was an earnest womanly compassion for me in her new affection. "Believe this: when she first came to me, I meant to save her from misery like my own."

"Well, well!" said I. "I hope so."

"But as she grew, and promised beauty, I gradually did worse, and with my praises, and with my jewels, and with my teachings, I stole her heart away and put ice in its place."

"Better," I could not help saying, "to have left her a natural heart, even to be bruised or broken."

"If you knew all my story," she pleaded, "you would have some compassion for me and better understand me."

"Miss Havisham," I answered, delicately, "I believe I may say I have known your story since I first left this neighbourhood. It has inspired me with great commiseration, and I hope I understand it and its influences. May I now ask a question concerning Estella? As she was when she first came here?"

She was seated on the ground, her arms on the ragged chair. She looked at me and replied, "Go on."

"Whose child was Estella?"

She shook her head.

"You don't know?"

She shook her head again.

"But Mr Jaggers brought her here, or sent her here?"

"Brought her here."

"Will you tell me how that came about?"

She answered in a low whisper: "I had been shut up in these rooms a long time, when I told him I wanted a little girl to rear and love, and save from my fate. He told me that he would look about for such an orphan child. One night he brought her here asleep, and I called her Estella."

197

"Might I ask her age then?"

"Two or three. She herself knows nothing, but that she was left an orphan and I adopted her."

So convinced I was of that woman's being her mother, that I wanted no further evidence.

What more could I hope to do by prolonging the interview? I had succeeded for Herbert, Miss Havisham had told me all she knew of Estella, I had said and done what I could to ease her mind. Therefore we parted.

Twilight was closing in when I went downstairs. I called to the woman who had let me in, that I would walk round the place before leaving. For, I had a feeling that I should never be there again.

I made my way to the ruined garden. I went all round it; round by the corner where Herbert and I had fought our battle; round by the paths where Estella and I had walked.

Taking the brewery on my way back, I raised the rusty latch of a little door and walked through. I was going out at the opposite door when I turned my head to look back. I fancied that I saw Miss Havisham hanging from the beam. So strong was the impression that I stood under the beam shuddering from head to foot.

As I came out between the open wooden gates, I hesitated whether to call the woman to let me out, or first to go upstairs and assure myself that Miss Havisham was as safe and well as I had left her. I took the latter course and went up.

I looked into her room and she still sat in the ragged chair close to the fire. As I turned to leave quietly, I saw a great flaming light spring up. In the same moment, she came running at me, shrieking, flames blazing all about her, soaring high above her head.

I got off my caped great-coat, and threw it over her; I dragged the great cloth from the table for the same purpose, and with it dragged down the heap of rottenness in the midst. We were on the ground struggling like desperate enemies, and the closer I covered her, the more wildly she shrieked and struggled.

Then, I looked round and saw the servants coming in with breathless cries at the door. I still held her down with all my strength.

I was afraid to have her moved, or even touched. Assistance was sent for and I held her until it came, fearing unreasonably that the fire would

198

break out again and consume her. When the surgeon came with other aid, I was astonished to see that both my hands were burnt; for, I had not felt it happen.

It was pronounced that she had received serious hurts, but the danger lay mainly in the shock. Her bed was carried in and laid upon the great table: which happened to be well suited to the dressing of her injuries.

Though her dress was burnt, she still had something of her old ghastly bridal appearance for they covered her to the throat with white cotton wool, with a white sheet loosely overlying that.

I discovered that Estella was in Paris, and the surgeon promised that he would write to her by the next post. Miss Havisham's family I took upon myself; intending to communicate with Mr Matthew Pocket, and leave him to do as he liked about informing the rest. This I did, through Herbert, as soon as I returned to town.

There was a stage, that evening, when she spoke lucidly of what had happened. Towards midnight she began to wander and she said innumerable times in a low solemn voice, "What have I done!" And then, "When she first came, I meant to save her from misery like mine." And then, "Take the pencil and write under my name, 'I forgive her!'" She never changed the order of these three sentences.

As I could do no more there, and as I had my own problems, I decided that I would return by the early morning coach. At about six in the morning, therefore, I leaned over and touched her lips with mine, just as they said, "Take the pencil and write under my name, 'I forgive her'."

CHAPTER 47

My hands were dressed two or three times in the night, and again in the morning. My left arm was burned to the elbow, and, less severely, to the shoulder. It was very painful. My right hand was not so badly burnt; it was bandaged, of course, but my left hand and arm I carried in a sling; and I could only wear my coat like a cloak. My hair had been caught by the fire, but not my head or face.

When Herbert had been down to Hammersmith to his father, he came back to our chambers, and devoted the day to attending on me. He was the kindest of nurses.

At first, as I lay quiet on the sofa, I found it painfully difficult to forget the glare of the flames, and the fierce burning smell. If I dozed for a minute, I was awakened by Miss Havisham's cries as she ran at me with the flames above her head.

My first question when I saw Herbert had been, of course, whether all was well down the river? He replied cheerfully in the affirmative, so we did not resume the subject until later. But then, as Herbert carefully changed the bandages, he went back to it.

"I sat with Provis last night, Handel, two good hours. He was very communicative, and told me more of his life. You remember his breaking off here about some woman that he had had great trouble with. – Did I hurt you?"

I had started – his words had given me a start. I shook my head. "I had forgotten that, Herbert."

"Well! He went into that part of his life, and a dark wild part it is. Shall I tell you?"

"Tell me by all means. Every word."

"It seems that the woman was young, and jealous, and revengeful; revengeful, Handel, to the last degree."

"To what last degree?"

"Murder."

"Whom did she murder?"

"It was a stronger woman who was the victim – in a barn," said Herbert, "but, she was tried for it, and Mr Jaggers defended her, and the reputation of that defence first made his name known to Provis."

"Was she found guilty?"

"No; acquitted. She and Provis had a little child of whom Provis was exceedingly fond. On the very night when the object of her jealousy was strangled, the young woman presented herself before Provis, and swore that she would destroy the child and he should never see it again; then, she vanished."

"Did the woman keep her oath?"

"There comes the darkest part of Provis's life. She did."

"That is, he says she did."

"Why, of course, my dear boy," pursued Herbert, "they had shared some four or five years of life, and he seems to have pitied her. Therefore, fearing he should be called upon to talk about this destroyed child, and so be the cause of her death, he hid himself, keeping out of the way of the trial, and was only mentioned as a certain man called Abel, out of whom the jealousy arose. After the acquittal she disappeared, and thus he lost her and the child."

"I want to ask – "

"A moment, my dear boy, and I have done. That evil genius, Compeyson, knowing he kept out of the way and why, afterwards used this knowledge as a means of keeping him poorer, and working him harder."

"Did he tell you when this happened," said I.

"His expression was, 'a round score o' year ago, and a'most directly after I took up wi' Compeyson'. How old were you when you came upon him in the little churchyard?"

"I think in my seventh year."

"Ay. It had happened some three or four years before, he said, and you reminded him of the little girl so tragically lost, who would have been about your age."

"Herbert," said I, after a short silence, in a hurried way. "Look at me."

"I see you, my dear boy."

"Touch me. You are not afraid that I have a fever, or that my head is much disordered by the accident of last night?"

"N-no, my dear boy," said Herbert, after taking time to examine me. "You are rather excited, but you are quite yourself."

"I know I am quite myself. The man we have in hiding down the river, is Estella's Father."

CHAPTER 48

After our momentous conversation, I was convinced that I ought to see Mr Jaggers, to get the truth. I don't know whether I did this for Estella's sake, or whether to transfer to the man about whose safety I was so concerned, some rays of the romantic interest that had so long surrounded her.

Herbert barely stopped me from going to Gerrard Street that night. If I did, he pointed out, I should probably be stricken useless, when our fugitive's safety would depend upon me. On the understanding, again and again reiterated, that I would go to Mr Jaggers tomorrow, I at length submitted to have my hurts looked after, and to stay at home. Early next morning we went together, and at Smithfield, Herbert went his way into the City, and I went to Little Britain.

I had already sent Mr Jaggers a brief account of the accident, yet I gave him all the details now. My appearance with my arm bandaged and my coat loose over my shoulders, favoured my object. While I described the disaster, Mr Jaggers stood before the fire. Wemmick leaned back in his chair, staring at me.

My narrative finished, and their questions exhausted, I then produced Miss Havisham's authority to receive the nine hundred pounds for Herbert. Mr Jaggers handed it over to Wemmick, with instructions to draw the cheque for his signature.

Mr Jaggers, swaying himself on his well-polished boots, looked on at me. "I am sorry, Pip," said he, as I put the signed cheque in my pocket, "that we do nothing for *you*."

"Miss Havisham asked me," I returned, "whether she could do nothing for me, and I told her No."

"I should not have told her No, if I had been you," said Mr Jaggers; "but every man ought to know his own business best."

"Every man's business," said Wemmick, rather reproachfully towards me, "is portable property."

I thought the time was right for pursuing the theme I had at heart. I turned to Mr Jaggers. "I did ask Miss Havisham, however, to give me some information relative to her adopted daughter, and she gave me all she possessed."

"Did she?" said Mr Jaggers. "Hah! I don't think I should have done so, if I were Miss Havisham. But she knows her own business best."

"I know more of the history of Miss Havisham's adopted child, than Miss Havisham. I know her mother. I have seen her within these three days."

"Yes?" said Mr Jaggers.

"And so have you, sir. And you have seen her still more recently."

"Yes?" said Mr Jaggers.

"Perhaps I know more of Estella's history than you," said I. "I know her father too."

Mr Jaggers stopped in such a way that assured me that he did not know her father. This I had strongly suspected from Provis's account of having kept himself dark; added to the fact that he himself was not Mr Jaggers's client until some four years later, and when he could have no reason for claiming his identity.

"So! You know the young lady's father, Pip?" said Mr Jaggers.

"Yes," I replied, "his name is Provis – from New South Wales."

Even Mr Jaggers started when I said those words. How Wemmick received the announcement I cannot say, for I didn't dare look at him, lest Mr Jaggers detected that there had been some communication unknown to him between us.

"And on what evidence, Pip," asked Mr Jaggers, very coolly, "does Provis make this claim?"

"He does not make it," said I, "he has no knowledge or belief that his daughter lives."

My reply was so unexpected that Mr Jaggers folded his arms, and looked sternly at me.

Then I told him all I knew, and how I knew it; but I left him to infer that I knew from Miss Havisham what I in fact knew from Wemmick. Nor did I look towards Wemmick until I had finished, and had for some time met Mr Jaggers's look. When I did at last look in Wemmick's direction, I found that he was intent upon the table before him.

"Hah!" said Mr Jaggers at last, moving towards papers on the table, " – What item were we on, Wemmick, when Mr Pip came in?"

But I would not be thrown off in that way, and I made a passionate appeal to him to be more frank with me. I reminded him of the false hopes into which I had at length lapsed, and the discovery I had made. Surely I was worthy of some little confidence from him, in return for what I had just now imparted. I said that all I wanted was the truth from him. And if he asked me why I wanted it, I would tell him, little as he cared for such poor dreams, that I had loved Estella dearly and long, and that, although I had lost her, whatever concerned her was still nearer and dearer to me than anything else in the world.

Seeing that Mr Jaggers stood quite still and silent under this appeal, I turned to Wemmick, and said, "Wemmick, I know you to be a man of gentle heart. I have seen your pleasant home, and your old father, and the cheerful playful ways with which you refresh your business life. I entreat you to say a word for me to Mr Jaggers, that he ought to be more open with me!"

I have never seen two men look more oddly at one another than Mr Jaggers and Wemmick. At first, a misgiving crossed me that Wemmick would be instantly dismissed; but, it melted as I saw Mr Jaggers begin to smile, and Wemmick become bolder.

"What's all this?" said Mr Jaggers. "You with an old father, and you with playful ways?"

"Well!" returned Wemmick. "If I don't bring 'em here, what does it matter?"

"Pip," said Mr Jaggers, smiling openly, "this man must be the most cunning impostor in all London."

"Not a bit of it," returned Wemmick, growing bolder. "I think you're another."

Again they exchanged puzzled looks, each apparently still distrustful that the other was taking him in.

"You with a pleasant home?" said Mr Jaggers.

"It don't interfere with business," returned Wemmick, "Now, sir, I shouldn't wonder if you might be planning to have a pleasant home of your own, one of these days, when you're tired of all this work."

Mr Jaggers nodded two or three times, and actually sighed. "Pip, we won't talk about 'poor dreams'; you have much fresher experience. But about this other matter, I'll put a case to you. Mind! I admit nothing. Put the case that a woman, under such circumstances as you have mentioned, held her child concealed, and was obliged to communicate the fact to her legal adviser, how the fact stood about that child. At the same time he held a trust to find a child for an eccentric rich lady to adopt and bring up."

"I follow you, sir."

"Put the case that all he saw of children, was their being generated in great numbers for certain destruction. And that he often saw children tried at a criminal bar, where they were held up to be seen; and that he knew of their being imprisoned, whipped, transported, and growing up to be hanged."

"I follow you, sir."

"Put the case, Pip, that here was one pretty little child out of the heap,

204

who could be saved; whom the father believed dead, and as to whom, over the mother, the legal adviser had this power: 'I know what you did, and how you did it. Part with the child. Give her to me, and I will do my best to bring you off. If you are saved, your child is saved too; if you are lost, your child is still saved.' This was done, and the woman was cleared."

"I understand you perfectly."

"Put the case, Pip, that the terror of death had shaked the woman's mind, and when she was freed, she was scared and went to her legal adviser to be sheltered. He took her in, and kept down the old wild violent nature, by asserting his power over her in the old way. Do you comprehend the imaginary case?"

"Quite."

"Put the case that the child grew up, and was married for money. That the mother and father were still living. That unknown to one another, were dwelling within so many miles, yards if you like, of one another. That the secret was still a secret – except that you had wind of it. Put that last case to yourself very carefully."

"I do."

"I ask Wemmick to put it to himself very carefully."

And Wemmick said, "I do."

"For whose sake would you reveal the secret? For the father's? For the mother's? For the daughter's? It would hardly serve her, to establish her parentage for her husband's information, and to drag her back to disgrace, after an escape of twenty years. Add the case that you had loved her, Pip, and had made her the subject of those 'poor dreams' which have been in the heads of more men than you think likely, then I tell you that you had better chop off that bandaged left hand of yours and then pass the chopper on to Wemmick there, to cut the other off, too."

I looked at Wemmick. He gravely touched his lips with his forefinger. I did the same. Mr Jaggers did the same. "Now, Wemmick," said the latter, resuming his usual manner, "what item were we at, when Mr Pip came in?"

I observed that the odd looks they had cast at one another were repeated several times: but now each seemed suspicious of having shown himself in a weak and unprofessional light to the other. They were now inflexible with one another; Mr Jaggers highly dictatorial, and Wemmick obstinately justifying himself over the smallest point. I had never seen them on such ill terms; for generally they got on very well together.

But, they were both happily relieved by the appearance of a client, Mike, who called to announce that his eldest daughter was taken up on suspicion of shoplifting. As he imparted this melancholy circumstance to Wemmick, Mike's eye happened to twinkle with a tear.

"What do you come snivelling here for?" demanded Wemmick.

"I didn't mean to, Mr Wemmick."

"You did," said Wemmick. "How dare you? You're not in a fit state to come here."

"A man can't help his feelings, Mr Wemmick," pleaded Mike.

"His what?" demanded Wemmick, quite savagely.

"Now, look here my man," said Mr Jaggers, pointing to the door. "Get out of this office. I'll have no feelings here. Get out."

So the unfortunate Mike very humbly withdrew, and Mr Jaggers and Wemmick appeared to have re-established their good understanding, and went to work again.

CHAPTER 49

I went to Miss Skiffins's brother, the accountant; and Miss Skiffins's brother went to Clarriker's and brought him to me. I then had the great satisfaction of concluding that arrangement. It was the only good and completed thing I had done, since first told of my great expectations.

Clarriker informed me that the affairs of the House were steadily progressing, that he could now establish a small branch-house in the East, and that Herbert in his new partnership capacity would take charge of it. I found that I must prepare for a separation from my friend.

But, it was worth the joy with which Herbert came home and told me of these changes, little imagining that he told me no news, sketching airy pictures of himself conducting Clara Barley to the land of the Arabian Nights, and of me going out to join them, and of our all going up the Nile.

It was now March. My left arm took so long to heal that I was still unable to get a coat on. My right arm was tolerably restored.

On a Monday morning, when Herbert and I were at breakfast, I received the following letter from Wemmick:

"Walworth. Burn this as soon as read. Early in the week, say Wednesday, you might do what you know of, if you felt disposed to try it."

When I had shown this to Herbert and had put it in the fire we considered what to do. For my disability could not be ignored.

"I have thought it over, again and again," said Herbert, "and I think we should take Startop. A good fellow, a skilled hand, fond of us, and enthusiastic and honourable."

I had thought of him, more than once.

"But how much would you tell him, Herbert?"

"Very little. Let him suppose it a secret jaunt, until the morning comes: then let him know it is urgent reason to get Provis aboard and away. You go with him?"

"No doubt."

"Where?"

It mattered little to me what port we made for – Hamburg, Rotterdam, Antwerp – as long as he was out of England. Any foreign steamer that would take us would do. As foreign steamers leave London at about the time of high-water, our plan would be to get down the river by a previous ebb-tide, and lie by in some quiet spot until we could pull off to one. The time when one would be due wherever we lay, could be calculated pretty nearly, if we made inquiries beforehand.

Herbert assented to all this, and we went out immediately after breakfast to pursue our investigations. We found that a steamer for Hamburg was likely to suit our purpose best, but we noted down what other foreign steamers would leave London with the same tide, satisfying ourselves that we knew the build and colour of each. I then went to get such passports as were necessary; Herbert, to see Startop at his lodgings. When we met again at one o'clock I, for my part, was prepared with passports; Herbert had seen Startop, and he was more than ready to join.

Those two should pull a pair of oars, we settled, and I would steer; our charge would sit and keep quiet. We arranged that Herbert should go to Mill Pond Bank that evening; that he should not go there at all, tomorrow evening, Tuesday; that he should prepare Provis to come on Wednesday, when he saw us approach, and not sooner; that all the arrangements with him should be concluded that Monday night; and that there should be no more communication until we took him on board.

CHAPTER 50

It was one of those March days when the sun shines hot and the wind blows cold. I took a bag, filling it with no more than a few necessaries. Where I might go, what I might do, or when I might return, were questions utterly unknown to me. My mind was wholly set on Provis's safety. I only wondered, as I stopped at the door and looked back, whether I should see those rooms again.

I had taken care that the boat should be ready. After a little indecision, we went on board and cast off; Herbert in the bow, I steering. It was then about high water – half-past eight.

The tide would be with us until three, so we intended to creep on after it had turned, and row against it until dark. We should then be well in those long reaches below Gravesend, where the river is broad and solitary, where lone public houses are scattered here and there, of which we could choose one for a resting-place. There, we meant to stay, all night. The steamers for Hamburg, and for Rotterdam, would start from London at about nine on Thursday morning. We should know when to expect them, according to where we were, and would hail the first – if by any accident we were not taken aboard, we should have another chance.

The crisp air, the sunlight, the movement on the river, and the moving river itself freshened me with new hope. I felt mortified to be of so little use; but there were few better oarsmen than my two friends, and they rowed at a steady stroke all day.

Early as it was, there were plenty of scullers going here and there that morning, and plenty of barges dropping down with the tide; the navigation of the river between bridges, in an open boat, was a much easier and commoner matter in those days than it is in these.

Old London Bridge was soon passed, and old Billingsgate market, and the White Tower and Traitor's Gate, and we were in among the tiers of shipping. Here, at her moorings was tomorrow's steamer for Rotterdam; and tomorrow's for Hamburg. And now I, sitting in the stern, could see Mill Pond Bank and Mill Pond stairs.

"Is he there?" said Herbert.

"Not yet."

"He was not to come till he saw us. Can you see his signal?"

"Not well from here; but I think I see it. – Now, I see him! Pull both. Easy, Herbert. Oars!"

We touched the stairs lightly for a single moment, and he was on board and we were off again. He looked as like a river-pilot as my heart could have wished. "Dear boy!" he said, putting his arm on my shoulder. "Faithful dear boy, well done. Thankye!"

Ever since the Stairs where we had taken him aboard, I looked warily for any token of our being suspected. I had seen none. We certainly had not been either attended or followed by any boat.

He had his boat-cloak and looked, as I have said, a natural part of the scene. It was remarkable, that he was the least anxious of any of us. He was not indifferent; he told me when danger came he confronted it, but it must come before he troubled himself.

"You see, dear boy, when I was on t'other side the world, I was always a-looking to this side; and it come flat to be there, for all I was a-growing rich. Everybody know'd Magwitch, and Magwitch could come and go, and nobody's head would be troubled about him. They ain't so easy concerning me here, dear boy – wouldn't be, leastwise, if they know'd where I was."

"If all goes well," said I, "you will be perfectly free and safe again."

"Well," he returned, drawing a long breath, "I hope so."

"And think so?"

He dipped his hand in the water, and said, smiling with that softened air upon him which was not new to me: "Ay, I s'pose I think so, dear boy. But we can no more see to the bottom of the next few hours, than we can see to the bottom of this river what I catches hold of!"

The air felt cold upon the river, but the sunshine was very cheering. The tide ran strong, I took care to lose none of it, and our steady stroke carried us on thoroughly well. By imperceptible degrees, the tide ran out, but was yet with us when we were off Gravesend. As our charge was wrapped in his cloak, I purposely passed within a boat or two's length of the floating Custom House. Soon the tide began to slacken, and the craft lying at anchor to swing, until they had all swung round, and the ships that were using the new tide to get up to the Pool, began to crowd upon us.

We got ashore among some slippery stones while we ate and drank what we had with us, and looked about. It was like my own marsh country, flat and monotonous, and with a dim horizon.

209

We pushed off again, and made what way we could. It was much harder work now, but Herbert and Startop persevered, and rowed until the sun went down. By that time the river had lifted us so that we could see above the bank. There was the red sun, on the low level of the shore, in a purple haze, fast deepening into black; and there was the solitary flat marsh.

As the night was fast falling, and as the moon would not rise early, we held a short council: we would lie by at the first lonely tavern we could find. So they plied their oars once more, and I looked out for anything like a house. Thus we held on, for four or five dull miles. It was very cold, and the night was as dark by this time as it would be until morning.

At length we descried a light and a roof, and presently afterwards ran alongside a little causeway. Leaving the rest in the boat, I stepped ashore, and found the light to be a public house. It was dirty, and I dare say not unknown to smuggling adventurers; but there was a good fire in the kitchen, and eggs and bacon to eat. Also, there were two double-bedded rooms – "such as they were," the landlord said. No other company was in the house than the landlord, his wife, and a grizzled male creature, the "Jack" of the little causeway.

With this assistant, I went down to the boat again, and we all came ashore, and hauled the boat up for the night. We made a very good meal, and then apportioned the bedrooms: Herbert and Startop were to occupy one; I and our charge the other. We considered ourselves well off, for a more solitary place we could not have found.

While we sat by the fire after our meal, the Jack – sitting in a corner, wearing a bloated pair of shoes, which he had exhibited as interesting relics that he had taken from the feet of a drowned seaman washed ashore – asked me if we had seen a four-oared galley going up with the tide?

"A four-oared galley?" said I.

"A four," said the Jack, "and two sitters."

"You thinks Custum 'Us, Jack?" said the landlord.

"I do," said the Jack.

"Then you're wrong, Jack."

"Am I?"

"What had they done with their buttons then, Jack?" asked the landlord.

"Chucked 'em overboard," returned the Jack. "Swallered 'em. A Custum 'Us officer knows what to do with his Buttons, when they comes betwixt him and his own light. A Four and two sitters don't go up with one tide and down with another, and both with and against another, without there being Custum 'Us at the bottom of it." Saying which he went out in disdain.

This dialogue made us all uneasy. The dismal wind muttered round the house, the tide flapped at the shore, and I had a feeling of being caged and threatened. A four-oared galley hovering about in so unusual a way as to attract this notice, was an ugly circumstance that I could not get rid of. When I had induced Provis to go up to bed, I went outside with my two companions (Startop by this time knew the state of the case), and held another council. We deemed it better to lie where we were, until within an hour or so of the steamer's time, and then to get out in her track, and drift with the tide. Having settled to do this, we went to bed.

I lay down with the greater part of my clothes on, and slept well for a few hours. When I awoke, the wind had risen, and the house sign was banging about, sufficient to startle me. Rising softly, I looked out of the window. As my eyes adapted to the moonlight, I saw two men looking into our boat. They then passed under the window, looking at nothing else, and struck across the marsh.

My first impulse was to wake Herbert, but, reflecting that he and Startop had had a hard day, I forbore. Returning to my window, I watched the two men moving over the marsh. In that light, however, I soon lost them, and feeling very cold, lay down to think, and fell asleep again.

We were up early. As we walked to and fro, I told them what I had seen. Again our charge was the least anxious of the party. It was very likely that the men belonged to the Custom House, he said quietly, and that they had no thought of us. I tried to persuade myself that it was so. However, I proposed that he and I should walk to a distant point, and that the boat should take us aboard there, at about noon. This being considered a good precaution, soon after breakfast he and I set forth, without saying anything at the tavern.

He smoked his pipe as we went along, sometimes stopping to clap me on the shoulder. One would have supposed that it was I who was in danger, not he. We spoke very little. I went ahead to reconnoitre the point, for it was where the men had passed in the night. There was no boat off the point, nor any sign of the men having embarked there. But the tide was high, and there might have been some footprints under water.

I waved my hat to him to come up, he rejoined me, and there we waited until we saw our boat coming round. We got aboard easily, and rowed out into the track of the steamer. It was ten to one, and we began to look out for her smoke.

It was half an hour before we saw her smoke, and soon after the smoke of a following steamer. As they were coming at full speed, we got the bags ready, and took that opportunity of saying good-bye to Herbert and Startop. Neither Herbert's eyes nor mine were quite dry. I suddenly saw a four-oared galley shoot out from under the bank a little way ahead of us, and row into the same track.

Now the steamer was visible, coming head on. I called to Herbert and Startop to keep before the tide, that she might see us, and I adjured Provis to sit quite still. He answered cheerily, "Trust to me, dear boy," and sat like a statue. Meantime the galley, which was very skilfully handled, had crossed us, and fallen alongside. She kept alongside, drifting when we drifted, and pulling a stroke or two when we pulled. One sitter held the rudder lines, and looked at us attentively – the other was wrapped up, much like Provis, and seemed to shrink, and whisper some instruction to the steerer. Not a word was spoken in either boat.

Startop could just make out the first steamer, and gave me the word "Hamburg," in a low voice. She was nearing us very fast, and the beat of her paddles grew louder. I felt as if her shadow were absolutely upon us, when the galley hailed us. I answered.

"You have a returned Transport there," said the man holding the lines. "That's him, wrapped in the cloak. His name is Abel Magwitch, otherwise Provis. I apprehend that man, and call upon him to surrender, and you to assist."

At the same moment, without an audible direction to his crew, he ran the galley abroad of us. They pulled one sudden stroke ahead, and were holding our gunwale before we knew what they were doing. This caused great confusion on the steamer, and I heard them calling to us, and the order was given to stop the paddles but I felt her driving down upon us irresistibly. In the same moment, I saw the galley steersman put his hand on Provis's shoulder, and both boats swung round with the force of the tide. All hands on board the steamer were running frantically forward. The prisoner started up, leaned across his captor, and pulled the cloak from the neck of the shrinking sitter in the galley. It was the face of the other convict of long ago. Still in the same moment, I saw the terrified face tilt backward, and heard a great cry on board the steamer and a loud splash in the water, and felt the boat sink from under me.

It was for an instant that I seemed to struggle with a thousand mill-weirs and a thousand flashes of light; then I was taken on board the galley. Herbert and Startop were there; but our boat and the two convicts were gone.

I could not at first distinguish sky from water or shore from shore; but the crew righted her quickly, and, pulling strong strokes ahead, lay upon their oars, every man looking silently at the water. Presently a dark object was seen. No one spoke, but the steersman held up his hand, and all softly backed water. As it came nearer, I saw it to be Magwitch, swimming, but not freely. He was taken on board, and instantly manacled.

The silent lookout was resumed. It was kept, long after all was still and the two steamers had gone; but everybody knew that it was hopeless.

At length we gave up, and pulled towards the tavern we had lately left, where we were received with no little surprise. Here I was able to get some comforts for Magwitch – Provis no longer – who had received a very severe injury in the chest.

He told me that he believed he had gone under the keel of the steamer. The injury to his chest, making his breathing extremely painful, he had received against the side of the galley. He added that in the moment of his laying his hand on his cloak to identify Compeyson, that villain had staggered up and back, and they had both gone overboard together. The sudden wrenching of Magwitch out of our boat had capsized us. He told me in a whisper that they had gone down, locked in each other's arms, and they had struggled underwater. He had finally disengaged himself, struck out, and swum away.

I never had any reason to doubt the truth of what he told me. The officer steering the galley gave the same account of their going overboard.

I asked to change the prisoner's wet clothes by purchasing any spare garments I could get at the public house. The officer gave permission, merely observing that he must take charge of everything his prisoner had about him. So the pocket-book that had once been in my hands, now passed to the officer. He further gave me leave to accompany the prisoner to London but declined to accord that grace to my two friends.

The Jack undertook to search for the body in the places where it was likeliest to come ashore.

We remained until the tide turned, and then Magwitch was put on board the galley. Herbert and Startop were to get to London by land, as soon as they could. We had a doleful parting, and I took my place by Magwitch's side, knowing it was my place henceforth.

For now, my repugnance had melted away, and in the hunted wounded creature who held my hand, I only saw a man who had meant to be my benefactor, and who had felt affectionately, gratefully, and generously, towards me with great constancy through the years. I saw in him a much better man than I had been to Joe.

His breathing became more painful as night drew on, and often he could not suppress a groan. I tried to rest him on the arm I could use, but it was dreadful to think that I could not be sorry at heart for his being badly hurt, since it was unquestionably best that he should die. There were, still living, people who could and would identify him. That he would be leniently treated, I could not hope. Since his trial, he had broken prison and been retried. He had returned from transportation under a life sentence, and had occasioned the death of the man who was the cause of his arrest.

As we returned towards the setting sun, I told him how grieved I was to think that he had come home for my sake.

"Dear boy," he answered, "I'm quite content to take my chance. I've seen my boy, and he can be a gentleman without me."

No. I understood Wemmick's hint now. Being convicted, his possessions would be forfeited to the Crown.

"Lookee here, dear boy," said he. "It's best as a gentleman should not be know'd to belong to me now. Only come to see me as if you come by chance alonger Wemmick. Sit where I can see you and I don't ask no more."

"I will never stir from your side," said I, "if I am allowed near you. Please God, I will be as true to you, as you have been to me!"

I felt his hand tremble as it held mine, and he turned his face away as he lay in the bottom of the boat, and I heard that old sound in his throat – softened now, like all the rest of him. It was a good thing that he had touched this point, for it reminded me that he need never know how his hopes of enriching me had perished.

CHAPTER 51

He was taken to the Police Court next day, and would have been immediately committed for trial, but an old officer from the prison-ship had to come to speak to his identity. Nobody doubted it; but Compeyson, who had meant to be witness to it, was tumbling on the tides, dead. I had gone direct to Mr Jaggers at his private house, to retain his assistance, and Mr Jaggers on the prisoner's behalf would admit nothing. But he told me that the case must be over in five minutes when the witness was there, and that no power on earth could prevent its going against us.

I imparted to Mr Jaggers my design of keeping him in ignorance of the fate of his wealth. Mr Jaggers was angry with me for having "let it slip through my fingers", and said we must try at all events for some of it. But I had no claim, and I finally resolved, and ever afterwards abided by the resolution, that my heart should never be sickened with the hopeless task of attempting to establish one.

There appeared to be reason for supposing that the drowned informer had hoped for a reward and had obtained some accurate knowledge of Magwitch's affairs. When his body was found, he was only recognizable by the contents of his pockets, notes folded in a case he carried. Among these were the name of a banking-house in New South Wales where a sum of money was, and the designation of certain lands of considerable value. Both these were in a list that Magwitch, while in prison, gave to Mr Jaggers, of the possessions he supposed I should inherit. He was convinced that my inheritance was quite safe, with Mr Jaggers's aid.

After three days' delay, the witness came, and he was committed to trial at the next Sessions, in a month.

It was at this dark time of my life that Herbert returned home one evening, and said: "My dear Handel, I fear I shall soon have to leave you."

His partner had prepared me.

"We shall lose a fine opportunity if I put off going to Cairo, and I am afraid I must go, Handel, when you most need me."

"Herbert, I shall always need you, because I shall always love you; but my need is no greater now."

"You will be so lonely."

"You know that I am always with him to the full extent of the time

215

allowed," said I. "And that I should be with him all day long, if I could. And when I come away, my thoughts are with him."

"My dear fellow," said Herbert, "let the near prospect of our separation be my justification for troubling you about yourself. Have you thought of your future?"

"No, for I have been afraid to think of any future."

"But it cannot be dismissed. I wish you to talk of it now, with me."

"I will," said I.

"In this branch house of ours, Handel, we must have a – "

I saw that his delicacy was avoiding the right word, so I said, "A clerk."

"A clerk. And I hope it is not at all unlikely that he may expand (as a clerk of your acquaintance has expanded) into a partner. Now, Handel – in short, my dear boy, will you come to me? Clara and I have talked about it again and again," Herbert pursued, "and she begged me only this evening, with tears in her eyes, to say to you that if you will live with us when we are married, she will do her best to make you happy. We should get on so well, Handel!"

I thanked them both heartily, but said I could not yet decide.

"But if you thought, Herbert, that you could leave the question open for a little while – "

"For any while," cried Herbert. "Six months, a year!"

"Not so long as that," said I. "Two or three months at most."

Herbert was highly delighted when we shook hands on this, and said he could now tell me that he believed he must leave at the end of the week.

On the Saturday, I took my leave of Herbert – full of bright hope, but sad and sorry to leave me – as he sat on the seaport mail coach. I wrote a little note to Clara, telling her he had left, sending his love to her over and over again, and then went to my lonely home.

On the stairs I met Wemmick. I had not seen him alone since the disastrous issue of the attempted flight.

"The late Compeyson," said Wemmick, "had slowly got at the bottom of half of the regular business now transacted, and it was from the talk of some of his people in trouble that I heard what I did. I kept my ears open, seeming to have them shut, until I heard that he was absent, and I thought that would be the best time for making the attempt. I can only suppose now, that it was a part of his clever policy, to deceive his own instruments.

You don't blame me, I hope, Mr Pip? I am sure I tried to serve you, with all my heart."

"I am as sure of that, Wemmick, as you can be, and I thank you most earnestly for all your interest and friendship."

I invited Wemmick to come upstairs for a glass of grog before walking to Walworth. He accepted. While drinking his moderate allowance, he said, with nothing to lead up to it: "What do you think of my meaning to take a holiday on Monday, Mr Pip? More than that; I'm going to take a walk and I'm going to ask you to take a walk with me."

I was about to excuse myself, when Wemmick anticipated me.

"I know you are out of sorts, Mr Pip," said he. "But if you could oblige me, I should take it as a kindness. It ain't a long walk, and it's an early one. Say it might occupy you (including breakfast on the walk) from eight to twelve. Couldn't you stretch a point and manage it?"

He had done so much for me at various times, that this was very little to do for him.

Punctually, I rang at the Castle gate on the Monday morning, and was received by Wemmick himself wearing a sleeker hat than usual. The Aged must have stirred with the lark, for I observed that his bedroom was empty.

We fortified ourselves with rum-and-milk and biscuits.

We went towards Camberwell Green, and Wemmick said suddenly: "Halloa! Here's a church!"

I was rather surprised, when he said, "Let's go in!"

We went up to it and stood in the porch a moment, while Wemmick dived into his coat-pockets, getting something out of paper there.

"Halloa!" said he. "Here's a couple of pairs of gloves! Let's put 'em on!"

As the gloves were white kid gloves, and as Wemmick was wearing the broadest smile, I now began to have my strong suspicions. They were strengthened into certainty when I beheld the Aged enter at a side door, escorting a lady.

"Halloa!" said Wemmick. "Here's Miss Skiffins! Let's have a wedding."

That discreet damsel was attired as usual, except that she now substituted her green kid gloves for a pair of white. The Aged was likewise occupied.

217

The clerk and clergyman then appeared. True to his notion of seeming to do it all without preparation, I heard Wemmick say to himself as he took something from his waistcoat-pocket, "Halloa! Here's a ring!"

I acted in the capacity of best man to the bridegroom; while a little limp pew opener pretended to be the bosom friend of Miss Skiffins. And the responsibility of giving the lady away devolved upon the Aged.

"Now, Mr Pip," said Wemmick, triumphantly smiling as we came out, "let me ask you whether anybody would suppose this to be a wedding-party!"

Breakfast had been ordered at a pleasant little tavern, a mile or so away upon the rising ground beyond the Green, and there was a bagatelle board in the room, in case we should desire to unbend our minds after the solemnity.

We had an excellent breakfast. I drank to the new couple, drank to the Aged, drank to the Castle, saluted the bride at parting, and made myself as agreeable as I could.

Wemmick came down to the door with me, and I again wished him joy.

"Thankee!" said Wemmick, rubbing his hands. "I say, Mr Pip!" calling me back, and speaking low. "This is altogether a Walworth sentiment, please."

"I understand. Not to be mentioned in Little Britain," said I.

Wemmick nodded. "After what you let out the other day, Mr Jaggers may as well not know of it. He might think my brain was softening, or something of the kind."

CHAPTER 52

He lay in prison very ill, during the interval between the committal for trial and the Sessions. He had two broken ribs, and his lungs were wounded. Breathing for him was painful. Speaking was therefore difficult, so he spoke less as time went on.

He was taken to the prison infirmary and I stayed near him as much as possible. I was allowed to be with him for a brief period every day, but each occasion was proof that his condition worsened. He wasted and became slowly weaker and weaker.

He was resigned, like a man tired out. From the odd whispered words I managed to hear I realised that he pondered over whether he might have been a better man under different circumstances, but he never justified himself or tried to bend the past. I never knew him complain.

The trial was very short and clear. He had returned, unlawfully, and it was impossible to find him anything other than guilty.

The Sentence of Death was given on a glorious April day. April rain glittered on the windows in the April sun.

Thirty-two people were to be sentenced at the same time. He sat foremost, seated to ensure he would live to hear the sentence.

The judge addressed all the prisoners, and singled out one who almost from his infancy had been an offender against the laws; who after repeated imprisonments, had been sentenced to exile for a term of years; and who had escaped and been re-sentenced for life. That miserable man seemed to have become convinced of his errors for a time and had lived a peaceable and profitable life. But in a fatal moment, he had returned to the land of his birth, leaving his haven of rest. He had evaded detection for a while and had then caused the death of his denouncer. The appointed punishment was Death.

"My Lord, I have received my sentence of Death from the Almighty, but I bow to yours," the prisoner managed to stand and softly say.

The prisoners were taken away, he last of all. He held my hand to the last.

I prayed that he might die before the sentence could be carried out.

The daily visits I could make were shortened now. Thinking that I was suspected of carrying poison to him I asked to be searched before I sat down with him. Nobody was hard with him or me.

As the days went on, I noticed that he would lie placidly looking at the ceiling. I continued to talk to him, and the occasional pressure of his hand on mine assured me that he could still hear and understand me.

Ten days after the sentence I saw a greater change in him. His eyes lit up as he saw me come up to his bed.

"You've never deserted me, dear boy. God bless you!"

I pressed his hand.

He lay on his back, breathing with great difficulty. Do what he could, and love me though he did, the light left his face, and a film came over the placid look at the ceiling.

"Are you in much pain today?"

"I don't complain of none, dear boy."

"You never do complain."

He had spoken his last words. He smiled and I understood his touch. He wished to lift my hand and lay it on his breast. I laid it there, and he smiled again, and put both his hands upon it.

My allotted time had run out, but looking round, I found the prison governor standing near me. "You needn't go yet," he whispered.

"Might I speak to him, if he can hear me?" I asked.

The governor stepped aside, drawing the guard with him.

Magwitch looked at me.

"I must tell you something, dear Magwitch," I said. "Do you understand me?"

A gentle pressure on my hand.

"You had a child once, whom you loved and lost."

A stronger pressure on my hand.

"She lived and found powerful friends. She lives now. She is a very beautiful lady and I love her."

With a last effort, assisted by myself, he raised my hand to his lips. He then let it sink to his breast again. The placid look came back, and passed away. His head dropped quietly to one side.

CHAPTER 53

Now that I was left wholly to myself, I gave notice to quit the chambers in the Temple. I was in debt, and had scarcely any money, and should have been alarmed if I had had strength to see beyond the fact that I was falling very ill. The late stress upon me had enabled me to put off illness, but not to put it away; now it was coming on me and I knew very little else.

For a day or two I lay on the sofa, or on the floor – anywhere I sank down – with a heavy head and aching limbs, with no purpose, nor power. Then there came one long night that teemed with anxiety and horror; and in the morning I tried to sit up in my bed, but found I could not do so.

As I lay on my bed, I saw two men looking at me.

"What do you want?" I asked, starting; "I don't know you."

"Well, sir," returned one, touching me on the shoulder, "this is a matter that you'll soon arrange, I dare say, but you're arrested. Jeweller's account, I think. Hundred and twenty-three pound, fifteen, six."

"What is to be done?"

"You had better come to my house," said the man.

I tried to get up and dress. When I next looked to them, they were standing a little off from the bed, looking at me. I still lay there.

"You see my state," said I. "I would come if I could; but I am quite unable. If you take me from here, I think I shall die."

Perhaps they replied, or argued the point, but as they hang in my memory by only this one slender thread, I don't know what they did, except that they didn't remove me.

That I had a fever and was avoided, that I suffered greatly, that I often lost my reason, that the time seemed interminable, that I passed through these phases of disease, I know of my own remembrance. That I sometimes struggled with real people, believing they were murderers, and that I would all at once comprehend that they meant to do me good, and would then sink exhausted in their arms, I also knew at the time. But, above all, there was a constant tendency in all these people, sooner or later, to settle down into the likeness of Joe.

After I had turned the worst point of my illness, I began to notice that this one consistent feature did not change. I opened my eyes in the night, and I saw in the great chair, Joe. I opened my eyes in the day, and, sitting on the window-seat, smoking his pipe, still I saw Joe. I asked for cooling drink, and the hand that gave it me was Joe's. I sank back on my pillow after drinking, and the face that looked upon me was the face of Joe.

At last, one day, I took courage, and said, "Is it Joe?"

And the dear old home-voice answered, "Which it air, old chap."

"O Joe, you break my heart! Look angry at me, Joe. Strike me, Joe. Tell me of my ingratitude. Don't be so good to me!"

Joe had laid his head down on the pillow at my side and put his arm round my neck, in his joy that I knew him.

"Which dear old Pip, old chap," said Joe, "you and me was ever friends. And when you're well enough to go out for a ride – what larks!"

After which, Joe withdrew to the window, and wiped his eyes. And as

221

my extreme weakness prevented me from going to him, I lay there, whispering, "O God bless him! O God bless this gentle Christian man!"

Joe's eyes were red when I next found him beside me; but I was holding his hand, and we were both happy.

"How long, dear Joe, have I been ill?"

"It's the end of May, Pip. Tomorrow is the first of June."

"And have you been here all the time, dear Joe?"

"Pretty nigh, old chap. For, as I says to Biddy when the news of your being ill were brought by letter, that how you might be amongst strangers, and that how a wisit at such a moment might not prove unacceptabobble. And Biddy, her words were, 'Go to him, without loss of time.'"

Joe stopped and told me that I was to have quiet, and to take a little nourishment at frequent times, whether I felt inclined or not, and that I was to submit myself to all his orders. So I kissed his hand, and lay quiet, while he proceeded to write a note to Biddy, with my love in it.

I asked Joe about Miss Havisham the next day.

"Is she dead, Joe?"

"Why you see, old chap," said Joe, "I wouldn't go so far as to say that, for that's a deal to say; but she ain't – "

"Living, Joe? Did she linger long?"

"Arter you was took ill, pretty much about a week," said Joe.

"Dear Joe, have you heard what becomes of her property?"

"Well, old chap," said Joe, "it do appear that she settled the most of it on Miss Estella. But she had wrote out a little coddleshell in her own hand a day or two afore the accident, leaving a cool four thousand to Mr Matthew Pocket. And why? 'Because of Pip's account of him the said Matthew'. I am told by Biddy, that air the writing."

This account gave me great joy, as completing the only good thing I had done.

By these approaches we arrived at unrestricted conversation. I was slow to gain strength, but I did slowly and surely become less weak, and Joe stayed with me, and I fancied I was little Pip again.

He would sit and talk to me with the old simplicity, and in the old protecting way, so that I would half believe that all my life since the days of the old kitchen was one of the mental troubles of the fever that was gone. He did everything for me except the household work, for which he had engaged a very decent woman.

We looked forward to the day when I should go out for a ride. And when the day came, Joe wrapped me up, took me in his arms, carried me down to the open carriage, and put me in.

Joe got in beside me, and we drove away together into the country, where the rich summer growth was already on the trees and on the grass, and sweet summer scents filled all the air. It happened to be Sunday, and when I looked on the loveliness around me, and thought how it had grown and changed, while I lay burning and tossing on my bed, the mere remembrance of having burned and tossed there, came like a check upon my peace. But then I heard the Sunday bells, and looked around a little more thankfully upon the outspread beauty.

We talked as we used to talk, lying on the grass at the old Battery. There was no change whatever in Joe. Exactly what he had been in my eyes then, he was in my eyes still; just as simply faithful, and as simply right.

At one point he spoke of Orlick, the man who had been his journeyman. He had gone down far in the world, and had been found robbing Pumblechook's house. When he was taken he was in a bad way and he inadvertently cleared up the mystery of the attack on my sister. It had been he who had hurt her, nearly killing her, meaning to kill her, all those years ago.

When we got back again he lifted me out, and carried me across the court and up the stairs. We had not yet talked of my change of fortune, nor did I know how much of my late history he was acquainted with.

"Have you heard, Joe," I asked him that evening, "who my patron was?"

"I heerd," returned Joe, "as it were not Miss Havisham, old chap."

"Did you hear who it was, Joe?"

"Well! I heerd as it were a person what sent the person what giv' you the bank-notes at the Jolly Bargemen, Pip."

"So it was."

"Astonishing!" said Joe.

"Did you hear that he was dead, Joe?" I presently asked, with increasing diffidence.

"I think," said Joe, after a long pause, "as I did hear tell how he were something or another in a general way in that direction."

"Did you hear anything of his circumstances, Joe?"

"Not partickler, Pip."

"If you would like to hear, Joe – " I was beginning, when Joe got up and came to my sofa.

"Lookee here, old chap," said Joe, bending over me. "Ever the best of friends; ain't us, Pip?"

I was ashamed to answer him.

"Wery good, then," said Joe, as if I had answered; "that's all right. Why go into subjects, old chap, which as betwixt two sech must be forever onnecessary? Think no more of it, and do not let us pass remarks upon onnecessary subjects. Biddy giv' herself a deal o' trouble with me afore I left (for I am almost awful dull), as I should view it in this light. Namely. You mustn't go a-over-doing on it, but you must have your supper and your wine-and-water, and you must be put betwixt the sheets."

The sweet tact and kindness with which Biddy – who with her woman's wit had found me out so soon – had prepared him for it, made a deep impression on my mind. But whether Joe knew how poor I was, and how my great expectations had all dissolved, like our own marsh mists before the sun, I could not understand. Another thing in Joe that I could not understand when it first began, but which I soon arrived at a sorrowful comprehension of, was this: As I became stronger and better, Joe became a little less easy with me. In my entire dependence on him, the dear fellow had fallen into the old tone, and called me by the old names, the dear "old Pip, old chap," that now were music in my ears. I too had fallen into the old ways, only happy and thankful that he let me.

It was on the third or fourth occasion of my going out walking in the Temple Gardens leaning on Joe's arm, that I saw this change in him. We sat in the bright warm sunlight, looking at the river, and I chanced to say as we got up: "See, Joe! I can walk quite strongly. Now, you shall see me walk back by myself."

"Which do not over-do it, Pip," said Joe; "but I shall be happy fur to see you able, sir."

The last word grated on me; but how could I remonstrate! I walked no further than the gate of the gardens, and then pretended weakness, and asked Joe for his arm.

How best to check this growing change in Joe? This perplexed me. I was ashamed to tell him exactly how I was placed, and what I had come down to; but I hope my reluctance was not quite unworthy. He would want to help me from his little savings, I knew, and I knew that he ought not to help me, and that I must not let him do it.

It was a thoughtful evening with both of us. But, before we went to bed, I resolved I would wait over tomorrow, Sunday, and begin my new course with the new week. On Monday morning I would speak to Joe about this change, I would tell him what I had in my thoughts; and why I had not decided to go out to Herbert, and then the change would be conquered forever. As I cleared, Joe cleared, and it seemed as though he had arrived at a resolution too.

We had a quiet day on the Sunday, and we rode out into the country, and walked in the fields.

"I feel thankful that I have been ill, Joe," I said. "It has been a memorable time."

"Dear old Pip, old chap, you're a'most come round, sir."

"We have had a time together, Joe, that I can never forget. There were days once, I know, that I did for a while forget; but I never shall forget these."

"Pip," said Joe, appearing a little troubled, "there has been larks. And, dear sir, what have been betwixt us – have been."

At night, when I had gone to bed, Joe came into my room. He asked me if I felt sure that I was as well as in the morning? "And are always a-getting stronger, old chap?"

"Yes, dear Joe, steadily."

Joe patted the coverlet, and said, in what I thought a husky voice, "Good-night!"

When I got up in the morning, stronger yet, I was full of my resolution to tell Joe all, without delay. I would dress and go to his room and surprise him; for it was the first day I had been up early. I went to his room, and he was not there, and his box was gone.

I hurried to the breakfast-table, and found a letter. "Not wishful to intrude I have departured fur you are well again dear Pip and will do better without Jo. P.S. Ever the best of friends."

Enclosed was a receipt for the debt and costs on which I had been arrested. Until then, I had vainly supposed that my creditor had withdrawn, suspending proceedings until I should be recovered. I had never dreamed that Joe would pay the money; but, he had paid, and the receipt was in his name.

What could I do but follow him, there to have out my disclosure to him, and my penitent remonstrance with him, and there to relieve my mind and heart of my innermost feelings, which had begun as a vague something and had formed into a settled purpose?

The purpose was, that I would go to Biddy, that I would show her how humbled and repentant I returned, how I had lost all I once hoped for, and would remind her of our old confidences in my first unhappy time. Then, I would say to her, "Biddy, I think you once liked me very well, when my errant heart, even while it strayed away from you, was quieter and better with you than it ever has been since. If you can like me only half as well once more, if you can take me with all my faults and disappointments on my head, I hope I am a little worthier of you than I was. And, Biddy, it shall rest with you to say whether I shall work at the forge with Joe, or whether we shall go to a distant place where an opportunity awaits me, which I set aside when offered, until I knew your answer. And now, dear Biddy, if you can tell me that you will go through the world with me, you will surely make it a better world for me, and me a better man for it, and I will try hard to make it a better world for you."

Such was my purpose. After three days more of recovery, I went down to the old place to put it in execution.

CHAPTER 54

The tidings of my high fortunes having had a heavy fall had reached my native place before I got there. I found the Blue Boar in possession of the intelligence, and it was exceedingly cool now that I was out of property.

It was evening when I arrived, much fatigued by the journey I had so often made so easily. The Boar could not put me into my usual bedroom, and could only give me a very indifferent chamber among the pigeons up the yard. But I had as sound a sleep there as in the most superior accommodation the Boar offered.

Early in the morning I strolled round by Satis House. There were printed bills on the gate announcing a sale by auction of the Household Furniture and Effects, next week. The House itself was to be sold as old building materials and pulled down. Stepping in for a moment at the open gate and looking around me with the uncomfortable air of a stranger who had no business there, I saw the auctioneer's clerk walking on the casks and telling them off for the information of a catalogue compiler. I then turned to go to Joe and Biddy.

The June weather was delicious. The sky was blue, the larks were soaring high, I thought all that countryside beautiful and peaceful.

The schoolhouse where Biddy was mistress I had never seen; but the little lane took me past it. I was disappointed to find that no children were there, and Biddy's house was closed. Some hopeful notion of seeing her busily engaged in her daily duties, before she saw me, had been in my mind and was defeated.

But the forge was now a short distance off, and I went towards it, listening for the clink of Joe's hammer. Long after I ought to have heard it, all was still. The chestnut-trees were there, and their leaves rustled harmoniously; but the clink of Joe's hammer was not in the midsummer wind.

Almost fearing to come in view of the forge, I saw it at last – it was closed. No gleam of fire, no glittering shower of sparks, no roar of bellows.

But the house was not deserted – white curtains fluttered in the window of the best parlour and it was open and gay with flowers. I went softly towards it, when Joe and Biddy stood before me, arm in arm.

At first Biddy gave a cry, but in another moment she was in my arms. I wept to see her, and she wept to see me; I, because she looked so fresh and pleasant; she, because I looked so worn and white.

"But dear Biddy, how smart you are! And Joe, how smart you are!"

"Yes, dear old Pip, old chap."

I looked at both of them, from one to the other, and then –

"It's my wedding day," cried Biddy, in a burst of happiness, "and I am married to Joe!"

Biddy held one of my hands to her lips, and Joe's restoring touch was on my shoulder. "Which he warn't strong enough, my dear, fur to be surprised," said Joe.

And Biddy said, "I ought to have thought of it, dear Joe, but I was too happy."

They were both so overjoyed to see me, so proud to see me, so touched by my coming to them, so delighted that I should have made their day complete!

My first thought was one of thankfulness that I had never breathed my baffled hope to Joe. How often, while he was with me, had it risen to my lips.

"Dear Biddy," said I. "You have the best husband in the whole world, and if you could have seen him by my bed – but no, you couldn't love him better than you do."

"No, I couldn't indeed," said Biddy.

"And, dear Joe, you have the best wife in the whole world, and she will make you as happy as even you deserve to be, you dear, good, noble Joe!"

Joe looked at me with a quivering lip.

"And Joe and Biddy both, as you have been to church today, receive my humble thanks for all you have done for me and all I have so ill repaid! I am soon going abroad, and I shall never rest until I have repaid the money with which you have kept me out of prison. Don't think, dear Joe and Biddy, that if I could repay it a thousand times over, I could cancel a farthing of the debt I owe you both!"

They both entreated me to say no more.

I sold all I had, and put aside as much as I could, for a composition with my creditors – who gave me ample time to pay them in full – and I went out and joined Herbert. Within a month I had quitted England; and within two months I was clerk to Clarriker and Co.; and within four months I assumed my first undivided responsibility. Herbert returned to marry Clara, and I was left in sole charge of the Eastern Branch until he brought her back.

Many a year went round before I was a partner in the House; but I lived happily with Herbert and his wife, and lived frugally, and paid my debts, and maintained a constant correspondence with Biddy and Joe. It was not until I became third in the Firm, that Clarriker betrayed me to Herbert; declaring that the secret of Herbert's partnership had been long enough upon his conscience, and he must tell it. Herbert was as much moved as amazed, and the dear fellow and I were not the worse friends for the long concealment. We were not in a grand way of business, but we had a good name, and worked for our profits, and did very well. We owed so much to Herbert's ever cheerful industry and readiness, that I often wondered how I had conceived that old idea of his inaptitude, until I was one day enlightened by the reflection, that perhaps the inaptitude had never been in him at all, but had been in me.

CHAPTER 55

For eleven years, I had not seen Joe nor Biddy, when, one evening in December, a little after dark, I laid my hand softly on the latch of the old kitchen door. I looked in unseen. There, smoking his pipe in the old place, as hale and as strong as ever though a little grey, sat Joe; and there, sitting on my own little stool, was – I again!

"We giv' him the name of Pip for your sake, dear old chap," said Joe, delighted when I took another stool by the child's side.

I took him out for a walk next morning, and we talked immensely, understanding one another to perfection. And I took him down to the churchyard, and set him on a certain tombstone there, and he showed me which stone was sacred to the memory of Philip Pirrip, late of this Parish, and Also Georgiana, Wife of the Above.

"Biddy," said I, when I talked with her after dinner, as her little girl lay sleeping in her lap, "you must give Pip to me, one of these days; or lend him, at all events."

"Dear Pip," said Biddy, gently. "You must marry."

"So Herbert and Clara say, but I don't think I shall, Biddy. I am already quite an old bachelor."

"You are sure you don't fret for her?" said Biddy.

"Oh no – I think not, Biddy."

"Tell me as an old, old friend. Have you quite forgotten her?"

"My dear Biddy, I have forgotten nothing in my life. But that poor dream has all gone by, Biddy, all gone by!"

Nevertheless, I knew even while I spoke, that I secretly intended to revisit the site of the old house that evening, alone, for Estella's sake.

I had heard she lead a most unhappy life, and was separated from her husband, who had used her with great cruelty. And I had heard of the death of her husband, from an accident consequent on his ill-treatment of a horse. This release had happened some two years before; for all I knew, she was married again.

I walked over to the old spot before dark. There was no house now, no brewery, no building whatever left, but the wall of the old garden. The cleared space had been enclosed with a rough fence. A gate in the fence standing ajar, I pushed it open, and went in.

A cold silvery mist had veiled the afternoon, and the moon was not yet up to scatter it. I could trace where every part of the old house had been. I was looking along the desolate garden walk, when I beheld a solitary figure in it.

The figure showed itself aware of me and stood still. I saw it was a woman. It was about to turn away, when it stopped, and let me approach. Then it faltered as if surprised, and uttered my name, and I cried out: "Estella!"

"I am greatly changed. I wonder you know me."

The freshness of her beauty was indeed gone, but its indescribable majesty and charm remained. These I had seen before; but what I had never seen before, was the saddened softened light of the once proud eyes. We sat down on a bench, and I said, "After so many years, it is strange that we should meet here again, Estella! Do you often come back?"

"I have never been here since."

"Nor I."

The moon began to rise, and I thought of the pressure on my hand when I had spoken the last words he had heard on earth.

Estella broke the silence.

"I have very often hoped to come back, but have been prevented. Poor, poor old place!"

The first rays of the moonlight touched the tears that dropped from her eyes. Not knowing that I saw them, she said quietly: "Were you wondering how it came to be left in this condition?"

"Yes, Estella."

"The ground still belongs to me. It is the only possession I have not relinquished. It was the subject of the only determined resistance I made in all the wretched years."

"Is it to be built on?"

"At last it is. I came here to take leave of it before its change. And you," she said, "you live abroad still? And do well, I am sure?"

"I work pretty hard for a sufficient living, and therefore – Yes, I do well."

"I have often thought of you," said Estella. "There was a long hard time when I kept far from me, the memory of what I had thrown away when I knew not its worth. But, since my duty has not been incompatible with the admission of that remembrance, I have given it a place in my heart."

230

"You have always held your place in my heart," I answered.

"I little thought," said Estella after a pause, "that I should take leave of you in taking leave of this spot. I am very glad to do so."

"Glad to part again, Estella? To me, parting is painful. To me, remembering our last parting has been ever painful."

"But you said," returned Estella, very earnestly, "'God bless you, God forgive you!' And if you could say that then, you will not hesitate to say it now – now, when suffering has been stronger than all other teaching, and has taught me to understand what your heart was. I have been bent and broken, I hope, into a better shape. Be considerate and good again, and tell me we are friends."

"We are friends," said I, rising and bending over her, as she rose from the bench.

"And will continue friends apart," said Estella.

I took her hand in mine, and we went out of that ruined place; the evening mists were rising, and in all the broad expanse of tranquil light they showed to me, I saw no shadow of another parting from her.